I0573805

GHOST HOUSE

A FAIRY TALE

JACQUELINE GREY

To Bun
Without you, there would be no Caius

And to mom
I really wanted you to see my book in print

CONTENTS

PART ONE
FAIRY TALE

ONE

◆•◆

Andrew stood in front of 34 Duke Street, otherwise known as Ghost House, and wondered what the hell he was doing there at one o'clock in the morning. The answer, of course, was that he couldn't say no to Charlie's crazy schemes. He'd tried—he and his best friend Jason always tried—but when faced with an excitement that could exhaust a ten-year-old, it was inevitable that they would fail. They'd learned that early on after meeting Charlie their first semester as freshmen.

"Here we are!" Charlie announced, gesturing needlessly. Based on personality alone, no one would ever guess he was the oldest of Andrew's friends by two years. He'd changed his major six times since Andrew had known him. At the rate Charlie was going, Andrew had a feeling he was going to graduate before Charlie did.

He shot Jason a pointed look. *Are we really doing this?*

The corners of Jason's sky-blue eyes crinkled with one of his "silently laughing at everyone" smiles. Andrew loved the way they sparkled when he did that. Even when it annoyed the shit out of him, like now.

Jason was the typical boy-next-door, clean cut and handsome. If he'd been a redhead, he could have given Archie Andrews a run for his money, but his sandy-brown hair made him look ready for the beach rather than a comic book. Andrew had been a sucker for his smile when they'd first met in second grade. Fourteen years later, that hadn't changed.

Jason shrugged. *Just go along with it.*

With a sigh, Andrew turned his attention back to Ghost House. It didn't look like much: a three-story, red brick box with boarded-up windows. Vines climbed the house's face, and the wood was in need of repair. Someone had spray-painted a "B" on the front door. Andrew had no idea what the letter was supposed to mean. The lawn was unkempt, which was to be expected of a building that had been abandoned for sixty years. The few times he'd passed it during the day, he hadn't considered it anything special, no matter what the rumors said. Yet standing in front of it now sent a shudder down his spine. The house loomed above him, as if daring him to enter.

Amanda, Charlie's girlfriend, wrinkled her nose. "We're really going to spend the night in *there*?" Jason's girlfriend, Marie, looked equally dubious.

"Come on," Charlie coaxed, throwing an arm around Amanda's shoulders. He was carrying a six-pack of beer in his other hand. "It's not that bad."

Amanda glared up at him. Even with her four-inch heels, she was still a good six inches shorter than him. What had made her think it would be a good idea to wear stilettos to an outing like this, Andrew didn't know for sure, but he wouldn't have been surprised if those shoes cost more than his iPhone.

A breeze stirred the curls on Andrew's neck and he

shivered, wrapping his jacket more firmly around his body. He refused to succumb to his imagination that it had been fingers brushing his skin instead of his hair.

"We look suspicious standing around here like this," he said. "How do we get in?" Anything to get them moving. Those windows were beginning to feel like eyes watching him.

"I've heard there's a loose board in one of the back windows," Jason said. "That's probably how everyone gets in."

Like any good urban legend, there were plenty of rumors about Ghost House, and they ran rampant on the town's university campus. It had become a tradition for students to sneak in and try spending a whole night in the old building. From the stories, some people succeeded and others didn't. The result didn't matter as long as there were new stories to be told. With all the gossip, Andrew wondered how it had taken this long for Charlie to convince them to join the lot.

They took the long way around the block to the back of the house in case any neighbors were up and snooping through their curtains. At one in the morning it was unlikely, but they didn't want to take any chances. The back of the building was even more neglected than the front. A chain link fence surrounded the property, but it had disconnected from its frame and sagged onto an untamed mess of dead weeds and sun-burnt grass. Andrew's skin itched as they skulked across the yard. He hoped ticks slept at night.

After a few moments of investigation, someone whispered, "Over here!" The sound felt overly loud in the silence of the night. With a prayer that no one had heard them, Andrew gathered with the others around the first floor window at the far corner of the house.

"Charlie, help me shift this," Jason said, gesturing to a plank braced in the window. It looked heavy but moved easily enough. Together, they lowered the wood to the ground.

"Ladies first," Charlie said tauntingly. Andrew was fairly sure Charlie had been the type of kid to pick on the girl he liked when he was younger. Apparently, he hadn't grown out of the habit.

"Not on your life," Amanda said. "I'm not going in there alone." Marie shook her head in agreement.

Andrew liked Marie. She was always willing to go along with dumb ideas like this one, which gave her points in his book. At first glance, she came off as the quiet, studious type. Where Amanda always looked ready for a camera, Marie dressed simply. Her black-framed glasses were the most stylish thing Andrew had ever seen her wear, but as he'd gotten to know her, he'd realized there was more to her than met the eye, evidenced by the tattoo she had hidden under her riot of curls. It was a tribal design in red and black and almost blended with her dark skin. He wanted to know what it was but had never found a reason to ask. Most importantly, she seemed to genuinely like Jason, and Andrew had never seen his best friend happier than when he was with her.

Jason put an arm around Marie and pulled her close. "Don't worry, hun," he said, "I'll protect you from the dark."

"But who will protect her from you?" Charlie teased with a wink. "I'll go in first."

Whether the window was open or empty, there weren't any loose shards of glass to hinder Charlie, and he slipped inside easily. He and Jason helped the girls through, then Jason turned to Andrew.

"Your turn."

"Hold this," Andrew said, handing Jason the six-pack he held. They had three in total and a bag of flashlights and batteries. Despite the impulsiveness of the night's venture, they had been smart enough to pick up supplies before heading over.

The window was a little high, but Charlie and Jason had used the board as a makeshift ramp for easier access. Andrew stepped up on the incline and slid inside. The room he entered was dark, but there was enough moonlight filtering in from outside to make out the vague shapes of furniture. He squinted until his eyes adjusted, and the layout of the room became a little clearer.

The floor was covered in a crazy geometric pattern. He wasn't sure, but he thought the design was what his mother referred to as art deco. Whatever it was called, it made his head hurt. There were booths along the far wall, and the rest of the room was sprinkled with square tables at various heights surrounded by brown leather stools or chairs.

"Is that a bar?" Andrew asked, peering into the darkness at the other end of the room.

"Yeah," Charlie answered. "I wonder if there's any liquor left on the shelves."

"Ew," Amanda said, taking a step back from her boyfriend. "You'd drink something that's been sitting in this dusty place for sixty years?"

"If there had been anything," Marie pointed out, "it was probably found by the students who've done this before."

Her logic did nothing to dissuade Charlie's enthusiasm. "Come on. Let's explore."

"Hey, a little help here!"

Startled by the sharp whisper, Andrew turned back to the window. Jason was sitting on the sill, precariously balanced with his hands full of beer and shopping bags.

Andrew hurried over to take the supplies and help him inside.

"Let's get the board back in place," Jason said.

"All right." Andrew set everything on a nearby table. He finished in time to see Jason hanging out the window as he reached toward the ground. Moonlight highlighted his jeans-clad ass, emphasizing the perfect curves of his rear end. Andrew was distracted by the sight until a grunt pulled him back to his senses. He squeezed into the window next to Jason and helped him lift the wood.

"Thanks," Jason wheezed out. They were both panting from the effort.

"Sure," Andrew said, his chest tight from more than the exercise. He mentally kicked himself for letting his imagination run away from him. At least it was better than the creepy thoughts that had been invading his mind outside.

"Are you guys coming or what?"

Startled again, Andrew stepped back. "Yeah," he called, grabbing the bags. Once they were gathered together, Andrew handed out the flashlights and batteries. No longer hindered by dim moonlight, they headed through a curtain-draped archway. Dust clouded around them as they pushed through, and it took a few moments for the coughing to stop. When Andrew could breathe clearly again, he saw they were in a large parlor. He supposed there was a better word for it, but he didn't know what it was.

It looked like someone's living room, if they were the type to throw fancy parties where people mingled with glasses of wine and held sophisticated conversations. Perhaps a few people would be listening to someone play the grand piano by the front windows. Andrew could imagine light shining into the room on a sunny day, if it weren't for the boards. The room would be full of music and laughter. For a moment, he could more than imagine it; he could almost see it. Lively people crowding the room, talking in intimate groups on the couches, or gathering around the piano to appreciate the player.

"I can't believe no one's stolen that chandelier." Amanda's voice snapped him back to reality. The room was once again dark and quiet, the air stale and unmoving.

Andrew looked up to see a monstrosity of iron and crystal hanging from the ceiling. "No one would be able to get it out of here," he replied.

"You could always take the pieces," Jason pointed out.

"Unless it's made of diamonds, I don't think chandelier pieces go for much without the rest of the chandelier."

"Why are we talking about furniture?" Charlie interrupted. "We're in a haunted house for fuck's sake."

He had a point. "So what is this place anyway?" Andrew asked. "Obviously, it isn't a regular house."

Charlie was grinning again, relishing the news he was about to share. "Before it shut down, this was the neighborhood whorehouse."

"Bullshit," Amanda said at the same time Marie muttered "yeah right" with an eye roll. "Like this neighborhood would have stood for such a thing," Marie added.

"It's not like you could tell from the outside," Jason pointed out.

"Seriously?" Andrew asked him.

Jason nodded, his eyes sparkling again. He may not have been as outspoken as Charlie, but he was enjoying this. "It's true. The story goes that one night the owner went crazy and killed a bunch of people."

Andrew looked around the room, trying to spot leftover blood stains. Out of the corner of his eye he caught Marie doing the same thing.

"The mysterious part," Charlie said, "is that by the time the police got here to investigate, the owner was gone and so were the bodies. There were no signs of a struggle, and no one could determine what had happened. Everyone had just vanished."

"If no one was left, who told the story?" Marie asked.

"A neighbor called to complain about a disturbance. They think he might have heard the murder."

"So the ghosts are supposed to be the victims?" Amanda asked, sounding skeptical.

"And the owner. He disappeared that night with the rest."

"Do you think they were killed in this room?" Marie's eyes darted around as if searching for the murderer.

"Probably," Jason said, putting his arm around her. She leaned into him, and he kissed the top of her head. Andrew turned away when she tilted her head up for another kiss.

"I guess we're sleeping down here then?" he asked.

"Of course!" Charlie exclaimed. "Best place to see the ghosts."

"And what are we supposed to sleep on?" Amanda asked, her voice dripping with disdain. Not for the first time, Andrew wondered what Charlie saw in her. If she hated doing things like this so much, why did she come along?

"I was thinking on the floor," Charlie replied, "but you can take a couch if you want."

Amanda looked horrified by the suggestion. Andrew shined his light on the chaise next to him. The cushion wasn't as worn as he would have expected, but he was sure it was full of dust and god only knew what else. He couldn't blame Amanda for her reaction that time.

"What about upstairs?"

"You think the beds up there will be any less dusty?" Jason asked.

"Down here it is," Andrew said.

"Speaking of upstairs"—Charlie grinned—"Let's check out the rest of the house."

They saw an alcove near the front door and headed for it. Inside, the foyer was decorated in a curlicue design that began on the floor before climbing the walls and sprouting leaves. A marble staircase wound up to the higher levels of the house, its metal railing decorated in a similar pattern.

"Hey, what's that?" They turned to where Marie was pointing her flashlight. A thick curtain marked the entryway to another room. Having learned from experience, they carefully shifted the fabric this time and found themselves in a small lounge. Couches lined the walls and various pillows littered the floor.

"I wonder what went on in here," Andrew said. "It doesn't look like much of anything."

"It's a private alcove," Charlie said. "What do you think went on in here?"

"Isn't that what upstairs is for?"

"You gotta get started somewhere."

"Do you ever think of anything but sex?" Marie asked.

"Nope."

Jason rolled his eyes. "I thought we were heading upstairs."

They mounted the stairs, treading carefully on the dusty stone. The second floor landing let out into a hallway that stretched the length of the house. Doors lined either side of it. They peered into the rooms but saw nothing out of the ordinary. Each had a bed, a small table, a chair, and a dresser. No bloodstains or dead bodies. Not even a whisper of a ghost.

The only excitement they encountered was when Amanda screeched, "Ew! Oh my god, how *disgusting* can people be?" They came running to her rescue, but it was nothing more offensive than a used condom on one of the bedroom floors.

"I guess not everyone is averse to sleeping on dusty sheets," Jason commented.

"They could at least clean up after themselves." Andrew agreed with her, though he couldn't imagine what sort of person would have sex in a room like this. Then again, was it that much worse than a sketchy motel when you really thought about it?

"Let's check out the third floor," he suggested.

"It's probably more of the same," Jason said.

"Doesn't hurt to look."

They did, and Jason was right. There were only two doors on the third floor, but the rooms inside were just like the ones downstairs.

"Does this hallway feel shorter to you?" Andrew asked.

Jason's brow furrowed. "Yeah, it does."

They looked around the hallway again, but it was just as plain as before.

"Maybe the third floor angles in at the back of the house? I didn't look up before entering."

"Maybe."

Not caring enough to speculate further, the group headed back downstairs.

"It's cold in here," Marie said sometime later. They had cleared a space in the center of the main parlor so they could stay close to each other. Beer cans were sprinkled around them in varying stages of emptiness. The flashlights

had been left on, and the play of light made eerie carica-
tures of their faces.

"I'll keep you warm," Jason said, wrapping his arms
around her and pulling her close.

Andrew was also feeling the chill as the night wore on
and the beer had lost its numbing effect. Only he didn't
have anyone to warm himself against. Charlie teased him
about how he never dated. Jason usually stepped in before
he got too carried away, but Andrew knew they both
wondered why he didn't have a girlfriend. He'd thought of
telling them a hundred times that he was gay, but each time
he'd chickened out. He didn't know how Charlie would
take the news, though he was sure Jason would be cool.
Jason wouldn't have a problem with it at all, yet Andrew
still couldn't bring himself to tell him.

He wasn't afraid they would find out he liked guys. He
was afraid they would find out which guy he had a
crush *on*.

He couldn't remember when he had started liking
Jason. It could have been a gradual thing. Or maybe he'd
fallen at the sight of that first smile. They'd become fast
friends, but it wasn't until eighth grade that Andrew realized how much he'd taken his best friend's presence for
granted. That was the year Jason got his first girlfriend, and
Andrew discovered what jealousy felt like. Ever since then,
he'd done his best to hide his feelings from Jason. It had
gotten easier over time. Perhaps it had just become a habit
he didn't know how to break.

"Has anyone left early?" Amanda's question broke
Andrew's train of thought.

"Why?" Charlie asked. "Are you giving up already?"

"I was just curious."

"Sure. One group only lasted an hour before they came

rushing out claiming to have heard strange noises and felt cold spots."

"That could be pipes, right?" Marie asked. "There aren't really ghosts in this house, are there?"

"Where would be the fun in that?"

"Don't worry," Jason told her. "Other groups have spent the whole night here without even hearing the creak of a floorboard."

Marie didn't look reassured, and she burrowed deeper into Jason's side. Andrew turned away so he wouldn't have to watch them cuddle.

"Maybe we should try to get some sleep," he said.

Charlie gestured with the can he'd been drinking. "We have to finish the beer first."

"We already did," Amanda snapped.

"Dude, what's crawled up *your* ass?"

"Look." Andrew raised his voice to cut across the argument. "I'm going to sleep, so keep the fighting down."

"What about the fucking?" Charlie asked, his good humor back to its normal, perverted setting given the opportunity.

"Not like you have to worry about that," Amanda muttered.

Andrew didn't want to worry about it either. Instead of answering, he turned away from the circle of light and lay down on the floor, using his jacket as a pillow. It was more effective at keeping dust mites away from his face than for supporting his head, but he bunched it up as best he could. Charlie and Amanda were still bickering as he closed his eyes and drifted off to sleep.

The sound of voices woke Andrew. He listened for a

moment, trying to remember where he was. There were more than four voices in the room. A lot more, and—was that a piano?

He opened his eyes and found himself standing in the middle of a room lit by various table lamps and a fireplace. People were scattered about, laughing in groups or talking intimately in pairs. Everyone had a champagne flute with bubbling, golden liquid, or a cigarette in a long, metal holder. Sometimes they had both. Something about the room—perhaps the cigarette smoke—made the whole scene feel blurry around the edges. Maybe the beer he'd drunk had taken a firmer hold than he'd thought.

Through the fog, Andrew noticed a man sitting alone on one of the couches. He was the only thing in focus, creating a sharp contrast to the rest of the room. When he looked at Andrew the corner of his mouth turned up in a wry smile. Andrew blinked. He really did feel tipsy. Maybe a little more than tipsy. When he could focus on the couch again, the man was gone. Startled, Andrew glanced around the room, a sudden urgency making his body feel steadier.

"Looking for someone?" a voice purred in his ear.

Andrew whirled toward the sound, but no one stood behind him, only more partygoers who were absorbed in their own conversations.

"Try again," the voice said.

Andrew turned, searching the room for the speaker. As his gaze passed over the couples and groups in the room, they flowed in and out of focus, making him feel dizzy.

"Perhaps over there."

This time his body moved on its own. When he tried, he found he could not look away either.

"Well? What do you think?" the voice asked.

Andrew felt like a mouse being played with by a cat. He

didn't like it, but his struggles were in vain. Finally, he gave up the fight and took a closer look at what was in front of him. He was facing a love seat upon which a couple was kissing. He was surprised to find that both of the participants were men. As he watched, the kiss went from lingering to passionate and a warmth flooded through him.

"Oh yes," said the voice. "That one has a *wicked* tongue."

Just think what he could do with it elsewhere on your body, came the unspoken thought. Andrew could imagine it, more clearly than he wanted to.

"Be careful though," the voice cautioned. "He's a *snake*."

The last word was stretched with venom, and it jerked Andrew's attention away from his fantasy and back to the couple. As their lips parted, he thought he saw the flicker of a forked tongue between them.

"Come," the voice called before Andrew could get a closer look.

Like a marionette, he was once again pulled against his will. He stumbled but didn't fall. When he'd regained his footing, he was looking at a man standing sentry against the wall. The man was a giant, broad shouldered and his thighs looked to be the size of Andrew's waist.

"Are you into strength?" the voice asked.

The man was intimidating. Andrew was accustomed to being average height, but he'd never met someone who towered over him so easily. The colossus turned and their gazes locked. Andrew was braced for intimidation or arrogance. He was surprised when he saw kindness instead. The man's dark brown eyes were warm and comforting, and Andrew could imagine his arms feeling the same way. An incredible yearning quickly grew in his chest as they looked at each other. He wanted to feel safe and warm, cared for.

"Don't be fooled," the voice warned. "He's a beast."

As if the word had called the transformation forth, the giant suddenly turned into a hairy monster. Long black fur covered him from head to foot, making his menacing size seem even bigger. His full, pink lips vanished and were replaced by a wide mouth with sharp, predator's teeth. Horns curved out from his head like Maleficent's, except these could have run Angelina through.

The vision was gone in an instant, but the spell had been broken. No longer pulled by longing, Andrew and the beast were just two men once more.

At the sound of a laugh behind him, Andrew's patience snapped. He whirled, glaring at the space where the voice always seemed to be. He came face to face with the stranger from the couch. He had the look of old Hollywood, with a long face, high forehead, and the kind of nose people paid for. His dark brown hair was neatly cut with a slight wave in the length at the top, the style framing small ears. The man was made to be immortalized in sculpture or on canvas, but despite his handsome looks, it was his eyes that caught Andrew's attention. They were a bright green and sparkled like freshly polished emeralds. Andrew opened his mouth to tell the guy off, but the appearance of an actual person left him at a loss for words.

The man looked smug, as if it had been his plan all along to throw Andrew so far off his balance. "Well? What would you like?" Andrew recognized his voice as the disembodied one that had accompanied him around the room. "They're all for sale for the night."

"Sale?" The question escaped Andrew as he tried to make sense of what was going on. Some impulse had him looking up, and the eyesore of iron and crystal above his head made everything click into place. Although it was lit and sparkling, Andrew recognized the chandelier. "I'm still in Ghost House."

"Ghost House?" the man echoed with a laugh. His eyes glittered with amusement.

Andrew could stare at those eyes for hours.

The stranger's merriment faded. "*I* am not for sale," he said sternly. Andrew opened his mouth to protest, but the man turned abruptly on his heel. "Perhaps you should leave until you've decided on what you want. This is *not* a place for loitering."

Unsure of how he could have offended a total stranger, Andrew tried to find the words for an apology. He was thwarted once again when the man glared at him. He froze, expecting a scolding or something more, but all the man said was, "Sleep," and Andrew was falling backward, scrambling for purchase as the world went dark around him.

A thud followed by throbbing pain near his temple brought Andrew back to his senses. He opened his eyes and looked around. The room was dark, but small traces of morning light filtered through the windows, allowing him to see the chandelier above him. It was dark with tarnish and some of the bulbs were missing. The polish and sparkle of the party was gone. It had all been a dream.

Of course it had been a dream. Nothing that confusing could be real.

He gingerly touched his head where he'd knocked it against the leg of a coffee table and winced at the pain. A bump was already forming. He sat up and leaned against a couch as he tried to soothe his aching head. His eyes

narrowed when he noticed a carved pattern on the edge of
the table. He'd seen that table in his dream. He glanced
around at the rest of the room. Aside from the piano and the
chandelier, most of the furniture had been different. That
should have been reassuring, but nothing about the dream
room's layout had felt familiar. Between the room and the
people, he'd felt like he'd been transported to the 1920s. It
was not at all the type of party he would imagine for
himself. Not to mention the annoying stranger—the
annoying but hot stranger. Where had his mind come up
with all that?

Contemplation was only making his head hurt more.
He lay back down. There was no point in trying to figure it
out, and it was too early for thought anyway. He closed his
eyes. Sleep wasn't long in coming, and he didn't dream
again.

TWO

—◆◆—

The next time Andrew woke it was fully day, and he wasn't the only one stirring. He could hear someone stretching and the sound of a kiss. He pointedly ignored the latter.

"Looks like we made it," he said.

After a moment, Jason lazily replied, "Yeah." He sounded happily distracted.

"Can we go home now?" Amanda asked from Andrew's other side. She was sitting up, her posture rigid as if one more speck of dust would send her over the edge.

"Yeah, I don't see why not." He pushed himself up from the floor. From that angle, he could see that Charlie was still fast asleep. "Who's going to wake prince charming?"

Amanda snorted and nudged Charlie none too gently with her foot. It took some work, but soon they were all awake and heading out of the house the same way they'd come in. In the light of day, the dust on their clothes couldn't have been more obvious. They brushed it off as best they could, but traces still clung stubbornly to fabric and hair. They hurried to their respective rooms for showers and to change before meeting at the dining hall for breakfast.

It was early in the morning by college standards for a Sunday, so there was plenty of hot water in Andrew's dorm. He took his time scrubbing his hair and soothing his muscles under the pounding stream.

"You took the good stall, didn't you?"

Andrew grinned, the water tracing the curves of his face as he ducked under the spray. "Yup," he called back. "If you hadn't taken your sweet time you would have gotten it."

"I had to say goodbye to Marie," Jason said.

"You're going to see her in twenty minutes."

"Doesn't matter when you're in love."

A sharp pang stabbed Andrew through the chest. He concentrated on rinsing the shampoo out of his hair until he was sure it was safe to speak again. "What about Amanda and Charlie?"

"Amanda couldn't move fast enough to find a shower. Charlie..."

"We'll be lucky if he makes it to breakfast," Andrew finished for him. "He's probably fast asleep."

Finished with his shower, he turned off the water and grabbed his towel. "We'll head over together when you're done?" he asked as he collected his things.

"Sounds like a plan."

Back in their room, Andrew quickly set about getting dressed. It wasn't like Jason would be put off seeing him in a towel, but standing around in one when they were supposed to be heading for breakfast was another matter. It would also keep him from thinking.

He hoped.

It didn't.

That had been the first time Jason had mentioned being

in love. It wasn't like he needed to tell Andrew or anything. Andrew wouldn't have been surprised if Marie and Jason had been saying it back and forth to each other for months now, but to hear it in person... That pang began in his chest again, and he roughly combed his hair to distract himself from it.

He didn't hold out any hope that he and Jason would one day be a thing. Jason was one hundred percent straight. Logically, Andrew knew nothing romantic could happen between them. He had come to terms with that knowledge a long time ago. His heart just needed a reminder in moments like these.

"Careful there or you'll go bald," Jason warned as he entered the room. He was naked except for a towel slung low on his hips. The planes of his upper body were damp and beads of water ran over his shoulders from hair Jason hadn't bothered to towel dry.

"You're going to catch a cold if you stand around like that," Andrew said, forcing his attention away from Jason's body.

"Yes, Mom," Jason teased. He whipped the towel from his waist and set about drying his hair.

Andrew bit the inside of his cheek as he felt his face grow warm. His nerves were on high alert, broadcasting just how close Jason's naked body was. He set his comb down, grabbed the water pitcher off their mini fridge, poured himself a drink, and choked it down. Maybe the real problem was that he needed to get laid. Aside from one random blow job at a party Charlie had dragged him to, he hadn't gotten any. Ever.

"You almost ready?" he asked, wincing when his voice sounded rougher than normal.

"Yeah, let me just grab my shoes."

Shoes. That was something Andrew needed to do too. He reached for his sneakers and made quick work of slipping them on.

"OK," Jason said. "Let's go."

Signs of life were beginning to show in the cafeteria when Andrew and Jason arrived, but they still had their pick of the tables and chose one close to the food and far from the bathrooms. They'd already started eating by the time Marie join them. A few minutes later, Amanda entered, leading a grumpy-looking Charlie.

"What's wrong with you?" Jason asked.

"Such a waste of time." Charlie kicked a chair out from under the table and plopped down, scowl firmly in place.

"What was?" Andrew asked.

Charlie rolled his eyes. "Ghost House. What do you think?" He shifted in his chair with an annoyed huff. "Nothing happened. We could have been drinking in a bar instead."

"We do that all the time," Marie said.

"We were drinking," Jason pointed out. "At least this time we had a more interesting setting."

"An empty house is not an interesting setting."

Amanda whirled on Charlie, her eyes narrowed dangerously, her lips pursed. "We just spent the night in a dust-infested rat hole, all at your insistence. Don't be so disappointed because you didn't see any ghosts."

"Did you really think we'd see a ghost?" Andrew asked.

"No," Charlie admitted, his shoulders slumping, "but *something*. We were in a haunted house and none of us were even scared."

The beast in Andrew's dream had been plenty scary,

but he didn't mention it. Charlie would think he was trying to appease him by making up a story. Besides, no one in the group really believed in ghosts, and he wasn't in the mood for their teasing if they thought he did.

As he thought about it, more details of his dream came back to him. Usually, his dreams had a blurry quality about them. Not visually, but in the way he remembered the details after waking. Even if he knew who a person was supposed to be in a dream, he couldn't ever remember the details of their face once he was awake. This time, he could clearly recall the people he'd seen, like the snake couple or the beast man. Most of all, he remembered the alluring stranger who'd taunted him. There was something about him that kept bringing him to mind, despite his frustrating nature. Maybe it had been the shine in those beautiful green eyes.

Belly full and running on not enough sleep, Andrew was in the mood for a nap. Luckily, Jason had planned to spend the afternoon with Marie, so he had their room all to himself. He'd almost made it to the door when his phone rang. A glance at the screen informed him that "Home" was calling. *Fuck.* He could toy with the hope that it was his mother checking up on him, but he knew better. He immediately pressed the button to send the call to voicemail, but it was too late. A familiar feeling of dread settled over him.

Andrew's dad was an ambitious man who'd built a consulting firm from scratch, and he dreamed of leaving his legacy in the hands of his son. To accomplish his goal, he planned to have Andrew work at Hollenbeck Consulting after graduation. That was all well and good, except Andrew didn't want to be a business management consultant. He didn't know what he wanted to do for a career, but he was fairly certain that working in a corporate office was not it. On top of that, constantly being around his father, day in and day out, was a disaster waiting to happen. He loved his dad, but they had very different views on many things, and Mr. Hollenbeck was reluctant to listen to what he didn't want to hear.

That was one of the reasons Andrew hadn't yet told his father he didn't want to work for the company. Even if he could manage to get his father to listen to him, the conversation would only end in disappointment. Lately, it seemed like all their conversations ended that way. Hearing the dismay in his father's voice was worse than being scolded or yelled at. If that was the inevitable outcome, he'd rather not talk to his dad until it was unavoidable. That didn't keep anxiety from settling onto his shoulders in the meantime though.

He unlocked his door, dropped his phone and keys on the desk, and face planted onto the bed. It made an alarming creak—possibly a crack—but held. With a sigh, he attempted to push the oppressive feelings aside and nap. He must have succeeded, because the next time he opened his eyes sunlight was streaming into the room, which was weird, since his and Jason's dorm room faced east and was shaded by trees. Confused, he glanced around and recognized the off-white walls and pale art deco furniture. The light was pouring in from the big picture window, and it made the piano shine.

What the hell was he doing back at Ghost House?

He turned around and saw the stranger from his dream sitting on a couch reading a book. As he watched, the man reached for a delicate teacup and raised it to his lips. His hand froze midway to setting the china back onto its saucer as he noticed Andrew. Unlike the previous night, he clearly hadn't expected Andrew to be there.

"Hey," Andrew said lamely.

The man set his cup down and sat up properly, straightening his back to his full height. "It's rude to assume an invitation that wasn't given," he said.

Andrew shrugged. "It's not like I had a choice. Last thing I remember was going to sleep in my dorm room."

"You're a college student?" The question was immediately waved away. "Of course you are. Only college students would be stupid enough to sleep here hoping to get scared by a ghost."

Andrew did his best not to be offended. "Do college students usually visit you in dreams?"

The man tilted his head, curious. "You think you're visiting me in your dreams?"

Andrew hadn't really thought about it, but he supposed he was. "I've never had the same dream twice, and I don't usually interact with them so..."

"Consciously?"

"Sure, that works."

The stranger placed his book on the table. It was bound in brown leather, embossed with gold writing on the cover, and had gilded pages. It looked like a book Andrew might find in his father's study. He caught the word "shrew" in the title but couldn't make out more from where he stood.

"Would you like a cup of tea?"

"Can a person drink in dreams?"

"Only one way to find out."

True. Andrew sat and took the offered cup. The tea was hot and tasted sweet without sugar. "Cinnamon?" he asked.

"Yes. I find the flavor is the perfect touch of sweet once you've smoothed out the bitter edges. Tell me," the man said, lifting his cup and settling back on the sofa, "what are you studying? And please make it interesting. Dream or not, there is no reason to be boring."

Andrew's major was business management. He didn't know how to make it sound exciting, so he went with the simple truth.

"What made you choose it?"

Was this guy really interested? "My dad wants me to take over his business. He's going to train me after I graduate, but the business degree would give me a head start."

His host pursed his lips.

Andrew wasn't sure if the gesture was one of disapproval, but before he could be called boring, he said, "You know, I thought it was customary to introduce yourself before giving your guest the third degree."

The man gasped. "How rude of me!" he exclaimed. "But I suppose that makes us even." He extended a long-fingered hand toward Andrew. "Caius," he said. "My name is Caius."

"Andrew." Caius's grip was firm but not overbearing. "It's nice to meet you, Caius."

"Oh, the pleasure is all mine," Caius said, his tone sultry.

Andrew retrieved his hand, shifting uncomfortably in his seat, before retreating behind his teacup once more. "Have you lived here long?" He wondered if that was a strange question to ask given that they were talking in a dream.

"*Ages,*" Caius replied, relaxing his visual hold on Andrew by looking around the room. "I really did like the modern style of the 1920s. I'm sure you've noticed," he added with a wave at the decor. "I did update the design as tastes changed, but what's a little vintage when you have such style?"

He looked at Andrew expectantly, but Andrew had lost the thread of Caius's spiel after the fifth word. His sense of style was jeans and sports jerseys or t-shirts. When it became apparent that Andrew was at a loss for what to say, Caius wilted. Andrew found himself unwilling to disappoint him even though he was a perfect stranger.

"You owned this place when it was running?"

Caius perked up immediately, and Andrew knew he'd done the right thing by asking. "Yes. This building was a haven for men of ill repute for almost seventy-five years."

"I still can't believe there was a whorehouse in my hometown," Andrew said with a shake of his head.

Caius tsked. "Please. I may not be polite company, but we can *pretend* to behave with propriety at tea time."

"Huh?"

"*Whore*, my dear. It's a cheap word for a cheap tramp. My boys were nothing but the best."

"Boys," Andrew echoed. "There were no girl prostitutes?"

"You were here last night," Caius said. "Did you see any women about?"

Last night's dream was hazy—much hazier than this one —but Andrew didn't remember seeing any women in the room, which brought another point to mind. "You asked me if I would like anyone," he said. "How did you...?" His voice trailed off, unable to admit the fact out loud even in a dream.

Caius laughed. "You're not the first student to come here."

That didn't explain anything in Andrew's opinion. "What does that mean?"

Caius leaned forward, his eyes sparkling with mischief. Andrew was distracted by their bright green color until Caius spoke. "All the students have had one thing in common," he said. "Can you guess what it was?"

Andrew felt his face flush. His hand jerked and tea spilled onto his lap. "Oh crap!" he exclaimed as the hot liquid seeped into his pants and burned his thigh. He set the cup down and scrambled for a napkin.

"Easy now," Caius coaxed. He placed a hand over the mess, which confused Andrew yet again. Shouldn't he be getting something to cool Andrew's leg with and stop the burn?

The skin beneath Caius's fingers tingled. Andrew didn't see anything happening, but the throbbing in his thigh gradually disappeared and the dampness of his pants slowly vanished. Eventually, the strange sensation faded as well, but Caius's hand remained where it was, inappropriately high on Andrew's leg. Andrew couldn't stop staring at it, and other parts of his body were beginning to take notice.

"What did you do?" he asked, his voice rougher than he'd intended.

"I healed the burn for you," Caius said. "I dried your pants as well. I didn't think you'd like sitting with a wet spot on your jeans."

Andrew was mildly surprised Caius knew what jeans were. Did they even exist before 1950? Then again, Caius was a dream, and it didn't matter when jeans had been invented.

"Your hand is still on my leg," he said.

"I know."

There was a purr to his voice, and it made Andrew feel hot. He swallowed. "Why?"

"You don't like it?"

No, it wasn't that, but Andrew wasn't sure how he felt about it. Caius was certainly attractive, and no one had flirted with him so openly before. But Caius was a ghost, wasn't he? This was a dream. This wasn't real. Andrew didn't want to be hit on by a figment of his imagination. It made him feel pathetic. If he was going to be alone, he'd use his hand, not an imaginary person.

Yet Caius's touch felt very real as he brushed his thumb over the denim of Andrew's pants.

"I—" Andrew stuttered. "Isn't this a bit fast?"

Caius laughed, the sound warm and musical, yet somehow mocking. "From what I've seen, your generation takes no time at all," he said, but he removed his hand from Andrew's leg.

"You've done this with them?"

"No. They came like you did, at night, and chose one of the boys to bed."

There was something about Caius's manner that felt a little *too* casual, as if it were a mask. Andrew wondered what could be hidden beneath it. Sadness? Loneliness? Whatever it was, he didn't like it.

"You told me I couldn't buy you."

"You can't," Caius said bluntly.

"I don't want to," Andrew replied just as directly. "You're worth more than a one-night stand."

Caius laughed again. "And how would you know that?"

"You don't think so?"

Caius proudly raised his chin. "Of course I am. I'm worth more than money could ever buy." He studied Andrew for a moment before sitting back, his tone lightening once again. "Do you think you have what it takes to win me?"

Andrew thought back to the weight haunting Caius's

expression. He was sure he had seen it. He was sure there was more to Caius than his flighty exterior. Yet Caius was still a dream. He was insubstantial. There was no point in trying to "win" him. But now that the idea had been broached, Andrew felt like it couldn't hurt to go through with it. It wasn't like anyone would find out.

"Yeah," he said. "I do."

"And how will you go about doing it?" Caius asked, his voice back to its sultry purr.

Fuck it. This was Andrew's dream, and he'd do what he wanted in it. "I want to kiss you."

"Am I a damsel to be won by a kiss?" Caius asked.

"No, but it feels like an irresistible start."

Caius lifted his chin again, preening. "I accept."

Andrew shifted closer to Caius on the couch. He suddenly felt nervous, as if this was his first kiss with anyone, not just with Caius. He licked his lips and swallowed, trying to moisten his dry mouth. Reaching out, he cupped Caius's chin in one hand, caressing his thumb over his cheek. Caius's emerald eyes drifted closed, and his chin lifted in anticipation. Andrew took a moment to admire his full lips before leaning forward and pressing their mouths together.

Caius's lips were warm and soft. When Andrew brushed his tongue along the seal of Caius's mouth, it opened, but he did not rush to claim it. He teased Caius, tracing his lips and letting their breaths mingle. Caius's tongue met Andrew's, and the kiss went from slow and lingering to a delicate tangle as they explored the taste of each other. Seeking more, Andrew deepened the kiss, and Caius melted beneath him. Their mouths sealed together, and all the world vanished except for Caius and their kiss.

THREE

◆◆◆

Andrew could still feel the wet heat of Caius's mouth. He could also feel someone roughly shaking his shoulder.

"Dude, come on. You're going to be late."

Andrew groaned and rolled over. With the return of reality came the realization that he had a significant erection. Thank god he'd rolled onto his stomach, so Jason couldn't see it.

"I'm up." He waved a hand weakly to prove it. "I'm up."

"Yeah? Not even five seconds ago you were dead to the world," Jason said, but he'd finally stopped shaking Andrew. "Did you take something to knock you out like that?"

Andrew jerked his head up from the pillow. "No."

Jason shrugged. "You ready to go?"

"Yeah, just..." Andrew dropped his head back down. "Give me a minute, okay?"

Concern furrowed Jason's brow before Andrew's position gave him a clue. He grinned. "Good dream, huh?"

The memory of Caius's mocking green eyes and the

taste of his mouth returned, as vivid as they had been in the dream. "Yeah," Andrew admitted quietly. Shit.

Both Andrew and Jason liked to play sports, but they didn't want to devote all of their free time to them. Luckily, their college had a hockey club on campus. Practices were three times a week with a game every Sunday. The games were competitive but friendly, and it left enough of their schedule open for other interests, like going to the bar or sleeping in haunted houses. They had tried to convince Charlie to join the team, but he had adamantly proclaimed that the only exercise he cared to do was in bed or at a gym.

There wasn't a rink on campus, so they had to take a bus to the local ice center for practices and home games. Andrew's mind was in a fog as he boarded. The fact that he'd dreamed of Caius and Ghost House twice now weighed on his mind. Reoccurring dreams weren't a good sign, were they? He didn't think he was going crazy, but he also didn't think insane people were aware of their situation. No. Repetitive dreams were a sign of something being on a person's mind. It was the subconscious trying to work out a problem that the conscious mind couldn't solve or some- thing like that. Somewhere in that dream was a clue to what his problem was and a way to solve it, but what could be on his mind that would make him dream of a 1920s brothel and its owner?

The bus passed South Main Street, the road that would take them down to Ghost House. The street went by quietly, like all the others. What had he been expecting? He felt like he'd given his phone number to a cute guy and was waiting for him to call. Maybe he was going crazy. Or maybe he really did need to get laid. If a kiss with a dream could get him this hung up, he was obviously overdue.

He pulled his attention from the window and turned

toward his teammates. Jason had left Andrew to his thoughts and was engaged in conversation near the back of the bus. A freshman named Derek beamed at him from a few seats over. "We're gonna kick ass today, yeah?"

An answering smile spread across Andrew's lips as he let himself get psyched for the game. "Yeah."

"All right, man!" Derek reached over to high five him. By the time the bus pulled into the rink parking lot, Andrew was fully energized and ready to win.

"Are we meeting Charlie for dinner when we get back?"

Jason nodded. "I think the girls are joining us too."

"OK." Andrew leaned his head back against the seat, relaxing his muscles and listening to the bus roll on. He was still pumped from the game. They had won 5 to 1, effectively "kicking ass" as planned. "I'm taking a shower before we head over," he added.

"You better," Jason advised. "They'll kick you out of the cafeteria before they let you spoil the food."

"I do not smell that bad."

Jason grinned. "Wanna bet?"

"How could you tell? You smell worse than I do."

"That's a lie."

"Try going to dinner without a shower then."

"I wouldn't go that far," Jason said, raking back the strands of light brown hair plastered against his forehead. Even sweaty, he was hot.

Back at the dorm, Andrew turned the water all the way to cold once he'd finished washing. He ducked his head under the spray hoping to wash away inconvenient thoughts of Jason in his hockey uniform. Memories of his dream came back to him to fill their place, and he laughed. Fantasizing about a sixty-year-old ghost was worse than crushing on his best friend. No, Caius was older than that if the details he'd mentioned about the building's design were to be believed. Not that it mattered. He was still a dream, and therefore, not real.

"Are you okay over there?" Jason called, his voice slightly muffled by the spray.

"Yeah." Andrew sighed. "I think I need to get laid."

Jason laughed. "Charlie and I have been saying that for how long now? What made you finally get on board with the idea?"

"I've been having some weird dreams lately. They probably have nothing to do with getting laid, but I don't know what else to think." He didn't want to consider that he was losing his mind.

"Dirty dreams?"

"No. Actually..." Andrew turned off his shower. Jason did the same, and the room was suddenly too quiet. "Nothing weird happened to you when we were at Ghost House, did it?"

"What do you mean?"

Andrew shrugged. "The weird dreams started when we were there. It's been..."

"Creeping you out?"

More like confusing. "Sort of. Yeah."

"Hey, I woke up in the middle of the night thinking that a snake was crawling on my leg. That place is creepy."

"Really? Charlie was so upset that nothing scary happened when we were there."

"Charlie was drunk, and even sober, he could sleep through a monsoon. Trust me, you weren't the only one who was spooked."

Andrew was relieved to hear that. Even if their experiences hadn't been the same, knowing Jason had also been affected by Ghost House made him feel a little better.

They collected their things and returned to their room. Once the door closed behind them, Jason asked, "So what does Ghost House have to do with you needing to get laid?"

Shit. Andrew had hoped Jason would forget he'd mentioned that. "It's dumb," he said as he grabbed a second towel to dry his hair. He was a fan of low maintenance, but his hair was curly and had a tendency to puff out if he didn't dry it before heading outdoors. Add in humidity, and it looked like dirty blond dandelion fluff. Those were the days he never left home without a hat.

"So? You can tell me. You know you can tell me anything, even the stupid shit."

True, but that didn't make Andrew feel any less embarrassed. "In my dream, I keep getting hit on."

"I thought you said this wasn't a dirty dream."

"It isn't. We talked mostly. Flirted. We kissed, but that's it."

"Sounds more like a date than a dirty dream."

"Yeah, it does."

"Maybe we were wrong. Maybe what you really need is a girlfriend."

More like a boyfriend, but Andrew didn't correct him.

Andrew wasn't surprised when he found himself back at Ghost House that night after he'd gone to sleep, but it was worrying. This was his third dream of the place. Good or bad, these dreams were now a thing.

The room was crowded, much like the first time he'd been there. He searched the room for Caius and found him on a stool at the end of the bar in the back room.

"Mind if I join you?"

Caius shrugged, his attention remaining on the bottles behind the bar.

"Is something wrong?"

"No," Caius replied shortly.

Andrew had never been in the doghouse before, but he recognized the signs. He searched his memory for what he could have done. The last thing he remembered was Caius's lips against his own. Then he realized that was the problem.

"I'm sorry," he said.

Caius turned to look at him, one eyebrow raised in a perfect arch.

"For disappearing," Andrew added, "after I kissed you."

"You mean during," Caius corrected. "I graciously accepted your kiss, and you vanished in the middle of it."

"I know. My roommate woke me up."

"I take it you're in one of those shared dorm rooms?"

For someone stuck in the past, Caius knew a lot about the present. "Yeah. My roommate and I have been best friends since we were kids."

"Hmmm..." Andrew squirmed beneath Caius's gaze. "Would this also be the person you're in love with?"

"Wha—?" Andrew spluttered. "What are you talking about?"

"It's written all over your face, my dear," Caius said. "The man must be *blind* not to see it."

"He doesn't— He's not gay," Andrew protested.

"What does that have to do with your feelings?" Caius asked. "Though I must say, I am rather surprised to find that you're taken when you were so prettily spouting words of courtship only hours ago."

"What? I— It's not like that."

"Not like what?"

"I wasn't trying to lead you on," Andrew said. "I—"

"You just wanted my kiss," Caius interrupted. "For all that you've been offered here so far, it's a wonder you protested anything. Or do you prefer winning what you take by your own merits? Is manipulation more exciting than gifts?"

"No, I'm not trying to manipulate—"

Caius's eyes narrowed, and Andrew's words caught in his throat. The world around them darkened, and the noise of the gathering became muted. Caius's voice was perfectly clear in contrast.

"I will not be played the fool by you, little boy," Caius said coldly. His words cut through Andrew, making him shiver. "Go play with your roommate and your little college escapades. You will not be welcome here again."

Andrew felt pressure against his chest. It pushed against him, and he slipped off the stool. He didn't hit the floor as expected. Instead, he kept falling. The unending sensation made his heart hammer as if he were plummeting from a great height. He never felt himself land before his mind fell to darkness.

FOUR

—◆•◆—

Andrew woke with a start, his arms flung out as if to break his fall, but he wasn't falling. He was safely on his mattress, although his racing heart clearly thought otherwise. He lay staring up at the ceiling until the organ slowed to its normal pace. What had just happened? Obviously, he'd had another dream of Ghost House, but something about this one felt different. Caius had been angry with him, and he wasn't sure why. As he remembered the dream, indignation filled his chest. What right did Caius have to be angry with him for having a crush? Jason was his best friend. Caius was a figment of his imagination. There was no contest.

Yet there was something about the dream that nagged at him. As he'd fallen from the stool, he'd had one last glimpse of Caius's face before blackness took him. What he'd seen in Caius's expression hadn't been anger. It had been pain.

What did that mean?

Andrew forced himself to push the thoughts away. There was no use analyzing. At least if what Caius had said was true, he wouldn't have to worry about dreaming about

Ghost House again. Hopefully any possibility of his going crazy was now over and done with. As for the getting laid theory... that had been dumb. He didn't need his subconscious to tell him he was overdue for sex. He knew that all on his own.

Unless Jason was right and what he really wanted was a boyfriend. It wasn't like he could easily find a date when he was always hanging out with friends and hiding that he was gay. The only place he was free to date was in a dream. If that were true, what did getting rejected by a dream mean? Even a figment of his imagination thought he'd make a shitty boyfriend.

He sighed, rubbing a hand over his face. Dreams didn't change reality. He'd just have to hope they were gone for good and get on with his life. Though getting laid wouldn't hurt. He'd have to figure out a way to work on that. In the meantime, he had to get up for class. He pushed the tangled sheets from his legs and got out of bed. He'd feel better once he splashed some water on his face. Soon he'd forget all about Caius and the dreams, and life would go back to normal.

He was right. As the week passed, he didn't have time to think about dreams he was no longer having. He was too busy worrying about things that were real. His dad had left a voicemail the day he'd called, and Andrew had yet to listen to it, let alone return it.

He was also stressing about the final project for his operations management class. He had to select a running business, research changes that had been made over the course of the company's life, and study the effects those changes had had on the business. Then he had to devise his own management plan and explain what he would keep from the current business model, what changes he'd make and why. Andrew was supposed to write a proposal stating what business he'd decided to use and his plan of study, but he hadn't decided what to do yet. He knew he could easily use his father's company as his topic, but he wanted to do something he'd be interested in. The problem was, he didn't know what that was, and he was running out of time to figure it out.

"You look like you're carrying the weight of the world. What's wrong?" Jason asked him one night while they were getting ready for dinner. Instead of answering, Andrew picked up his phone and thumbed to the missed call list. He showed the list to Jason. It didn't take his friend long to find the number he was looking for.

"You haven't called him back? It's been *days,* Andrew. He's probably fuming by now."

"And another few days won't make it any worse. He can only kill me once, and he can't do that through the phone."

"You're going to give him a coronary, you know that, right? Worse yet, think about what you're doing to your poor mother. She's the one who has to live with him while he's angry with you."

Ouch. That one hurt as Jason knew it would. Andrew loved both his parents, but he was much closer to his mother. She was a kind woman who loved gardening and always had something delicious cooking on the stove when he came home. He hated the thought of his father's temper causing her trouble because of him. Not that his mother couldn't handle it. When she was fired up on a topic, nothing could stand in her way.

"Call him," Jason said.

"I will."

"When?"

"Can we talk about this after dinner?" Andrew asked, hoping the mention of food would save him. It did, but the look Jason shot him meant the conversation was far from over. For a moment, Andrew wondered if he'd picked up that expression from his mother. Jason had spent many evenings at the Hollenbeck house for dinner and sleepovers. Andrew's mother treated Jason like a second son. He'd heard the argument about nature versus nurture. If Andrew needed proof that facial expressions were born from the nurture side of things, that look of Jason's was it.

"I already know what he's going to say. He wants me to get an internship at some corporate office so I'll have worthy experience before I go work for his company."

"And you don't want to, right?"

Andrew nodded.

"So call him back and tell him so."

"It's not that easy and you know it."

"Easy or not, you still need to do it."

"I know." Andrew sighed. "Can we leave it for now? We're supposed to be eating dinner, and I'm hungry."

"You're the one who brought it up."

A gurgling from Jason's stomach interrupted their conversation. They looked at each other and laughed.

"Come on," said Jason. "Let's go eat."

At dinner, Charlie had his own piece of news to share. "Amanda broke up with me."

Andrew and Jason both flinched. "Was it Ghost House that did it?" Andrew asked, trying for gentle but knowing it wouldn't matter either way.

"Ghost House was just an excuse. She's been harping

on me since we started dating, asking me when I'm going to graduate and what I'm going to do for a *real job*." Charlie worked a few nights a week at a bowling alley handing out rental shoes and freeing trapped pins from the machines. It wasn't the classiest of jobs, nor something Andrew could imagine doing for the rest of one's life.

"You have been here for six years," Jason pointed out.

"Not you too." Charlie groaned. "Look, I don't know what I want to do with my life. I'm still figuring it out. Is that such a bad thing?"

"No," Jason admitted, "but you can't take forever to decide. Eventually your parents aren't going to pay for college anymore. What will you do then?"

Charlie seemed to hunch in on himself at the question. For someone who was always bright and boasting, it was a weird thing to see. He looked like one of those insects that curled up when you touched them.

"You could always go for something and change it later if you don't like it," Andrew suggested. "It'll probably give you a better perspective once you're in the job too. You can only learn so much in school."

"Yeah, but where do I start? I have no idea what I want to do for a job."

He was preaching to the choir on that one. Andrew knew the job he'd have after college and was already planning on leaving it, and like Charlie, he didn't know where else to go.

"What do you like to do besides date girls?" Jason asked. Andrew assumed the "date girls" part was to cut off any joke Charlie may have been tempted to make more than an assumption that there was nothing else to his life.

"Go to the gym. Drink beer."

There had to be more to Charlie than that. "Ever

consider becoming a physical therapist? Or a personal train-er?" Andrew suggested.

Charlie shrugged. Now he was just being petulant. Andrew and Jason threw out a few more suggestions, but they knew they were speaking to deaf ears. Charlie would have to get out of his mood before he'd take their advice.

"Am I like Charlie?" Andrew asked as he and Jason walked back to their dorm after dinner.

"What do you mean?"

Andrew felt bad for his friend's breakup, but the part of the conversation that had stuck with him was how lost Charlie had seemed. Andrew felt the same way. "Do you think six years from now I'll still be undecided on what I want to do with my life?"

"Your situation is different than Charlie's."

"Not really. I mean, I can't be taking college classes forever, but if I work for my father's company, I'll still be stuck somewhere trying to figure out what to do with my life and how to do it."

"I thought you weren't going to work for your father's company."

"How can I not if I can't think of something else to do?"

"Then you better think harder." Jason put a hand on his shoulder. "I know you, man. You'll think of something. You're not going to end up like Charlie."

Jason's touch and his words didn't chase Andrew's worries away, but they were more comforting than he wanted to admit. "I feel bad for him," he said.

"Me too."

"What does he see in Amanda anyway?"

"To hear it from him, it's all about the sex."

Andrew stopped walking. "Seriously?"

Jason shrugged. "If it was, I don't think he'd be this upset that she broke up with him."

True. And if she was pushing so hard for him to think about his future, there had to be more to her than just bitchiness and an inability to enjoy the silly things in life. For Charlie's sake, Andrew hoped so.

Andrew had almost escaped the confines of Boyle Hall when he heard his name being called.

"Mr. Hollenbeck!" came the voice again.

With carefully hidden reluctance, he stopped walking and turned to face his professor. "Yes, Mr. Brumbaugh?" he asked, though he knew exactly what this was about.

"I haven't seen your proposal for your final project yet, Mr. Hollenbeck. This is going to count for a good portion of your grade. I expect to have it in hand by the end of the week."

"Yes, Mr. Brumbaugh."

"Do you know what business you are going to focus on?"

Andrew's stomach clenched. He could either admit that he still didn't have any idea what to do his final project on or make the easy choice and go with his father's business. "I had considered doing the report on my father's company. He wants me to work with him after I graduate, and this would help me become familiar with the way the business works before then."

The professor nodded. "Utilizing your course work toward your future goals. That sounds like a very good idea. You should have no problem getting a proposal to that effect to me by Friday."

Andrew felt like prison bars were closing on him the more he thought about it. "Yes, sir," he managed to say.

He spent the next few moments reminding his body how to breathe. When his attention returned to the world outside himself, he realized his professor was still standing there, although now he was staring at the wall beside Andrew.

"Have you ever wondered why a set of Shakespeare plays would be in a building devoted to business classes?" Professor Brumbaugh asked.

Andrew turned to see what he was looking at. There was a glass case mounted on the wall. Inside was a matching set of books. Andrew had seen them in passing every time he'd entered and left the building. He'd always assumed they were on business related topics and never paid them much attention. Now that he looked, he could see the books were definitely not the boring textbooks he'd first imagined. He didn't recognize all of the titles but *Romeo & Juliet* was familiar, as well as *Hamlet* and *Macbeth*. He'd never been a fan of Shakespeare, but he'd seen some of the revamped, modern movies and had read *Romeo & Juliet* in high school for class.

It wasn't until he spotted a book titled *The Taming of the Shrew* that a shiver ran down his spine, and his body broke out in a cold sweat. Suddenly, he recognized the books. They were brown leather with gold lettering and gilded edges. The book Caius had been reading from the second time they met *had been from this set*. As he looked closer at *The Taming of the Shrew,* he could have sworn that had been the very book Caius had been reading.

"Where are these books from?" he asked, his eyes glued to the literature behind the glass.

His professor shrugged. "I don't know. Donation, I suppose. Have a good day, Mr. Hollenbeck."

Andrew paid no attention as his teacher left. He was too busy trying to wrap his head around the fact that a bunch of books he'd never noticed before had been in a random dream he'd had. What did that mean?

"There you are!" Jason's voice cut across his thoughts, startling him. How long had he been standing there like an idiot? "I've been looking for you. I got out early today and thought we could do a smoothie run."

Andrew didn't need anything cold at the moment. He wanted a warm blanket and reassurance that he wasn't losing his mind. "Hey, Jase, have you ever had a dream that included something you'd never seen before, but you later found out it was real?"

Jason eyed him as if he was wondering if aliens had taken over Andrew's body. "What?"

"Someone was reading a book in a dream I had." He gestured toward the case. "And it was one of these books."

"So? You pass this thing every day, man. It's not like you've never seen them before."

"Yeah, but I'd never looked at them before. Up until today, I had no idea they were a bunch of plays by a dead guy instead of a bunch of dusty tombs from some live guys with no life in them."

Jason laughed. "Supposedly the subconscious notices more than we do. That's why it's in charge of ordering your thoughts while you sleep. I'm telling you, man, you've seen these books every day, you just didn't notice them consciously. It's not that big a deal."

Jason was probably right. "I suppose. It was just surprising."

"This have something to do with Ghost House?"

Andrew looked at him in alarm. "What makes you say that?" he asked, his voice not as casual as he'd have liked.

"You mentioned that dream you had when we were there and that it freaked you out. Figured this would be part of that."

"Oh," Andrew said with an uneasy laugh. "Yeah. Every time I think I'm over it, something weird reminds me about it."

"That sucks, dude. So, smoothie run?"

Andrew nodded. "Smoothie run."

FIVE

— ◆•◆ —

Jason may have reassured him that the books being in his dream were perfectly normal, but Andrew couldn't get his dreams with Caius off his mind. Passing those books every day on his way to and from class didn't help. He was still busy, but in the quiet moments, especially when he lay in bed at night before he fell asleep, he'd remember the last time he'd seen Caius and that pained expression on his face. Had he really seen it? If so, what had it meant? And why was he so worried about someone that didn't even exist?

Andrew knew why. Caius may not have been real, but he had enjoyed their brief time together. He had liked being attracted to someone who actually liked him back, and that kiss they had shared... He could still remember the feel of Caius's lips and the taste of his mouth. Even more than the kiss, he missed being honest with Caius. Hell, Caius had seemed to know all of his secrets without being told what they were. Andrew hadn't realized how much he'd appreciated that or how much easier it had been to be with someone he wasn't hiding from.

He shook himself from his musing. Thoughts like this were going to land him in the loony bin. He needed to find someone new, someone who was attracted to men and lived in the real world. There had to be a gay bar or club somewhere around campus or in a nearby city. He preferred the latter. The last thing he wanted was for Jason or Charlie to find out about him visiting a gay club. He wasn't ready for that conversation yet.

One night when Jason was out on a date with Marie, Andrew sat on his bed, stretching his legs out in front of him and pulled his laptop onto his lap. He fired up a browser but hesitated before entering his search. Instead of "gay clubs," he found himself typing "ghost house" into the search bar. The results yielded a bunch of articles about the local legend. Most of them seemed to deal with rumors and ghost stories. He even found the article that had probably inspired Charlie to suggest they all sleep there, but he wanted factual information. Calling himself all sorts of crazy, he kept digging.

From what he could glean, Ghost House was really called The Cut Sleeve. It had opened in 1882 on the cusp of an economic recession and managed to stay open even after brothel prostitution had been outlawed in the United States in 1949. It closed unexpectedly in 1955. Andrew thought it would have been difficult for a gay establishment to go unnoticed during that time period, but none of the articles said anything about the patrons being gay. Perhaps Caius had been teasing him when he'd alluded to that detail.

And there he went thinking of Caius as a real person again. Fuck.

Andrew searched for a little longer but couldn't find anything more. There were no details about the owner of the bordello, nor were there pictures except for some of the building's exterior. He didn't believe that his dreams had been filled with facts, but the articles didn't help to prove or disprove anything from them. One thing he did find strange was an aerial view of the building he found on Google. Even from the top, it looked like a box, yet when they had been inside it, the top floor had felt shorter. Could it have been his imagination or was part of that hallway blocked off? If so, why?

He shook himself from his musings. He could not keep letting himself get hung up on a dream that happened almost two weeks ago. Nor was he going to start acting like the main character in an amateur detective novel.

His thoughts were interrupted by a text message alert on his phone. Glancing down, he saw Jason's number on the screen. *Be prepared. Charlie is on a mission. He's rounding us up for Karaoke at the Keg.*

Double fuck. This was even worse than losing his mind.

Like a harbinger of doom, there was a knock on the door. Andrew braced himself before answering. Charlie stood in the hallway, grinning like he had the night he'd suggested they sleep at Ghost House.

"I heard you want to sing karaoke," Andrew said.

"Yeah! We haven't gone since that time last year."

"That's because they almost kicked you out."

"What are you talking about? We didn't cause any trouble that night."

That was true, but what Charlie didn't realize was that he sounded like a bag of cats screaming whenever he sang. The bar patrons hadn't appreciated the sound, and it didn't bode well for a welcoming return.

"Whatever, man," Andrew said. "I could use a beer."

"That's the spirit." Charlie slapped him on the back. "Jason and Marie are going to meet us there."

"What brought this stroke of inspiration on?" Andrew asked as they made their way toward the parking lot and Charlie's car.

"I'm free, man. Free as a bird, and I'm ready to party."

Andrew assumed this meant Charlie was over his breakup with Amanda. He was surprised at the quick turn-around. Charlie had been so down after it had happened, he hadn't thought he would recover so quickly. "That's great, man," he said.

"Yeah. Tonight's going to be a blast!"

It wasn't. The singing was as bad as Andrew had antici-pated, but thankfully, most comments were kept away from Charlie's ears. It also helped that Jason had a good singing voice and Marie looked cute when she sang a duet with him. Andrew gave her points for bravery, since he could tell she was embarrassed when she was on stage. The crowd cheered Jason and Marie on though. They'd even given a nice round of applause the few times Andrew had been brave enough to take the mic. The alcohol helped too.

The worst part of the evening was Charlie's choice of songs. Every one was about heartbreak and being left by his lover or something along those lines. It was clear he wasn't over Amanda like he pretended to be. Andrew felt bad for him, especially if his pain was enough that he was willing to sing—badly—about it in public.

Andrew, on the other hand, was happy to get out of the dorm. Now that he was doing something, his mind had cleared of freaky dreams. He was even amused when Charlie tried to hook him up with a pretty blond that he'd sworn was checking Andrew out from across the room. This was how things were supposed to be. Time with friends, and no more weird dreams.

It wasn't until someone got up to sing "Save Me" by Remy Zero that the evening dimmed for him. The pleas of the chorus brought back to mind that last image of Caius, and no matter what he did he couldn't shake it.

That was how he ended up stumbling along with Charlie at three o'clock in the morning, drunk off his ass. Thankfully, Jason had been much more lenient with his use of alcohol and drove them all back to campus safely, dropping Marie at her dorm before herding Andrew and Charlie toward theirs.

"Are you sure you want to go back to your room?" Jason asked Charlie. "Your roommate will kill you if you get in at this hour and start banging into things."

"And where'm I s'posed to sleep?" Charlie slurred. "Your floor?"

"We have a sleeping bag," Andrew offered. He didn't remember where they had put it but was pretty sure they had one.

Charlie was quiet for a few moments. Whether he was considering the offer or his thought process had shut down completely, Andrew couldn't tell. Finally, he said, "A'ight," and they altered course to Andrew and Jason's room.

It was a bit of a circus as they arranged the sleeping bag and sorted themselves for the night, but by four in the morning, they were dead to the world.

The next morning when Andrew's alarm went off, he regretted two things. First was the alcohol and the pounding headache that had resulted from it. His mouth tasted like dried mud, and sunlight was now his sworn enemy. So was noise, which brought him to the second thing he regretted: forgetting how badly Charlie snored when drunk. His friend only snored after a serious drinking binge—which last night definitely counted as—but when he did, he could wake the dead.

Resisting the temptation to smother Charlie with a pillow, Andrew popped two pills for the headache and brushed his teeth until all he tasted was minty freshness. Then he hunted for a pair of sunglasses and zombie-shuffled his way to class.

He had managed to tame the hangover by the time he had to get ready for practice. Lunch had helped, as had lots of water.

"How are you feeling?" Jason asked when he entered their room.

"I feel like I've been hit by a Mack truck."

"We should convince Charlie that bar nights shouldn't be before Friday. It would save us from karaoke night."

Andrew nodded and then regretted the action. His headache was mostly gone, but he was afraid it was only waiting to reassert itself with a vengeance at the slightest sign of weakness.

"What made you drink so much last night anyway? That isn't like you."

Before Andrew could answer, his cell phone rang. "Oh fuck." He squeezed his eyes shut as if that would make his father's number disappear from the screen, but it was still there when he opened them again. Could this have come at a worse time? As he answered, Jason motioned to him that they needed to catch the shuttle. Andrew waved him on. There was no way he was going to make practice now. Even if the conversation didn't take an hour, he could already feel his headache preparing for its revenge attack.

"Hello?"

"Why haven't you called me? I left a message for you two weeks ago."

"Sorry, Dad. I've been busy."

"If this is how you treat family, I shudder to think how you'll respond to work calls. Have you been looking into internships?"

Andrew considered lying, but he didn't have the energy to do so. "Not yet."

"I thought so. That's why I've prepared a list of options for you. I've emailed them to your school address. Look them over and decide which you'd like to apply for. You need to do this soon. Internships like these will vanish instantly, and you *do not* want to be stuck scraping the bottom of the barrel."

"Yes, Dad. I'll look them over this weekend." He had no idea when. He was dreading the internships almost as much as he was dreading working for his father.

"How is your schoolwork going? That hockey club of yours isn't conflicting with your studies, is it?"

Andrew refrained from mentioning how he was supposed to be heading to practice right then. "It's not conflicting. Practice and games are set every week so I have plenty of time around that and my classes to study. In fact," he added, hoping the news of his final project would be a breadcrumb to keep any more of his father's questions at bay, "I have a project this semester for my operations management class where I need to devise a business management plan. I thought I would do the report on your company." Now that he'd told his dad, there was no way he was going to be able to change the topic. Not that it mattered. He'd already handed in the proposal.

"That's a wonderful idea. It will give you ample opportunity to familiarize yourself with the company while still doing schoolwork. You'll have to drop by the office. You can't see how a business works without visiting it. I won't be able to give you a tour, but I can arrange for one of our interns to do it. I'll have one of them call you, so you can set up a time."

"Sounds great, Dad." No, it didn't. It felt like he'd swallowed a stone which had permanently lodged itself in the middle of his chest.

"Wonderful. Oh, and your mother wanted me to tell you that she misses you, and she wants to know when you're going to visit."

"Tell her I miss her too, and I'll come up for dinner soon."

"Try to give her a date sooner rather than later," his father advised. "You know she likes to have time to plan."

"Yes, Dad."

"Very good. Don't forget to look over that list of internship possibilities, and I'll have one of my interns call you tomorrow."

"OK."

"Have a good day, Andrew."

"You too, Dad."

His father hung up. Andrew took a deep breath and let it out slowly. That lump in his chest had loosened but hadn't gone away completely. He felt like invisible walls were closing in on him. He opened a window, suddenly finding it hard to breathe in the stuffy dorm room. A *ding* on his computer alerted him the email from his father had arrived. He shut the laptop, not wanting to look at it. He decided to go for a walk. Fresh air and exercise would help to clear his head. Yeah, it was to clear his head. He wasn't running away from anything, really.

He walked a lot farther than he'd originally anticipated and found himself standing in front of Ghost House. It loomed over him like it had the night he'd slept there. It was as if the house had adopted Caius's glare and was saying "go away." That was okay. He didn't plan on sneaking inside. He wasn't sure why he was even there, but since he was, he figured he'd indulge his curiosity. Taking the same route they had the other night, he made his way to the back of the house. Keeping to the far end of the property, he looked up. Just like the image from the internet, the house was square in the back.

So how was it shorter on the third floor? There had only been two rooms up there, and both had been similar in size to the rooms below. It wasn't possible for the house to be square on the outside without having more rooms on the inside, so where was the extra space?

And why was this bothering him so much?

"You're not freaking Sherlock Holmes," he muttered to himself. That was true. Sherlock would have figured out the mystery already. Or he would have stormed straight into the house to investigate if he needed more clues. Andrew wasn't going to do that. Breaking and entering into a haunted house was all well and good when he was with friends. Alone, the idea was intimidating.

With the thoughts still nagging at him, he left Ghost House and headed back to campus.

"Where have you been? Practice was over an hour ago."

"How was practice?"

"How did things go with your dad?"

OK, if they were going to have a question battle, that one definitely won. "Better than I expected," Andrew admitted. "I told him about that final project I have, and he sounded interested in it. I think that staved off the worst of his wrath."

"That's good. So when are you going to tell him that you don't want to take over his business?"

Andrew pursed his lips, attempting to look thoughtful. "When I'm dead?"

Jason smirked. "And deprive him of the pleasure of killing you?"

"*Exactly.*"

"You're going to have to do it someday, you know. Unless you really don't mind being miserable for the rest of your life."

Andrew collapsed onto his bed with a sigh. "I know. I just...don't know how to tell him."

"Words are a good start."

Andrew glared at Jason. "Thanks, Captain Obvious. I meant which words. I can't think of any way to tell him that he'll actually listen to me. He thinks I'm lazy and that I procrastinate. He thinks I have no motivation to do anything about my future. He even sent me a list of internships that I'm supposed to apply for. He couldn't wait for me to look anything up on my own. Waiting two seconds is too long for him. I'm supposed to be constantly working for my future. For the best future possible for me. It makes me tired just thinking about it."

"Are you thinking about your future at all?" Jason asked.

"Kind of. I'm too busy being inundated by what I don't want to do that I haven't found what I do want to do."

"That is difficult."

"That's the part I hate the most. I could probably figure out what I want to do if I was given half a chance, but I don't think I can get him to give me that chance unless I prove to him that I've already figured it all out and have a plan like he'd want me to."

"You don't think just being honest with him would help? I don't mean dump your frustrations on him but put them forward like legitimate, reasonable concerns. Maybe then he'll listen."

"Maybe. I'm too worn out from that phone call to think about it right now. Maybe I'll try talking to him when I visit."

"You're going up to see them?"

"Mom misses me and wants me to. Not sure when yet, but I'll also need to drop by to take a tour of Dad's company. Want to come with?"

"For dinner, yes. For the tour, no."

"Spoilsport."

"My friend duties only go so far, dude. Even between best friends, there are limits."

"Asshole," Andrew said, but he was smiling.

"Hey, you never answered my question from before. Why did you get so drunk last night?"

That killed Andrew's amusement. He knew Jason had been teasing about the limits on their friendship, but when it came to ghosts and imaginary men, he wasn't sure that line didn't exist. How much could he tell Jason? And the more he thought about it, he realized he wanted to tell Jason.

"I..." Andrew began. "I sort of met someone."

Jason's eyes widened. "Seriously? Why didn't you tell

me? Who is she? What's she like? Where did you meet her? Is she in one of your classes?"

Jason's barrage of questions made Andrew feel so much better. Though there were details about Caius he wasn't ready or able to share, it felt good to talk about him. "Slow down," he said with a laugh. "Can we take one question at a time, please?"

"This is the first time I've heard you talk about a girl. I can't help getting excited."

The sentiment warmed Andrew even as it stabbed through his heart. He'd never spoken about girls because he didn't like them like that. He still wasn't talking about a girl.

"So what's she like?" Jason asked.

How to describe Caius? Flirty? Mysterious? Annoying? Hot? It was hard to find the right adjectives for him. "Mischievous," he said.

"That's an unusual way to describe someone."

"It's the best word I can come up with."

"Is she pretty?"

Andrew nodded. "Classically, like an old-fashioned movie star."

"Where did you two meet?"

In a dream? "Around town. It was...unexpected. We ended up drinking tea and talking." That was partially true, at least.

"Tea?"

"Weird, right? It was good tea though. Cinnamon."

"I've never seen you drink tea in your life."

"Sometimes," Andrew protested. "At home with Mom."

"That doesn't count. That's on holidays when they're serving dessert and she's on a 'no coffee' kick."

"Don't tell her," Andrew said, "but the cinnamon tea

was better than any she's ever served. I might drink it more often if she served that one."

"Your mother would be crushed if she knew."

"That's why I said not to tell her."

"So why haven't I met this mischievous woman yet?"

How to answer that? Luckily, the truth worked in Andrew's favor. "We had a fight."

"You've known this girl long enough to have a fight with her and this is the first time I'm hearing about her?" Jason asked incredulously. Thankfully, he didn't launch into a lecture on what it meant to be a best friend, though Andrew could tell it was on the tip of his tongue. "What was the fight about?" he asked instead.

"I'm not sure exactly," Andrew admitted.

Jason laughed. "Women are like that sometimes. Give her time to cool off and then ask her how you can make it up to her. Even if you don't think it's your fault, it probably is."

"I don't think it's like that," Andrew said. For one thing, Caius was not a woman. For another, he wasn't even real. "I'm being given the silent treatment," he said. "Hardcore. I can't even get close enough to apologize."

Jason frowned.

Andrew loved how the corner of his mouth creased when he did that. Then he remembered Caius's accusations. "Does Marie ever get jealous?"

"What do you mean?"

"If you talk to another girl, does she get jealous?" Andrew clarified.

"Not really," Jason said. "Though it depends on how close I am to the girl. I mean, if someone you liked was close to another person, anyone would get jealous, wouldn't they?"

Andrew bit his lip. Perhaps that's what had set Caius

off, but it wasn't fair. He and Jason had known each other since they were kids. They were bound to be close. He wouldn't give his best friend up for a kiss, even if the person he'd kissed had been real.

"So she got jealous of another girl?"

"Not exactly..." How had Caius known about Jason anyway? Could he have seen something the night they'd all slept at Ghost House? That was impossible, though. No one had been there but them. And, he reminded himself for the thousandth time, Caius wasn't real. "It doesn't matter. We're not talking anymore."

"Are you so sure about that?" Jason asked. "You've seemed lost in the clouds lately. If you've been thinking of this girl that much, I don't think it's as over as you think."

"It's not my decision to make."

"I can't imagine a girl who can make this sort of impression would drop you that quickly. Go talk to her, man. Bang down her door if you have to."

"I can't."

"Why not? Her father has a shotgun and doesn't approve of you?"

Andrew laughed. "No," he said. "I don't have a door to knock on."

"You don't know where she lives?"

"I—"

He did know where Caius lived. Sort of. Still, it was where he used to live, and every time they'd been together it had been at Ghost House. Everything had started the night Andrew had slept there. Maybe he could find a way to talk to Caius again if he went there. He really hoped it wouldn't require sleeping alone in the house, but he'd give another visit a shot. The house had given him the feeling of Caius glaring at him earlier. Maybe the idea wasn't as far-fetched as he imagined.

"Thanks," he said to Jason as he grabbed his keys and jacket.

"I didn't mean right this second!"

"No time like the present," Andrew said. He wanted to go before he lost his nerve.

He lost it halfway to Ghost House.

What the hell am I doing? This is stupid. This is insane. He knew he wasn't going to find Caius. If he did, that would be even worse than the dreams. Then he'd be hallucinating. But Jason had been right. He had been thinking of Caius lately. He thought about him every time he walked through Boyle Hall. He thought about him even when he didn't have the freaky Shakespeare books as a reminder. The more he thought, the more he remembered little details, like Caius's knowing smile, his sparkling green eyes, and that look of pain the last time Andrew had seen him. No matter what he thought, his mind always returned to that moment, wondering if he'd seen it and what it meant. He wanted to see Caius again. Even if this trip ended up proving that Ghost House was filled with nothing but old furniture and dust, it was better than doing nothing at all.

Ghost House looked as abandoned as ever. Andrew stood on the curb and looked up at the three-story building. "There's nothing in there. This is ridiculous." And now he was talking to himself. That did not bode well. The boarded-up windows looked like eyes gazing down on him, but unlike the last time he'd been there, they felt empty. He hesitated. In the past, he'd felt unwelcome or watched when he'd been there. Now it was like the soul had been ripped from the place. Somehow that was even more frightening.

He found he could not move either toward the house or away. He was frozen.

A loud crash followed by the yelp of a cat startled him into movement. He quickly circumnavigated the yard until he was safely out of sight behind the building. From the back, the house was less imposing, and he climbed through the now familiar window. Inside, the bar was dark and silent. He cursed himself for forgetting to bring a flashlight. How was he going to see anything without one?

He carefully picked his way through the tables and past the curtain into the parlor. Enough light from the street lamp outside filtered through the cracks in the boards, letting him vaguely see the shapes of the furniture. He could just make out Caius's couch, the one he'd been sitting on when Andrew had visited him during the day. It was one of the few pieces of furniture that was the same in the dream as in reality. It was too dark to see if anyone was on it.

"Caius?" he called out. Carefully, he picked his way through the furniture toward the sofa. A deeper shadow made his heart skip a beat. There was someone—or something—on the couch. "Caius?" he repeated, his voice coming out as a whisper, as if afraid to be heard. His palms were sweating, and his heart raced. He knew it wasn't Caius on the couch, but if it wasn't him, who was it?

Maybe someone else was here. Maybe another bunch of kids had come from campus to try their luck at sleeping at Ghost House. Charlie had said many students did, and there was that website he'd found. This could be someone from school.

The chills running through his body said otherwise.

He couldn't make out any features, but someone *was* there. Andrew tried to call again, but his voice caught in his throat and refused to go any further. So did his feet. They were glued to the floorboards, nothing could will them any closer.

"H-hello?" he managed at last.

"And here I thought we were rid of you." The voice was raspy and definitely not Caius's. The cold sweat that had begun on Andrew's palms now covered his entire body. He shivered.

He didn't want to ask, but he had to. "Who...who are you?"

The figure on the couch shifted, and a beam of light fell across it. Andrew had never seen a face so angular, as if someone had grabbed hold of the chin and pulled until it had stretched long and thin like a stiletto. Andrew thought he saw the hint of scales on skin. He would have chalked the image up to his imagination, but this time he wasn't in a dream. He bolted for the bar, tripping over tables and chairs on the way. He scrambled to the window and fell through it, crashing to the ground and cutting his hand open on a rough piece of brick. Terror had him on his feet in an instant and vaulting the back fence. As he sprinted toward campus, he could have sworn he heard laughter echoing from the house behind him. It followed him for much longer than he thought possible.

SIX

—◆•◆—

Andrew's hands shook so badly when he finally made it back to his dorm it took him three tries to shove his key into the lock. Finally, the door opened, and he rushed inside, remembering at the last moment not to slam it behind him. Thankfully, Jason was sound asleep and wouldn't see him acting like an idiot in the middle of the night. Though the sound of the laughter no longer echoed in his ears, the remnants of his terror had not vanished completely. After cleaning and bandaging his hand, he slid into bed, but it was a long time before he felt safe closing his eyes. The sound of Jason's breathing on the other side of the room wasn't as reassuring as it should have been.

He must have dozed off at some point, because the next thing he knew, Jason was shaking him awake. "Wh-what?" He struggled to open his eyes, sleep threatening to take him back under at any moment.

"Why is there blood all over our door?"

"What?"

"Why is there blood all over our door?" Jason repeated, emphasizing each word.

"Oh." Andrew tried to process the question so he could give an answer. "I fell. Cut my hand." He tried to show Jason the bandage, but his arm felt like it was weighed down with bricks. "'m fine," he mumbled. "Tired."

He didn't hear Jason's response before sleep took him under again. The next time he opened his eyes, he was in Ghost House. Caius was sitting at his usual couch with a teacup in one hand and another of those Shakespeare books on the table. Andrew's chest tightened with a mix of excitement and apprehension at the sight of him. He hadn't realized just how much he'd missed Caius until that moment. A part of him hoped Caius would be as glad to see him as Andrew was.

"Before you, no one ever visited me during the day," Caius said. "You have done it twice now. Are you planning on making it a habit?"

Andrew was too relieved to see Caius to banter. "I'm sorry," he said. "I didn't mean to make you feel like I was trying to manipulate you. I like you, I really do, but you're right. I do have a thing for Jason. I've liked him for years. Nothing has ever happened between us and nothing ever will, but he is my best friend. I'm not going to do anything to change that, but we are nothing more than that."

Caius slowly set his cup down. The movement was purposeful and stretched the time before his reply. Finally, he looked at Andrew. "I prefer groveling to be done at my feet," he said, "but I suppose I can make an exception just this once."

Andrew felt his whole body unknot in relief. "Thank you."

"So tell me," Caius said, patting the couch beside him. "How miserable have you been while I've been giving you the silent treatment?"

Andrew almost laughed, but that would have ruined the effect of his groveling. "Ugh," he said, attempting to be dramatic, though he was sure he failed at it. "It was terrible. I feel like I haven't had a restful sleep in *days*. All I could do was think of you." He knew his words were cheesy, but Caius smiled, pleased with the flattery.

"How have things been here?" Andrew asked. It felt weird to make small talk about a business when it wasn't actually running, but he supposed the rules in dreams were different. Besides, he'd just apologized to a figment of his imagination. His definition of normal was in need of an update.

"Oh, the same old," Caius said with a wave of his hand. "There is never a shortage of people looking for an hour's worth of pleasure."

That made Andrew wonder once again if someone else had stayed in Ghost House since he had. He tried to be casual as he asked, "Oh? Meet anyone new?"

Caius gave him a look that made it clear he knew Andrew's ulterior motives. "If you're wondering if other students have been bold enough to take the challenge of sleeping here, then no. It's getting too cold out to camp in an empty house. They tend to appear in spring and summer. As for anyone else... I haven't noticed anyone of interest."

Andrew couldn't help smiling.

"Would you care for some tea?"

"Yes, please."

Caius fetched another cup from a nearby shelf and poured. While he served, Andrew studied the book on the table. It was definitely Shakespeare. A book of sonnets this time. "I saw these books in one of the buildings on campus," he said. "They have the whole set displayed in glass."

"Someone must have stolen them," Caius said. Andrew

was surprised he didn't deny the books were his or insist on the dream being real. He spoke of reality so casually and of the dream just as nonchalantly. The rules were definitely different here.

"Supposedly the books were donated," Andrew informed him. "At least they weren't sold for a profit."

"They were mine," Caius said. "It's still theft. Cream? Sugar?"

"No, thank you. Everyone thinks you're dead, or long gone at least."

"The building should still be in my name," Caius informed him as he handed over a cup and saucer. He didn't skimp on fancy China at tea time. "Therefore, I own it and everything in it."

Andrew wondered if that were true. Was there a way he could find out?

He flinched as he took the cup, and Caius noticed. "What happened to your hand?"

Andrew glanced down and saw the bandages he'd hurriedly wrapped around his hand when he'd come home. They were rumpled by sleep, and he was surprised to see them in the dream.

"I cut my hand last night," he explained. Suddenly, the memory of the night before came rushing back to him. "I...I was at Ghost House. I saw someone there."

"A student?"

"No. I don't know who it was." Or what it was.

"What were you doing there?"

Andrew shrugged, trying to shake off the memories of fear. "I'd been thinking of you. Next thing I knew, I was standing in front of the house."

"You know that's not where you'll find me."

"It's not like I was finding you here. You'd sent me away."

"With good reason."

"You didn't sense me when I was there?"

"Should I have?"

Andrew felt embarrassed. That had been a stupid thing to ask. Just because his dreams of Caius were at Ghost House didn't mean Caius was there in real life. Caius wasn't real, but for some reason, he kept having to remind himself of that. He kept wanting to ask questions as if Caius could really answer them.

"So what convinced you to let me back in?"

"Your begging. You wanted to see me, and so here I am."

Ah, yes. If his subconscious was really telling this story, it would be that easy to get what he wanted. For some reason, that thought made him sad. He didn't like being reminded that Caius was only a figment of his imagination. He decided to change the subject.

"I googled this place recently," he said. "The sites I found didn't have too much to say except that it was one of the longest-running brothels in the United States before it closed."

"Checking up on me, were you?" Caius asked.

There wasn't any warning in Caius's voice, but Andrew wondered if he should be cautious with this topic of conversation. "I was just curious," he said. "There are plenty of rumors as to why the building closed down, but nothing much to say about it when it was running. And no one knows the true story."

"You think I'm going to tell you if you ask politely? You'll have to work harder than that."

Andrew was curious, but he didn't want to think about

reality any more today. "What would I have to do to convince you?" he asked, teasingly.

"Oh no," Caius scolded. "I am not so easily seduced. You will have to sit here and have tea with me like a proper gentleman today."

That was disappointing. Andrew faked shock, going so far as to put a hand to his chest. "How dare you assume I would immediately resort to seduction," he exclaimed. "Do you think so little of me?"

Caius laughed, a bright ringing sound that lit up the room. "My apologies. I am a bit rusty when it comes to having gentleman callers."

Andrew didn't think Caius made apologies very often, even when they were for innocuous things. "I suppose you can be forgiven," he said, "but in exchange, you have to tell me something about yourself."

"Like what?"

"Why did you open a bordello?"

Caius settled into the couch cushions, his teasing countenance vanishing for a more serious expression. Andrew held his breath, realizing Caius was going to give him a rare gift: a piece of his past. "We were entering an age of depression," he said. "Not the Great Depression, of course, but economic downturns are bad enough when you're in them. Some things never go out of style no matter how bad things get. In fact, those are the things that become more popular when desperation runs rampant."

"So you did it for the money?"

"Partially."

Andrew waited to see if Caius would elaborate.

There was a long pause and a sigh before he continued. "I used to be a romantic," Caius admitted. "I still am, I suppose. I love watching people come together with that look in their eyes. It's like the only person they can see is their lover, and they make each other so happy."

"I don't think that's the type of thing you find in a place like this," Andrew said.

"No," Caius agreed. "It's not the type of thing you find often at all."

Andrew wondered how the two points connected. "Have you ever been in love?"

"Oh *yes*," Caius said, "a few times."

Andrew hadn't. "What was it like?"

"It never seemed to work out for me. My first love, for example, was *deliciously* handsome, big in every way you could imagine and an absolute sweetheart. I thought we would always be together." He sighed. "Unfortunately, he turned out to be the political type. He decided to marry a pretty little thing that would bear him beautiful children—a duty I was unable to perform—and broke up with me. I must admit, I didn't take it at all well. I turned him into a beast and ran away. Never saw him again."

Caius had to be kidding about that last part. "What are you," Andrew asked with a laugh, "a witch?"

"Sorcerer, my dear," Caius replied. "There's a difference."

Andrew gaped at him. "You're serious."

"Of course. I would have thought it was obvious after I healed your burn the other day."

"Yeah, but, I thought that was...I don't know. Part of the dream."

"In a way, it was. My powers aren't as effective in dreams."

"But you're telling me that you're a witch? Like, for real? You not only ran a brothel, but you can also do magic?"

"Sorcerer, darling. Let's keep the titles in their proper place. And yes, that is what I'm telling you."

"But..." Andrew began, "no one does magic. I mean, there are Wiccans and other people who believe in it, but that's not the same. You're talking about fairy tale, Harry Potter type stuff here."

"Harry Po— Oh. That. Yes, someone mentioned that one to me."

"And you're like that?"

"If I have to repeat myself one more time, I am going to send you away and no amount of groveling will get you back in here, so shut up and listen. For the third time, I am a sorcerer, not a witch. I didn't have to learn anything or go to some school hidden in the clouds like your Harry Potter. I was born this way. I will something and it happens, and if you don't stop asking inane questions, I'm going to will you onto your school football field in nothing but your underwear during a big game."

Andrew ignored the threat and interrupted whatever else Caius might have said by asking, "What else can you do?"

Caius looked taken aback by his interest. "You're not going to doubt me?"

Andrew probably should, but... "We're in a dream," he said. "I'm allowed to believe anything I'd like in a dream. If we ever meet in the real world, you'll have to prove it to me then."

Caius considered this for a moment. Then he nodded. "I can do anything, really. I've used my power for odds and ends, but the real impressive things have always been curses."

"Like your ex," Andrew said.

"Yes, exactly so."

"I guess I should be thankful that you only gave me the silent treatment when you were angry with me."

"You're welcome to kiss my feet in gratitude."

Speaking of kisses... Andrew shifted closer on the couch. "I'd prefer to kiss you elsewhere. We were interrupted last time."

Caius eyed him but didn't move away. "If you vanish on me again, I won't be forgiving," he warned.

"Understood." Caius was cute when he was grumpy.

He began with gentle kisses on Caius's mouth, then trailed them over Caius's jaw and down his neck.

"Oh, that's new," Caius said, his voice breathy. Andrew could tell he liked it. He changed direction, kissing a path up to Caius's ear where he took the soft lobe between his lips and sucked on it. Caius gasped when he scraped his teeth over skin. Andrew spent a few minutes lavishing attention there, savoring each noise he received in return.

When Caius curled his fingers into Andrew's shirt and pulled him closer, Andrew went willingly. He wrapped his arms around Caius, half lifting him into his lap to reach him better. This time when they kissed, it was open mouthed and deep as if they would devour each other. When they finally drew apart, they were both panting.

"I'm still here," Andrew said.

"My wrath is a terrible thing. You are wise not to test it."

They separated so Caius could pour Andrew another cup of tea and refill his own. Andrew searched for something to talk about, but he couldn't think of anything to say. He picked up his cup, stalling for time as he drank. The silence stretched, but he found it comfortable.

"You still didn't explain how you cut your hand," Caius said.

"I fell out the window when I left and landed hard on the brick."

Caius flinched in sympathy. "Do you want me to heal it?"

He'd forgotten Caius could do that. He held his hand out for Caius to take. There was a tingling sensation like the last time, and the ache in his hand vanished.

"That's amazing," he whispered.

Caius gave him a small smile. It was almost bashful. "Will you come back tonight?"

"I'm not sure how much control I have over when I show up," Andrew said, "but I hope so."

Andrew was smiling when he went to dinner that night. He couldn't help it.

"Look who finally got out of bed," Jason teased. "What time did you get home last night?"

Andrew shrugged. "I didn't look at a clock."

"I'm guessing things went well. Your girl forgave you?"

Andrew's grin only widened in answer.

"Girl? What girl?" Charlie asked, coming up behind them, his tray laden with food. "Andrew's got a girlfriend?"

"Supposedly she's mischievous and looks like an old-fashioned movie star, but that's all I know," Jason said. "Maybe you can get more out of him."

Andrew's happiness turned to dread at the impending interrogation. Charlie, only too happy to dig for details, asked, "Have you banged her yet?"

Andrew laughed in relief. If that was the route Charlie was taking, he was probably safe. "No."

"What the hell are you waiting for? Marriage?"

"Not everyone is like you, Charlie," Jason said. "Some

people like to go on a date or two before they run to the bedroom."

Charlie tsked in disgust. "We're in college, the prime of our youth. If we're not having sex, we're wasting our education."

"What does one have to do with the other?" Andrew asked.

Charlie scoffed and rolled his eyes as if that was the dumbest question he'd ever heard. "So who is this girl anyway? I've never seen you talk to anyone long enough to arrange a date."

"We haven't been on a date. We've just...talked."

"Talked?"

"We...kissed," Andrew admitted

"That's more like it!" Charlie said, clapping him on the shoulder. "A little slow for my taste, but it's a foot in the door."

Jason rolled his eyes at Charlie. "I'm glad things are going well for you," he said.

"Thanks." There was that dumb grin again. He couldn't make it go away.

"By the way," Jason continued, "what happened to your hand? You mentioned something about falling?"

Yes, his hand. Under the table, Andrew flexed his fingers. The ache of injury was missing. After waking, he'd taken the bandage off to find the wound completely healed. The sight of his unblemished skin had frightened him almost as much as the monster he'd encountered the night before.

Which made him wonder why he had kept what had happened to him from Caius. It hadn't been a student. Why hadn't he told Caius the truth?

He knew why. Too many things were making him feel

like he was losing his mind lately. Between the dreams, the details of Ghost House, Caius's books, the monster last night, and now the mystery of his healing hand, it was getting to be too much. He knew he'd cut himself. Jason had seen the blood, so that had to have happened. Did that mean the monster had been real as well? What the hell was going on with him?

"Yeah," he said to Jason. "I tripped and cut my hand on some brickwork. Dumb, I know." He held up his hand to stall Jason's inevitable questions. He'd rebandaged it that morning, not wanting to have to explain the inexplicable to his friends. "Don't worry. I cleaned the cut and bandaged it before going to sleep last night."

"Are you sure you don't need stitches?"

"I'll check on it when we get back to the dorm, but I think I'll be okay. No need for your mother hen routine."

"I am *not* a mother hen," Jason said.

"Dude, you totally are," Charlie put in. "Remember when I broke my ankle after falling off your back deck?" he asked Andrew.

Andrew nodded. It had been at his parents' annual summer barbecue. That had been his parents' first impression of Charlie. They hadn't invited him back since.

Charlie turned to Jason. "You gave Andrew's mom a run for her money with all your fussing the following week."

"I— well…"

Andrew laughed, feeling a little better. Jason couldn't protest because he knew it was true, and Andrew's mom was a champion at fussing over her boys.

"Enough about that," Charlie said. "Let's get back to Andrew's girl. You haven't told us anything about her."

"Yeah," Jason agreed. "Mischievous is not a lot to go on."

It wasn't, but how could he describe a man like Caius?

A man who—if he was to be believed—had just revealed to Andrew that he was a witch! Correction: sorcerer. The more Andrew learned about Caius, the more unbelievable he seemed, which should not have been a surprise given he was a dream.

"It's like perpetually being outside when a storm is on the way," he said. "That moment when the wind is rustling, and there's this energy crackling in the air, but it hasn't been let loose yet. You're just anticipating it, and excited, not knowing what's going to happen next, but you know it's going to be thrilling."

"What are you, a poet now?" Charlie asked.

"Would you rather I list off adjectives?"

"Yes."

Andrew ignored him.

"You really like her, don't you?" Jason asked.

"We haven't known each other that long."

"That doesn't matter when you like someone."

What about when the person you liked wasn't real? Did it matter then?

"That must have been some kiss," Jason said.

Andrew remembered the feel of Caius's lips against his. Real or not, he wouldn't have traded it for the world. "Yeah," he said, "it was."

Every night Andrew dreamed of Caius. It began to feel normal to close his eyes in his dorm room and open them in Ghost House. He looked forward to it, and he didn't spend his time solely with Caius. He'd spoken to a bunch of the prostitutes and some of the random guests. Once, he even met a kid he could have sworn was a student on his campus. He did his best to ignore any doubts of what this meant for his sanity. He enjoyed his time with Caius too much to waste time worrying about what it all meant.

He probably would have slept more often, but real life kept him busy. His classes were demanding, and his father's intern had emailed him a list of dates for his tour. Andrew decided it would be best to get it over with, so he agreed to come up the first weekend on the list. It would make his mother happy to see him, and he wouldn't have to worry about his dad harping on him to stop procrastinating. Jason agreed to accompany him. He was glad to have company for the three-hour drive. Jason was also a great buffer to have around his parents.

He wondered if he would still dream of Ghost House when he was farther away. Did distance matter with the dreams? He couldn't imagine not seeing Caius when he went to sleep. Maybe he needed a break from his dreams if he was worried about not seeing his imaginary... He couldn't call Caius his boyfriend. They hung out every time he was there, but it was always in a group setting. Usually, he and Caius mingled with the crowd or played card games in the bar. They didn't get much "alone time" when he visited. He'd been tempted to take a nap or two during the day just so they could be alone, but he hadn't had the time.

By the time his weekend trip to his parents rolled around, he was a mix of anticipation, worry, and dread. Having Jason in the car helped, as did the promise of a home-cooked meal. The best part about going home was his mother's cooking. Andrew's mouth watered every time he thought about it.

Jason's mind must have been following the same train of thought. "What do you think she's making?" he asked when they were about an hour into the trip.

"No idea, but I can't wait."

"Neither can I. Did you tell her I'm coming? She usually makes chocolate cake when she knows I'm coming."

"She could make that for me, you know." He glanced at Jason and saw the pitying look his best friend gave him.

"You keep thinking that, Andrew," Jason said, "but we all know it's me she makes the cake for."

He was probably right. "She makes the lasagna for me."

It didn't matter who the food was for as long as they were in time for dinner. They'd left after their Thursday classes, but it hadn't been early enough to completely miss rush-hour traffic. They were currently in a stop-and-go patch, but no amount of congestion was going to keep Andrew from eating his mother's lasagna. He probably would have visited more often if campus had been closer and he didn't have to worry about the inevitable nagging from his dad every time he showed up.

When they finally made it, the smells of dinner greeted them at the door along with his mom. "Andrew Michael! How dare you keep away from this house for so long! After all the years I spent raising you, you'd think you could spare a little time for your mother," she scolded as she herded them into the house.

"Sorry, Ma. I've been a little busy on the weekends."

"And you, Jason? What's your excuse? You know you're welcome to visit without my son when he's too 'busy.'"

Ouch. Point taken.

Jason smiled. "Semester's been hectic for both of us, Mrs. Hollenbeck. We'll be sure to make a point to drop by more often."

"You better. And what about that girl you were dating? Are you still seeing her?"

"Yes, ma'am."

"Good. Bring her next time too. I liked her. She needs to

learn to speak up, but she's very nice." Her attention focused on Andrew like a laser beam. "And what about you, young man? When are you going to bring home a nice girl for me to meet?"

Hard to bring someone home to meet your mother when he was a figment of your imagination. Andrew wondered what his mother would think of Caius if she met him. She'd freak out about the brothel, but Caius did have a certain charm to him when he decided to employ it. They'd probably get on like a house on fire.

"I know that look," his mother teased, interrupting his thoughts. "Who is she?"

"There is no 'she,' mom."

"Don't lie to me, Andrew. I've known that look since your first heartbreak in eighth grade."

Andrew felt his body break out in a cold sweat. How did she know about that? How much did she know about that?

"She's a mystery to all of us," Jason said. "He hasn't let anyone meet her."

"Even you, Jason?" His mother was wide-eyed.

Jason nodded.

"I'm not sure I like this. It's one thing to keep a girl from your parents until the time is right, but I don't like the idea of someone you can't even introduce to your best friend. Who is this girl, Andrew?"

Fuck. How the hell was he going to get out of this conversation?

Luckily, they heard the front door open. "I got the marshmallows you asked for, Margie, but they were out of heavy cream," Andrew's father called. He entered the kitchen and saw Andrew and Jason.

"Hello, boys. I see you managed to arrive at a decent hour. Traffic wasn't too bad, I take it?"

"We made sure to leave enough time to get here," Andrew said.

His father nodded. "Jason, it's been a while. How are your studies going?"

"Fine, sir."

"Still interested in economics?"

"Yes, sir."

"I look forward to seeing what you do with your degree." Andrew noticed his father wasn't concerned about their hockey club keeping Jason from studying.

"All of you get out of my kitchen and go sit at the table," Mrs. Hollenbeck ordered. "Dinner will be ready in five minutes."

Dinner was a casual affair. For a while, Andrew's mother dominated the table by filling Andrew and Jason in on all of the local gossip. She loved to keep him up to date about people he'd known from high school, whether they had been his friends back then or not. Andrew welcomed the reprieve from her curiosity about Caius, but it didn't last forever. Eventually, the grapevine ran out of fruit to share, and he could see her gearing up for an interrogation. Andrew did the only thing he could think of to avoid the questions. He turned to his father and asked about the following day's tour. His father looked surprised but pleased by his interest, which made Andrew feel guilty about his impure motives.

"We're starting early tomorrow morning. You'll come to the office with me at six, and my assistant, Melody, will give you a tour of the building. Once that is completed, I have arranged for you to meet with Chandra Clarke who you can interview for information on the history of the company as well as our current goals and focus." Andrew was surprised his father wasn't planning to give that information to him himself. As if reading his mind, his father said, "This will be an opportunity for you to practice networking. You will have to get to know and work with various people in the company. It will be beneficial for you to start making those connections now."

"Sounds good." What else could he say? His father's logic wasn't wrong.

"Are you planning on joining them, Jason?" his mother asked.

"No, I was planning on catching up with some old friends and stopping by my parents' place."

"They don't mind you staying here before you see them?"

"I haven't told them I'm coming yet. I thought it would be a nice surprise."

Mrs. Hollenbeck smiled. "I'm sure your mother would like that."

Yes, Jason's parents would get a surprise, and Andrew would be left to deal with his father alone. Andrew glared at his friend. *Traitor.* Jason's answering grin said he wasn't bothered in the least about abandoning him.

Andrew's worry about his dreams of Ghost House was put to rest that night. He stood in the parlor, the usual nightly crowd surrounding him with its familiar laughter and smoke. He took a moment to survey the sights and sounds before scanning the room for Caius.

"Lookin' for some company, sugar?"

The man who had spoken was a smarmy-looking guy with dark, oily hair that matched the rest of his appearance.

Andrew recognized him as one of the prostitutes, but not one he'd conversed with before. The hooker was standing closer to Andrew than necessary, and Andrew stepped back to put some distance between them.

"I'm looking for Caius," he said.

"Caius?" the man asked, confused.

"The owner?"

"Oh! Him. I'm sure he's around somewhere. Why don't you wait with me until he shows up?"

"No, thank you." Before the prostitute could hit on him again, he added, "Excuse me," and moved on.

He headed toward the bar. This room was noisier, filled with laughter and clinking glasses, but Caius wasn't among the throng. He turned back the way he'd come and spotted the archway to the foyer at the front door. He hadn't ventured past the parlor since the night he'd slept at Ghost House and had forgotten about the alcove there. He weaved his way through the furniture and people toward it, giving a wide berth to the man who'd propositioned him. Hopefully, he'd find Caius in the alcove instead of having to venture upstairs. For all the nights he'd visited, they'd never been higher than the first floor.

Unlike the rest of the house, the setup in the alcove was pretty much the same in the dream as in reality. Couches lines the walls and a bunch of pillows were scattered on the floor. The main difference was the fabric that draped from the ceiling, giving the space a tent-like atmosphere, and the tall, fancy glass bottles set around the floor. Caius lounged on a chaise, a haze of smoke above his head. In his hand, he held the end of a hose which connected to one of the fancy bottles. The bottle was topped with tinfoil and charcoal.

"What is that?" Andrew asked.

Caius brought the hose to his lips and inhaled deeply.

When he exhaled, a cloud of smoke billowed in front of his face. "A hookah pipe."

Andrew had heard of them but had never seen one in person before. "You have a hookah lounge in here?"

Caius nodded.

"Why?"

"People like the exotic." Caius offered the pipe to Andrew. Now that he was closer, he could see there was a mouthpiece at the end of the tube. Having never smoked before, Andrew was careful as he took a drag. The smoke that gathered in his mouth had a sweet hint of apple in it. He laughed as he exhaled.

"You like?"

"Yes." Andrew settled back against the pillows next to him. It was the first time in a long while since they'd been alone together. He took advantage of it by sitting close and putting an arm around Caius's shoulders. "Tell me more about your life before you owned this place," he said.

"Isn't it your turn to share something?"

"You're the interesting one here," Andrew pointed out. "My life isn't nearly as glamorous."

"Oh no," Caius said. "That won't do. I must be courted by somebody exciting. Make something up if you have to."

Making up stories wasn't Andrew's forte. He was majoring in business, not English. "I'm a member of the university hockey club. Ice hockey."

To his surprise, Caius perked up at the news. "You're on a team?" he asked. "Do you wear uniforms and compete?"

"Yes. It's not as intense as some of the other sports on campus, like the football team, but our games can get pretty heated."

"Wait a moment," Caius said as he took the pipe from Andrew. "I want to imagine you all sweaty after a game."

He sucked on the pipe and closed his eyes. They remained closed as he exhaled.

Andrew waited a beat before asking, "Are you done yet?"

Caius sharply held up a hand. "Hold on. I'm enjoying this."

"And what about me?" Andrew asked, taking the pipe back. "Don't I get to imagine you all sweaty after doing something?"

Caius's mouth curved wickedly. "If you'd like," he purred. He opened his eyes and turned a heated gaze on Andrew. "I only get sweaty after one thing."

Andrew held Caius's stare for a moment before inhaling a mouthful of smoke. He set the pipe aside and leaned forward, crawling his way over Caius's body. Caius waited, tilting his chin when Andrew was close enough for their lips to meet. Andrew blew the smoke into Caius's mouth. A few wisps escaped but the majority was caught by Caius. They stared at each other as Caius held it. Instead of releasing it, Caius reached up and brought their mouths back together. Their tongues tangled in a smoky kiss that soon made them forget about the hookah.

Eventually, the pipe burnt out, but Andrew didn't care. Caius was lying half on top of him, and their legs were entwined amongst the pillows. He was lazily threading his fingers through Caius's hair, which was softer than he'd expected. He was easily becoming addicted to the sensation and to the comfortable way they fit together.

"I think it's your turn for sharing," Andrew said.

"I think it's high time you asked me to take you upstairs."

"No."

Caius pushed up from where he'd been resting his head

on Andrew's chest. "Why not?" he asked, his voice incredulous.

"Because I will not have sex with you in a dream." Andrew couldn't bring himself to do it. A wet dream was one thing, the dreamer had no control over the events. This would be on purpose. "I want the real thing."

"That's impossible."

"Is it?" Andrew asked.

Caius was silent for a moment before he lowered his head back down with a sigh. "I suppose it would look like you bought me, and we can't have that."

Andrew was glad Caius couldn't see his face. He hadn't realized how much he'd wanted their meeting in the real world to be possible until he'd said it out loud. "No, we can't."

They lay quietly for a while, and Andrew wondered if Caius was just as disappointed as he was. He'd already known it was impossible. Caius had said as much once, but that hadn't stopped the flicker of hope burning in Andrew's chest. It was a spark that burned brighter every time he looked into Caius's captivating green eyes. His own prickled, and he closed them, waiting until the tightness in his chest had eased before opening them again.

"I once cursed a man for being a slimy toad," Caius said suddenly.

Andrew appreciated the diversion. "What did you do? Turn him into a frog?"

"A *toad*, I said. The punishment must fit the crime."

Andrew laughed. "When was this?"

"Oh, a long time ago," Caius said with a lazy wave of his hand. "It's not like I go cursing people willy-nilly. Usually, they're spread out by a few years."

"How many people have you cursed?"

"That's akin to asking how many people I've slept with. Darling, you don't want to know."

"You'd be the villain in every fairy tale," Andrew said.

"I wouldn't be surprised if certain fairy tales were inspired by me. Though I'm not the only sorcerer who's worked a curse or two."

"No one sides with the villain in stories," Andrew pointed out.

"That's because the story is always told by the ones who were cursed. What is that saying? There are three sides to every story?"

"Yours, mine, and the truth."

"Exactly."

"So what's yours?"

"They deserved what was coming to them."

"That's not much of a defense without an explanation," Andrew said.

Caius pushed himself up into a sitting position. Andrew followed suit, sensing this was one of those few times Caius would talk plainly. "One thing you must understand about curses, Andrew, is they can always be broken. There is no point in punishing someone if they cannot learn from their mistakes and take action to fix it. Whether they do so and whether they manage to break the curse is solely on their shoulders."

"You don't take responsibility at all?" Andrew asked. "Do you even look to see if they've succeeded?"

"I'm not a teacher, Andrew. I'm a sorcerer. Their rehabilitation is not my problem. Their punishment is."

"And what if they can't break the curse?"

"You've never heard of a life sentence? Some people get out for good behavior, others don't."

"You're comparing life as a toad to a jail sentence."

Caius shrugged. "A body is a cage of sorts."

Was Caius serious? Andrew hadn't *really* believed Caius was a sorcerer when he had mentioned it. Sure, he'd healed Andrew's hand, but that was...different somehow. Yet, hearing Caius talk about the curses he had performed so nonchalantly made Andrew wonder. Real or not, Caius believed he was a sorcerer. Caius believed he had done these things and didn't think there was anything wrong with doing them. Andrew didn't want to imagine that Caius was evil, but the more he thought about it, the more the possibility grew. Evil wasn't always done with intention. In history, many people who were seen as evil had believed they were doing the right thing at the time. Caius, with his nonchalance, could be the same. Andrew had learned that Caius's flippancy was often a mask to hide how he was really feeling, or to avoid a topic he did not want to talk about, but this was different. He was volunteering the information. This was not a mask or a misdirection. For the first time, Andrew wondered if his pleasant dreams were something else entirely. Maybe they were really nightmares.

Maybe the monster Andrew had seen the other night had been Caius.

SEVEN

—◆•◆—

Andrew's feelings of unease did not go away after he'd woken up. It didn't help that he had to be up at the ass crack of dawn to be ready by six. He had a hard time swallowing down breakfast even though his mother's pancakes were his favorite, but he did his best. He didn't want his mother asking him questions.

He wasn't staying the whole day at his father's office, so he and his dad had taken separate cars. Andrew was grateful for the small reprieve.

When he entered the lobby, he found a tall woman in a grey business suit waiting for him. She looked to be only a few years older than him, and although her clothes were impeccable and her red hair had been combed to a smooth shine, she already looked frazzled.

"You must be Andrew. You look just like your father."

Andrew smiled. If she was stressed this early in the morning, she could use a friendly face. "And you must be Melody. My dad told me you would be giving me a tour of the place."

"I suppose he thought I was the only one with free time

on my hands." There was a sharp bite underlying her words. So much for making things easier on her. "Let's get started."

"Sure."

The tour wasn't so bad. He'd loved visiting his dad's place of work as a kid, but as a teenager, the appeal had worn off, and he'd found excuses to avoid it. It was bigger than he remembered. Melody pointed out all the different departments and gave Andrew a little insight into what they did and how they helped other companies. She was very knowledgeable and polite, but there was something behind her demeanor that irked Andrew. He couldn't put his finger on what it was until they'd gotten coffee in the break room.

While they made up their cups, Melody asked, "I hear you're going to work here after you graduate."

"That's the plan."

"Must be nice having daddy pull strings for you."

Andrew almost dropped his coffee. As it was, he jerked and some of the scalding liquid sloshed over his hand, burning him. "What did you say?"

"Not all of us are lucky enough to have those kind of connections. So where will you be starting? A nice little head manager job or are you jumping straight to VP?"

Andrew had no idea what Melody was talking about. Jump to VP? Why the hell would he do that? "I'll be starting at the bottom when I come here," he said. "I may even work under you."

Melody didn't look convinced, but she let the subject drop. "Come on. Let's finish this stupid tour."

She may have thought the tour was stupid, but Andrew had collected a lot of information for his final project, and he still had the interview to do. When the tour was over, Melody headed off to do what he assumed were important things, and he was left to wait in the coffee room. He didn't mind. He used the time to jot down notes, happy to no longer be subject to her accusatory attitude.

"Melody told me you were in here," his father said, entering the room. "How did the tour go?"

"Pretty good. I hadn't realized there were so many different areas inside the company, and such a variety of jobs too."

"You thought we were all stuffy old men in suits?"

"Kind of?"

He father laughed. "The suit is a requirement, I'm afraid, but the stuffiness isn't. We have some pretty interesting people working for this company. Speaking of which, what did you think of Melody?"

Andrew didn't know enough about her to form an opinion. "She seems like a hard worker," he said. "By the way, what did you tell her about me?"

"I told her you were my son and that you will be working here after you graduate."

"Nothing else? No details about what I would be doing when I work here?"

"No, why?"

Andrew shook his head. "Nothing. I was just wondering." Melody hadn't been the nicest person he'd met, but there wasn't any reason to get her in trouble over incorrect assumptions. "After this interview, what's on the menu?"

"I was going to suggest we go for lunch, and I'll answer any questions I can for you, but something's come up. After the interview, you can go home. We can talk over dinner."

"Mom doesn't like it when you talk business over dinner."

"This isn't business, this is your schoolwork. She'll make

an exception." His dad glanced at the clock on the wall. "Time to go."

The manager his dad brought him to was on the phone when they first arrived. Her expression was stern as she hung up and waved them inside, her dark brows pulled down in thought, but she smiled as she stood to shake Andrew's hand. He was nervous about interviewing someone—it was the first time he'd ever done something like that—and he hoped his hand wasn't sweaty.

"Nice to meet you, Mrs. Clarke," he said, noting the ring on her finger.

"The pleasure is mine." Her words held the touch of an accent. "Now, what can I do for you?" she asked, gesturing for him to sit in one of the chairs facing her desk.

"I'll leave you two to it. Once you're done here, head back to my office."

"Got it, Dad."

His father left and closed the door behind him. For all that his dad intimidated him—especially when angry— Andrew was already missing the security of his presence. Now that he was gone, Andrew was unsure where to begin.

"What is this project that you're working on?" Mrs. Clarke asked.

"It's for my operations management class. For our final we have to study a business and then devise our own management plan for it."

"Sounds like more fun than sitting in your dorm reading stuffy books."

"We do that too."

Mrs. Clarke smiled again, and Andrew relaxed.

"So what exactly do you do here?" he asked.

. . .

After the interview, Andrew stopped by his father's office to let him know he was done and then headed back to his parents' house. No one was home when he arrived, so he let himself in and began typing up the notes he'd taken. He started formulating them into an outline for his paper and wrote down some questions for when he spoke to his father later that night. The whole day had been a lot less grueling than he'd anticipated. It had helped that he hadn't had any pressure from his dad. In fact, what his dad had done for him had been incredibly helpful. He didn't think managers at a company that size made room in their schedule for student interviews, especially on a Friday.

Being at the office was a completely different experience than hearing his dad talk about it. Like he'd told his father, he'd originally pictured a building full of stuffy old men his father's age. Many of the employees were much younger than he'd imagined. There was a big mix of ages, sexes, and races in the company as well, but despite the nice variety, he still hadn't felt comfortable there. The place was too big, too impersonal, and although they helped people on some level, Hollenbeck Consulting was first and foremost a corporate entity that helped other corporate entities. Andrew wanted to help *people*.

He heard the front door open. From the sounds coming from the foyer, his mother was home. He shut his laptop and headed downstairs to greet her.

"Oh good," she said when she saw him. "Help me with these?" She gestured with arms laden with shopping bags. "There's more in the car."

He helped her bring the bags into the kitchen and then went to get the rest before helping her put the groceries away.

"You still haven't told me anything about this girl you're

interested in," his mother said as she put cans of beans in the pantry.

Andrew almost dropped the eggs he was holding. "There's really nothing to tell."

"I don't believe that for a second. I know you're hiding something from me, Andrew. A mother can always tell."

Andrew sighed. "There's nothing to tell, Mom."

His mother set the cans on the shelf and turned to look at him. "You're a good boy, Andrew. You're smart and kind, but you have a tendency to keep things to yourself. I won't push you anymore if you really don't want to tell me, but don't lie to me. Whatever is on your mind is weighing you down. I can see it. I want you to know that I am here for you. I'm willing to listen to you any time you're ready to unload."

"Thanks, Mom." He did appreciate it even if he wasn't going to take advantage of her offer. There were too many secrets on his plate to figure out what to unburden. His most pressing, he realized, was his dreams of Caius. Ever since Caius had forgiven him, he'd looked forward to visiting Ghost House whenever he went to sleep. After what happened last night, he was dreading it.

Caius was at a table playing poker when Andrew arrived that night. For once, Andrew was grateful for the crowd. He didn't want to be alone with Caius. As they played, Caius acted no differently than he had in any of the other dreams. He was sociable and charming and didn't seem to notice the churning emotions in Andrew's gut. It was difficult for Andrew to reconcile the smiling face in front of him with the horrors that Caius had spoken of the night before. He was distracted as they played and consistently lost each hand he was dealt. Thank goodness he was in a dream. Some of the pots he'd lost were more than his college tuition.

Eventually, he needed a break. He waved off the dealer and stood from the table. "I'm going to get a drink," he announced. Perhaps some space would help him ease his nerves.

"Be a dear and bring me a margarita," Caius said, his eyes on his newest hand. He had won the pot Andrew had just lost and looked like he wouldn't be moving from the table any time soon. Andrew nodded and headed toward the bar. He ordered a beer and took a seat on one of the stools. While he sipped his drink, a man slid onto the stool beside him. Andrew glanced over and his stomach clenched with unease. Although the man didn't look like the creature he had seen on the couch at Ghost House, there was a sharpness to his features that reminded Andrew of that terrifying night. This was also the person Caius had called a snake the first night Andrew had dreamed of the brothel. Andrew hadn't found cause to refer to him as anything else. He hadn't spoken with the man much, but there was something about him that made Andrew wary.

"Enjoying yourself?" Andrew wondered if he'd heard the elongated 'S' in the man's speech or just imagined it.

"Yes." He hoped short answers would encourage the snake to go away. No such luck.

"I'm surprised you're still here."

Andrew turned to him in confusion. "What do you mean?" An echo of the creature's words came to him. *I thought we were rid of you.*

"You didn't think you were the first one to enter these dreams, did you?"

That was unexpected. Other than Caius, no one had

mentioned they were in a dream. Then again, his conversations with the rest of the guests had been more sociable than serious. Even so, he was surprised to hear someone referring to Ghost House in a way that made it not real.

"Caius told me I'm not the first," Andrew said.

"Your Caius isn't the man you think he is. I wouldn't be too complacent if I were you. Who knows what you'll become when he's done with you."

It took a moment for Andrew to recognize the sneer on the man's face. It was the same look he'd seen on Amanda when she was relishing a secret. Andrew only knew one thing about Caius that could be that big of a secret. He hoped he was correct, otherwise Caius would be pissed at him for spilling the beans.

"You mean how he turned his ex into a beast?" he asked.

The snake's eyes widened in surprise, but he smoothed the reaction into another oily smile. "He told you he's a sorcerer? And you believed him?"

Andrew shrugged. "Why not?" Even if he wasn't sure if Caius was evil, he wasn't going to let a stranger know that.

"Oh, I see. This is just a dream to you, so it doesn't matter." The snake leaned forward, and Andrew had to resist leaning away and falling off his stool. "Let me tell you something, little boy. Many have suffered at the hand of your Caius." He waved a hand to indicate the rest of the room where patrons and prostitutes mingled. "This isn't some party. It's an echo of the past, and every one of those boys are his victims."

Andrew couldn't help looking around at the crowd. He saw the smarmy man who'd hit on him and remembered Caius's story about the toad. He saw the man Caius had referred to as a beast and the other prostitutes he'd spoken with.

"Caius cursed them all?" There were at least a dozen prostitutes in the building.

The snake's smile was triumphant. "Yes."

Caius had been right. It was like hearing how many people your boyfriend had slept with. Twelve was a big number when they were talking about people Caius had cursed. Who knew? There could have been more than that. The snake hadn't said these were the *only* people Caius had cursed. Andrew felt like he wanted to throw up. "Why are you telling me this?"

The snake raised his eyebrows in an attempt to look innocent. "I'm only here to warn you. I would hate to see you end up like the rest of them."

Andrew would believe that when hell froze over. "Them," he repeated, the word catching his attention. "What about you?"

The snake's expression darkened, and for a moment, Andrew saw a glimmer of the creature from the couch. Fear rocketed through his body, and his pulse quickened. "Be careful, boy. It isn't wise to cross a sorcerer."

He left, but Andrew's nerves were shot. Chills marched like ants over his spine. Now he knew that this was a nightmare, and if Caius was a monster, he wasn't the only one in it. It was the snake he'd seen when he'd gone to Ghost House, but how could he have been there? Had that been a waking dream or had that been real? The questions Andrew had been working so hard to avoid came rushing back in a flood, threatening to choke him. What the fuck was going on? The only person who could tell him was Caius. He downed the rest of his beer and called the bartender over. After ordering another beer for himself and Caius's margarita, he returned to the poker table.

"What took you so long?" Caius asked when Andrew arrived. "I'm parched."

Andrew handed him his glass, trying his best to keep his hand from shaking. A new player had taken his chair, and he didn't have a place to sit. Not that that was the biggest loss. The bar was the one place where the differences between the dream and reality were greatest. In the real world, there were comfortable brown leather stools, booth seating, and square tables. In the dream, the tables were circular and the chairs that surrounded them looked like short, fabric-covered tubes with a cushion shoved halfway down their length and one side cut out so a person could sit. They were red, trimmed in gold, and not at all comfortable. The knowledge of the disparity only served to heighten Andrew's need for answers, but Caius was still winning and looked like he'd settled in for the long haul.

"Would you mind if we went somewhere else?" Andrew asked.

Caius laughed. "And where would you like to go?"

"I meant, somewhere we wouldn't be in the middle of a crowded bar."

"I think he wants to be alone with you," one of the players chimed in.

"Go with him," said another. "Give us a chance to win some money for a change."

Caius considered. "I suppose I could give you gentlemen a break." He gathered his chips onto a tray and handed them to the beast to count. "You can all pay me later." To Andrew he added, "Even you."

Andrew didn't know how Caius expected him to pay, but there was a glint in the other man's eye that made him think it wouldn't be with money.

After a few more teasing exchanges with the group,

Caius stood with his drink in hand and gestured for Andrew to follow him. He led the way into the foyer and through the curtain to the hookah lounge. A topless couple kissed amorously among the cushions. Caius cleared his throat to get their attention.

"Perhaps you should take this upstairs?" he suggested.

The couple gathered their shirts and left.

"There. Now we're alone," Caius announced, lounging back among the newly vacated pillows.

Yes, now they were alone. Doubts swirled like murky water in Andrew's mind. The snake had scared the shit out of him, but he wasn't sure what to think about Caius either. He paced in front of the couch, not caring about the annoyed purse of Caius's lips.

"Caius, this whole...thing," he said, waving a hand to include the building and everyone in it. "It's not my subconscious creating a story for me, is it? We're really here, aren't we?"

Caius's annoyance turned to surprise. He raised a single eyebrow, a talent Andrew had only heard of before meeting him. "What do you think?" he asked.

"A part of me thinks you're real." The part of him that still wanted to believe that Caius was fun and mischievous and flirty, not an evil sorcerer that'd cursed people. "But if you're real, why are we here? What is this dream we're in?"

Caius took a sip from his drink before answering. He looked thoughtful as he did so. "This dream," he said finally, "is a spell. A curse, to be more precise."

"Someone cursed you?"

Caius nodded. "The concept of getting what is coming to you is an old one, I'm afraid," he said with a sigh. "This is the result of someone thinking I should be taught a lesson for all of my wicked ways."

"I'm not sure being trapped in a place like this would turn anyone away from their wicked ways."

Caius smiled, but it didn't reach his eyes. "There are many ways to get a point across."

"Like being haunted by your past?"

Again, he'd managed to surprise Caius.

"That snake guy said something to me when I got our drinks."

"Ah, so that's where these questions stem from."

"Who is he?"

Caius shrugged. "Another facet of my past. One who doesn't like me much."

"He doesn't seem to like me either."

"He doesn't like how you keep coming back to me," Caius said.

"Am I really the only one who's been here more than once?"

"No, there have been others."

A sharp pang twisted in Andrew's chest. Maybe the snake had been right. Maybe he wasn't as special as he'd wanted to believe.

"Do you remember the day you healed my hand?" Andrew asked. "I had told you I'd seen someone at Ghost House. It was him."

Caius sat up sharply. "You saw him? In the real world?"

The concern in Caius's voice made fear prickle on the back of Andrew's neck. "He was sitting on the couch, your couch. I don't know if it was a dream, but I had left the dorm. If I'd been sleepwalking, I'm sure Jason would have said something."

Caius's eyes narrowed, and his lips pressed into a thin line. Andrew hadn't seen that expression on his face since the night he'd been banished. He was glad it wasn't aimed at him this time. "I don't like this," Caius said. "I don't like this at all."

"He can't do anything, right? It's not like he's Freddy Kreuger."

"Who?" The look of utter bafflement on Caius's face would have made Andrew laugh if he hadn't been so terrified.

"He's a horror movie character. He haunts people's dreams, and the more people know about him, the stronger he gets until he can kill people in their sleep."

"That sounds terrifying." Caius didn't look frightened though. He looked fascinated.

"If we had a way to watch movies I'd show them to you. They're old by now, but from your point of view it probably won't matter."

"Are you calling me old?"

"No, I'm saying you haven't seen a TV in over sixty years. This would be a good way to ease you into the experiences of HDTV."

"I'm going to pretend I know what that is and look offended."

"You do that."

Their banter had eased Andrew's nerves slightly. He didn't want to talk about curses and ghosts anymore. He wanted to talk about trivial things and pretend there was nothing to be scared about.

"Are you really going to make me pay you back for the money I lost in the poker game?"

"Oh yes." Caius eyed Andrew like a predator stalking his prey. "Every cent."

"Last time I checked, I don't carry cash in my dreams."

Caius laughed and beckoned him with a finger. "Silly boy. As if I'd want money from you."

Despite his lingering doubts, one look at those irresistible green eyes and Andrew was more than happy to pay.

With Andrew's obligations for his school project over with, he and Jason headed back to campus on Saturday. After extracting promises from them to visit for her birthday in two weeks, Andrew's mother sent them off with plenty of food to hold them over for the week.

Andrew had Jason drive them back. He was too distracted. After his conversation with Caius, he couldn't stop thinking about the curse and how he may have seen the snake in the real world. If the snake could be there, did that mean that Caius could as well? Weren't they sharing the same dream? And if so, didn't that mean that Caius had to be sleeping somewhere in the real world? But where was he? The only place that Andrew could think of was the shortened hallway on the third floor of Ghost House. Could Caius be behind that wall?

So much for not being an amateur detective.

Not that it mattered. He couldn't go destroying someone's house, even if the building had been abandoned for decades. Hell, even if he found Caius, that didn't mean he could wake him up. The man had been sleeping for over sixty years. (He didn't want to think about what that meant for what Caius might look like.) And if he did wake him, what would he be unleashing onto the world? Caius wasn't anything like the snake, but that didn't mean he wasn't evil. Lucifer had been the most beautiful of God's angels, and he was supposed to be the evilest of all creatures. Though that depended upon what mythology you looked at for him. It was the same with Caius. He had done bad things in his past. Did that mean he would still do them? Did that mean he was inherently evil?

Caius had said the dream was a curse. He'd also said that curses were made to be broken, that the person who'd been cursed would be released if they learned something. If Caius was cursed, wouldn't it work the same for him as well? If he woke from the dream, didn't that mean he'd learned something?

The thoughts kept swirling round and round in Andrew's head throughout the day. He couldn't eat a thing at dinner, too lost in thought.

"What's up your butt?" Charlie asked when he'd been silent for too long.

"Huh?"

"I get more conversation out of my morning cereal than I am from you right now. What's wrong with you today?"

Andrew shrugged. "I have something on my mind."

"Is this something to do with that girl you're seeing?" Jason asked.

"Yeah." Andrew wasn't in the mood to deny it.

"Did you get into another fight?"

"No."

"Then what's the problem?" Charlie insisted.

Andrew sighed. "I want to see him."

He missed the surprised looks Charlie and Jason exchanged over his head before Jason said, "Then go. If it's bad enough that you can't even eat your dinner, go. What's stopping you?"

Andrew blinked. What was stopping him? Caius might not be in the house, but it wouldn't hurt to check. He could always decide what to do if and when he found him. It was better than obsessing over it. On the heels of that thought came a sudden urgency, a need to see Caius for real. He shot to his feet, almost knocking his chair to the floor. "I'll see you guys later," he called as he grabbed his jacket and headed for the door.

In his hurry, he didn't hear Charlie ask Jason, "Him?"

An autumn wind swirled crisp leaves around Andrew's ankles as he walked to Ghost House. Wisps of clouds drifted across the moon, and he half expected to see a witch fly by on her broom. At this point, it wouldn't have surprised him. It was almost Halloween. What better time to wake a ghost?

When he arrived, however, Ghost House was dead.

He'd expected an atmosphere like the night he'd slept there, when he'd felt watched, dared to enter. He'd thought the house—that Caius—would be waiting for him. Yet, whatever soul the building possessed was gone.

He'd felt this once before: the time he'd visited when Caius had been angry with him. The emptiness terrified him.

Andrew continued to the back of the building and carefully picked his way through the overgrowth. The makeshift ramp he'd used the night he'd snuck in alone was just as he'd left it. Despite his worry about Ghost House's silence, he was relieved no ghostly laughter echoed from the open window above it. That changed as soon as he slipped inside.

Like a beast waking with a roar, the air around him became charged with anticipation, as if the house knew his intended purpose and eagerly waited for the result. The abrupt shift was nerve-wracking, and he wondered if he were dreaming. He couldn't be. He knew he was awake. Was this a waking dream? Or worse yet, had he finally succumbed to hallucinations and madness?

The light of the moon and streetlamps didn't reach the bar, and his mind threatened to succumb to the natural fears of the dark. He'd remembered a flashlight this time, but as he scrambled to turn it on, a voice hissed, "Sneaking in, are we? That's not very heroic of you."

Startled, he dropped the flashlight and whirled toward the sound, but he couldn't see anything in the darkness. "Where are you?" he asked, fighting to keep his voice steady. Even without seeing him, Andrew knew it was the snake. His presence made Andrew shiver, and he searched the dark blindly, trying to find him.

A dim light suffused the room, allowing Andrew to make out the furniture around him and the creature standing next to the window. The snake's skin was pale and there was definitely a sheen from scales on his cheeks and neck. He must have had hair at one time, but now only a few dry strands clung to his otherwise bald pate. His eyes were the color of sewage and slitted like those of the creature he resembled. Had Caius really known this monster?

The snake moved closer and a vile odor assaulted Andrew's nose. He backed away, covering his mouth with his hand as his stomach lurched. He didn't know what a rotting corpse smelled like, but it was the only thing that came to mind to describe the stench.

Bile burned his throat, and he swallowed. "Don't come near me."

The snake smiled, his mouth stretching unnaturally wide. A chill ran down Andrew's spine at the sight of it.

"Why are you here?"

"Because you're here," the snake replied. "A hero can't have a story without a villain."

"Who said anything about me being a hero?"

"You're here to save the damsel in distress. That makes you the hero of the story, doesn't it?"

"Save him?" Andrew asked, confused.

The snake looked baffled. "Of course. Why else would you be here?"

"I wanted to see him. In person."

"How do you know he's here? You've only met him in dreams. What makes you think he even exists?"

"Because you're here," Andrew said, throwing the snake's words back at him. As he spoke, hope bloomed in his chest. If the snake was in the real world, it had to be possible for Caius to be as well. Andrew wanted to know if that were true. He needed to know.

The snake leered at Andrew, and Andrew had to force himself not to take a step back. "You do remember that the princess you are rescuing is not a princess at all, yes?" he hissed. "He's a *sorcerer*. The demons you see here are of his own creation."

"Even you?" Andrew asked before he could stop himself.

The snake's smile widened. "Especially me."

The light around them drifted away toward the bar. Not wanting to be stuck in the dark with the snake, Andrew followed its lead. As he walked, he noticed the tables and chairs around him were covered in a haze. Upon closer inspection, he realized they were like a double exposure. He could see the furniture from the house, but he could also see the tube-like chairs from his dreams.

The bar was similarly foggy, but its differences weren't as drastic. On the end of the wooden counter sat a large toad. Unlike everything else in the room, the animal was clear to see, like him and the snake.

"Recognize him?"

Andrew flinched. He turned so the snake was no longer at his back. "Should I?" he asked, but they both knew the answer. This was the man Caius had cursed. "Is it real?"

"Pick him up and find out."

Andrew reached for the amphibian carefully, but it made no move to escape. It hung limply when he lifted it, its short back legs dangling. Its skin was dry and bumpy, and its body felt delicate in his hands. It was definitely real.

"Does he know he's a toad when he's in this state?"

"Of course," the snake said. "It wouldn't be much of a curse otherwise."

"And he's stuck like this? Forever?"

"It's a familiar story by now. He's stuck like that until someone is kind enough to kiss him." The snake tilted his head. "Would you like to do the honors?"

Andrew looked at the toad again. It stared back at him, unblinking. Could he really leave someone trapped like that when it would only take a simple kiss to save them?

"It's up to you. You're the only one who can free him."

No, he wasn't. It was the toad's job to save himself, to learn. Andrew remembered the smarmy prostitute from his dreams. If that was the man in this frog's body, then Andrew didn't think he had learned much.

"No," he said, setting the toad back on the bar. "I won't kiss him."

"Suit yourself." The snake shrugged and turned toward the curtained archway to the next room. Before the curtain stood a young man. Andrew recognized him as another of Ghost House's workers. Seeing him so plainly made Andrew pause. This was a ghost he'd dreamed of many times before, but the room they were in was dark and dusty and real. His worlds really were colliding.

"Who are you?"

"He can't answer you, I'm afraid," the snake replied. "Your precious Caius was displeased with him and took his voice away. I'm surprised he didn't cut out his tongue. Perhaps he was feeling kind that day."

The mute opened his mouth as if to speak, but nothing came out. He looked at Andrew with pleading eyes, but Andrew had no idea what he was asking for. Even if he had, he wasn't there to rescue a stranger. Steeling himself, Andrew pushed past the young man and into the next room.

"You can be heartless when you want to," the snake remarked as he followed. "No wonder you're a match for the sorcerer."

Andrew didn't reply.

This room was just as hazy as the bar had been. The only pieces that were clear were the ones that had existed in both places, like the piano and Caius's couch. He hadn't expected Caius to be on the sofa, but he still felt disappointed to see it empty.

The light moved on, leading them toward the alcove by the front door. As Andrew neared the foyer, the mysterious light suddenly vanished. Andrew let out an involuntary squeak before slapping his hand over his mouth to prevent any other undignified sounds from escaping. He had no idea where the snake was, and that only made his pulse race faster. He moved carefully forward, reaching for the railing of the staircase to center himself. Instead, his fingers closed over the firm muscles of an arm. He recoiled, thinking it was the snake he held.

"My apologies," came a voice in the dark. It was a normal man's voice without serpent-like accents, which was reassuring, but Andrew still didn't like being lost in the dark.

"Sorry," Andrew said. "I didn't see you there."

The man laughed softly. "I can't see anything."

That distracted Andrew from his fear. "You're blind?"

"Yes. My sight was taken from me."

Tension returned to Andrew's shoulders as he realized that this was another of Caius's victims. "Why?"

"The sorcerer did it to punish his lover. The curse he placed on his lover wasn't enough to appease his wrath, so he cursed me as well."

There had to be more to the story. Even if he hadn't wanted to think better of Caius, the story had too many holes to be believed at face value. Before he could ask for more details, the dim light returned. Andrew looked around for the blind man, but instead, he came face to face with the snake. He retched. He hadn't realized the stench had vanished along with the light. He only noticed now that it had returned with a vengeance.

"Are you going to stand here all night?"

"No," Andrew snapped. "And I thought you were the villain here. Aren't you supposed to be stopping me?"

"I don't have to. The ghosts will do that themselves."

"They haven't so far."

"You haven't met all of them yet."

As if on cue, an unfelt breeze billowed the curtains to the hookah lounge. With the snake's words fresh in his mind, Andrew wasn't sure he wanted to meet this ghost. He looked toward the stairs. He could easily walk by the alcove and continue on. His goal was to reach the third floor where he thought Caius was. There was no reason to go into the lounge.

"I thought you were here to rescue the fairytale princess," the snake said. "You can't do that in a hallway."

He was right, but fairy tales were not complete until the

hero had faced the challenges set before him. All of the challenges. Andrew stepped through the curtain.

This room was the least changed from the dream to reality. The biggest difference was a pile of fabric on the couch to his right. It shifted, and he realized that it was a figure swathed in rags and a veil. He couldn't tell if it was a man or a woman, though he hoped it was at least a person.

"You are wondering who I am."

Yes. "You're one of the ghosts that haunt this house," Andrew replied. "Someone who has been cursed."

"Yes."

"What did he do to you?"

"Something too terrible to speak of."

What could be worse than what Andrew had already encountered? He didn't want to know, but he couldn't move on until he'd heard. "Tell me."

Slowly, the figure lifted the veil. Andrew was braced for all kinds of horrors, but what he saw was a beautiful young woman. Even he could appreciate her looks in an aesthetic sense. Charlie would have been all over her.

"I don't understand," Andrew said. "What did Caius do to you?"

"He did the worst thing he could possibly think of," the woman said. She leaned forward. "Think about it, *boy*."

Andrew thought back to his first visit to Ghost House. Caius had told him what the place had been in the past, what it was in the dream. He had told Andrew that he knew Andrew was gay and why.

"You were here last night. Did you see any women about?"

Andrew gasped. "You're a man."

"'Were' is the operative word." The ghost leaned back

against the wall. "Did you know there are people who treat women worse than they would treat an unwanted dog?"

Andrew thought of Jason and Charlie. Sure, Charlie could be vulgar, but neither of his friends were like that. When he said as much, the woman laughed.

"You never know what people are capable of until they show you. The sorcerer made sure to make me beautiful. There was no way I wouldn't catch their eye."

Andrew had a sudden vision of the parties he'd been to on campus, the bars he went to with his friends. He'd seen men grope women and blame it on the alcohol. How many of them backed off when the girl told them to stop? How many of them didn't?

Caius had ensured this woman—no, this man—would encounter the type that didn't take no for an answer. Andrew felt his stomach turn. He wanted to be sick.

His horror must have shown on his face, because the woman started laughing again, a high cackling sound that pierced his ears. Andrew turned and ran through the curtain. He would have continued straight out of the house if it hadn't been for the snake catching him by the arm. Andrew shook off his grip, the revulsion of the snake's touch only adding to his nausea. His knees buckled and he retched. His stomach was empty but bile burned his mouth and throat, and his stomach ached before he was done.

The snake laughed. It was a soft hissing sound that chilled Andrew to the bone. "Has the brave hero decided to turn tail and run back home?" he taunted. "I knew we should have been rid of you, but this is even better."

"I—" Andrew began. He wanted to run away. He wanted to leave and never set foot in Ghost House again.

"He can see you, you know. Every look of disgust reaches him in his dreams. He knows what you're thinking, and if you run away now, he will know you left him behind."

Andrew remembered the hurt look on Caius's face when he'd been banished. Caius had done that over a simple misunderstanding. If Andrew walked away now, there would be no misunderstanding his actions. This time he'd be leaving of his own choosing, and Caius would never forgive him.

"Does it matter?" the snake asked. "He's a sorcerer. He's evil. I'm sure you've thought so yourself. Why should you care to save him? He's a monster set in his ways. Do you really think a college boy like you could change him?"

"What does it matter to you?"

"I told you, I'm the villain of this story."

"You're not being very villain-like."

The snake moved toward him in a flash. His face was inches from Andrew's, and the stench made gray spots appear before Andrew's eyes. "Do you want me to be your villain? I can be. I have enough power to turn you into a dust mite if I so chose. I could kill you, rip you to pieces, and trust me, boy, nothing would bring me greater pleasure. Nothing, that is, unless you left him on your own. You will, you know. Eventually. No one can stay with a creature like that for long. And whether you want to leave first or not, he will destroy you."

It was hard to hear the snake's words when Andrew was trying not to faint. He shook his head to clear it and tried not to breathe through his nose. The smell was cloying in his mouth and didn't make him feel any better. He tried to concentrate on what the snake was saying instead.

"He hurt you." Andrew understood that much. Then he made the connection. "You're the one who did this to him. You're the one who wanted to punish him."

The sneer on the snake's face twisted further, making him even uglier. "*Yes*," he hissed, "I locked him up and threw away the key, and *you*, little boy, are going to be his last hope. If you will not break the curse, then he'll sleep for all eternity."

A cold rush of fear washed over Andrew. The snake was not a ghost, he was a sorcerer, and if he was powerful enough to curse Caius, then he would have no problem turning Andrew into another toad for the bar, or a dust mite like he'd said.

"What's it going to be boy?"

"In fairy tales, after the hero rescues the princess, they live happily ever after. If you hate him so much, you wouldn't want that."

The snake laughed again, the horrible sound making Andrew shiver. "Fairy tales are stories. They have endings and can easily have their future chalked up to a line or two. You forget, you live in the real world. There's no such thing as happily ever after in the real world. If anyone knows that, it's your precious *Caius*."

No. Andrew didn't want to believe that. Real life wasn't as simple as "happily ever after," but people could still be happy. Caius could still be happy, and if this whole curse was to punish him, then what was the point if he couldn't try to redeem himself?

He pushed himself up from the floor. Dizziness threatened to topple him, but he braced himself until he was steady on his feet. Then he walked past the snake and began climbing the stairs. The snake didn't follow. Halfway up, the staircase turned. At the top of the flight, a frame had been mounted to the wall and covered with a piece of cloth. He reached out to tug the fabric off, but a gentle hand on his wrist stopped him.

"The live version is always better than the portrait, don't you think?"

Andrew turned to find a handsome young man standing next to him on the landing.

"You like what you see?"

Given the invitation, Andrew gave him a once over. "Yeah."

"You can see more if you'd like."

"I don't think..." Andrew's protest trailed off as the ghost stepped close and caressed the side of his face.

"You're so handsome."

"Thank you," Andrew whispered. His body responded to the other man's proximity, making his jeans feel tight. The stranger noticed and smiled.

"What say you and I detour into somewhere more private?"

"I..." Andrew swallowed. "I can't." He stepped back, and his shoulders hit the wall. "I have somewhere to be."

"Oh?" The ghost closed the space between them. "And where is that?"

Andrew couldn't remember. He pressed his hands against the wall to help him resist the temptation to touch and tried to think. "I..." His fingers curled with the effort to keep them against the wall. Fabric brushed his skin, and he gripped it tightly. "I really have to go."

"No one's stopping you."

He was right, and yet Andrew couldn't move. He pulled the fabric closer to him, as if it were a security blanket that could protect him in his immobility. The material tumbled from the frame it covered and fell to the floor.

"No!" the man screamed, turning away from Andrew and hiding his face. "Don't look at me!"

Bewildered, Andrew looked at the painting. It was an oil portrait of the young man.

"It's a very nice portrait," he said. "Why do you hide from it?"

The ghost was silent for a moment. Then he spoke from behind his hands, his voice slightly muffled. "If I look at the painting, my true face will be revealed."

Who was he? Dorian Gray? Still confused, Andrew said, "But they look the same."

The man paused. Slowly, he raised his head, though he still looked at the floor. "What?"

"The painting and your face are the same," Andrew said. "Are they not supposed to be?"

The model looked at him, then turned to the picture. Realizing what he had done, he brought a hand to his face. "I'm not changing?"

Andrew shook his head.

"And I'm not ugly?"

"Far from it."

"He said he would make me beautiful," the ghost said softly.

Andrew considered this. "Maybe he thought you already were."

Moisture gathered in the man's eyes, and a single tear rolled down his cheek. Andrew gave him a moment to compose himself.

"I'm sorry for being such a tart," the young man said.

Andrew smiled. "I was flattered by the attention."

"You wouldn't...?"

Andrew shook his head. "I have to keep going."

The ghost nodded. "Good luck." In a blink, he was gone. Andrew looked around. The painting had also vanished. Taking a deep breath, he continued climbing the stairs. There was a shelf mounted to the wall on the third floor landing. It hadn't been there the night he'd slept at Ghost House. Taking it as a sign, he moved closer. On the shelf was a golden mirror. It looked like a golden plate at first. The edges were decorated in a starburst pattern, but when he stepped closer, he could see his reflection in the center. He looked tired and worn, and his hair was a mess. He tried to brush a few strands back into place with his fingers but stopped when the image shimmered and changed. When it finished, Andrew was looking at a bedroom. It was spacious and furnished in mahogany and tan. The picture shifted to the large bed on the far side of the room. The sheets were still but someone lay beneath them. Andrew could just make out Caius, his face peaceful in sleep. He gasped.

"That mirror was spelled to show you what you most desire."

Andrew reluctantly turned away to face the snake.

"That's him then? That's where he's sleeping?"

"It's what you desire. That doesn't necessarily mean it's true."

"It's true." Andrew was determined to believe it was true.

"See for yourself then."

He would. Andrew brushed past the snake and into the hallway. He passed the doors leading to empty bedrooms and stopped at the end of the hall. It was short like he remembered, and the wall in front of him was plain. He still believed there had to be something there. The room from the mirror had to be behind the plaster and paint. He brushed a hand over the smooth surface, trying to find a hidden catch or mechanism. The wall shimmered beneath his fingers, and a door appeared.

"Magic," Andrew whispered in awe. He turned the doorknob and stepped forward. The room he entered was dimly lit, but not by the ghostly light that had led him before now. The first hint of dawn filtered through the windows. Andrew examined what he could see of the room, willing his eyes to adjust faster. There was a bookcase in one corner and two couches faced each other in the center of the room. A dark rug took up much of the space on the floor. No matter how hard he looked, he did not see a bed, and he did not see Caius.

Movement made him look once more at the furniture. A giant shadow rose from the cushions, and Andrew couldn't help taking a step back into the doorway. The shadow was massive and covered in long black fur from head to toe. Andrew could make out claws the size of his fingers on each of the monster's hands.

"You're the Beast," he whispered.

"I am." The Beast's voice was a slow, deep rumble. It fit the shape of the creature and made Andrew all the more reluctant to move closer to him.

"I was told Caius would be here," he managed to say.

"He is."

Had the Beast eaten him? Thankfully, Andrew was too frightened to ask the question out loud. "Where is he?"

The ghost pointed. Off to Andrew's left were curtains, much like the ones dividing the hookah lounge from the rest of the hallway downstairs.

"Are you going to let me see him?"

The Beast nodded.

Andrew took a step toward the curtains, then hesitated. "What will I find in there?"

"That, I cannot tell you."

"Shouldn't you be trying to eat me or something?" Not that he wanted to give the Beast any ideas.

"I am not the enemy here," the Beast said.

Yes. Andrew knew who that was. He glanced back to see if the snake had followed him. He hadn't, and when Andrew turned around, the Beast had vanished as well. Andrew listened to the silence until he was sure he was truly alone. Then with a deep breath, he entered Caius's bedroom. The curtains were even dustier than the ones downstairs. His eyes watered, and he coughed until his lungs were clear.

It was dark in the room, but he could see a sliver of light on one wall. He made his way to the window and carefully pulled back the drapes. Early morning light shone into the room. It pooled on the bed, highlighting the figure sleeping there. Just like in the mirror, Caius lay still beneath the sheets.

"Shit." The word escaped Andrew in a whisper.

Even after all of the phantoms and the dreams, he hadn't been sure Caius truly existed, yet here he was, lying on a dusty bed in the real world. Andrew moved closer. His eyes were glued to Caius's face, examining every pore to make sure it was the same as he'd seen in his dreams. If Caius had been asleep for sixty years, it didn't show.

"Caius," he whispered. If this were a fairy tale, the sleeping beauty would wake with a kiss. It seemed unfair for Caius to be sleeping during their first real kiss. Andrew leaned forward and whispered once more. "Caius. Wake up."

The man didn't stir.

Unable to think of another solution, Andrew slowly pressed his lips to Caius's. When he pulled back, nothing had changed. Before disappointment could set in, he saw movement beneath Caius's eyelids.

"Caius?" His heart began to pound, and a thrill ran through him. Had he really broken a sixty-year-old curse?

Caius's eyes fluttered open, and Andrew gasped. Elation filled him at the sight of those beautiful green eyes.

"Holy shit," he said. "You're real."

PART TWO
EVER AFTER

EIGHT

—◆◆—

Freedom! Caius widened his eyes, partially in surprise and partially just to see if he could. Yes, that was his face moving. His actual face and not a dream of one. Oh, how exhilarating it felt to be moving again! *Really* moving! Andrew had done it. He'd broken the curse. Caius had waited so long, unable to do anything, and now he was free. He grinned and grabbed Andrew by the ears, pulling the young man down for a ravishing kiss. He wasted no time prying Andrew's lips apart so he could delve into his mouth with an eager—yet parched—tongue. Oh, that wouldn't do. He sought deeper, seeking the wetness of Andrew's mouth to moisten his own. How lovely it felt to have real, warm lips against his. He moaned his appreciation, but before Andrew could get any ideas, Caius pushed him away, breaking the kiss, and sat up.

"Now, now," he said, his voice a rough whisper. He cleared his throat and tried again. "You'll be a dear, won't you, and get me some water? Sleeping for sixty years does terrible things to a person's hydration." He wiggled his feet, wondering if his legs had the strength to carry him.

"There's so much to do!" he exclaimed, throwing his arms out wide just because he could. And he could. That was wonderful. His arms worked perfectly right off the bat. "I'm going to have to get a new wardrobe. Obviously. I wonder if any of the current fashions are interesting." He eyed Andrew up and down pointedly. "My current example is quite lacking."

Lacking in the fashion department, but not in appeal. Caius was relieved to see that Andrew's appearance in reality was the same as it had been in the dream. He hadn't been sure that would be the case. The subconscious did like to embellish on occasion.

Tall and built like an athlete, Andrew had muscles in all the right places, especially his arms. Caius had loved caressing them in the dream, and he looked forward to feeling them wrap around his real body. It was a shame Andrew insisted on hiding the rest of his physique under such drab clothes.

"Let's see...Paris was always a good place for fashion. Is it still?" Andrew's expression of shock was unchanging. Oh well, he'd catch up eventually.

Throwing the covers back, Caius kicked up a cloud of dust that had them both coughing. With a wave of his hand, he made the dust in the room swarm into a giant cloud that floated near the ceiling. Another gesture and the window flew open. The dust gusted out the window and fell to the ground with a *poof.* That was fine. The gardener could take care of it. Which meant Caius would have to find a gardener. Perhaps he could get a butler too, or at least someone to keep the house clean. Doing it with magic all the time would become tedious.

He shook his head. "Before all that, I have to figure out what to do with this place." He also needed to get back into the habit of talking out loud to people. He added that to his list of things to do.

"If I rise, will you catch me if I fall?" he asked Andrew.

"Of course." Andrew took a step closer to the bed.

Caius smiled and caressed Andrew's cheek, relieved that Andrew was coming around. His blue eyes were clear and focused. "Not to worry, my dear. I haven't forgotten my prince."

Andrew blushed. Wasn't that adorable? "I didn't think you had," he said. Caius had a feeling he was more hung up on being called a prince than the thought that Caius had forgotten him.

"First things first: water and food. I'm famished."

"After sixty years, I'm sure you would be."

Oh good. Andrew had found his footing. It wouldn't do for him to falter now, not after being Caius's gallant knight. Caius owed the boy for waking him, and he planned on paying him back in full, particularly if payment included a reintroduction to Andrew's kissable lips. Caius wanted to taste them again and feel them in more intimate places. But before he could indulge in his imagination, there were necessities to take care of.

"Take me out for breakfast, Andrew," Caius said.

Andrew gave them both a once over. The dust had been cleared from their clothing, but they were not suitable for anything fancy. "Perhaps we should change before our first date?" he asked.

He had a point. Caius grinned. "Let's go shopping."

Despite being able to get a few sentences out in reply to Caius's rambling, Andrew was still in shock. The man from his dreams not only existed but was walking around beside him. He followed mutely as Caius led the way to the bank, talking volubly about how relieved he was that it had not gone out of business, because that would have just caused *so* much trouble. He insisted that Andrew wait for him in the lobby while he spoke with the bank manager. Andrew was fine with that idea, since it gave him a few minutes alone to sort his thoughts.

There had been enough dust on Caius to prove he really had been sleeping on a bed in an abandoned house for sixty years. It was like some twisted version of *Sleeping Beauty* where Caius was the princess. He wondered for a moment if Caius would mind being thought of as a princess and then reined his thoughts back in. He was starting to ramble like Caius, and they'd only known each other for ten minutes. In the real world, anyway.

Which brought up another thought. Had he really visited Caius in those dreams? Were they shared dreams? He supposed so, since Caius acted as if they knew each other and didn't seem at all surprised to have woken up with Andrew standing above him. Was this really like a fairy tale?

Fairy tales didn't exist. They might have been based on truth, but sorcerers and curses weren't real. Except Caius had admitted to being a sorcerer, and the way he'd cleared the dust from the room had definitely been by magic. Not to mention being asleep for sixty years without aging a day had to count for something in the fairy tale category.

But if that were true, did that also mean everything else was true? Had Caius run Ghost House before it had become Ghost House? How old did that make him? He looked like he could be anywhere between twenty and thirty-five, but none of those ages were right if he'd run a brothel for three-quarters of a decade.

More importantly, did that mean Caius had really cursed people in the past? He'd never concluded if Caius was evil or not, yet when he had seen him lying in that bed, all thought of repercussions had fled his mind. He'd only wanted to see those green eyes looking back at him again. Because of that, Caius was now awake and in the real world. Up until now, everything had been colored by the fact that it had all been a bunch of dreams. A part of Andrew still felt like he was in a dream, but he knew he wasn't. Caius was real, and his powers were real. If Caius was evil, whatever chaos he caused was going to be Andrew's fault.

Caius's return interrupted Andrew's thoughts. "Shopping time, my dear," he said, beaming happily. "I hope those strong arms of yours aren't just for show. I have a whole wardrobe to fill, and I am not going to waste time getting started on it."

"What about breakfast?" Andrew asked.

Caius waved a hand. "We'll find something. First, these old rags have *got* to go. After that, we'll have a nice brunch and see where the day takes us."

Andrew had a feeling the day would be taking them to plenty of clothing stores, and he didn't think any of them would be Walmart or the Gap. Five minutes into Caius's shopping spree, he found out he was right. Caius liked expensive things, and from the looks of the wad of cash he had in his pocket, he could afford them.

"You didn't rob the bank while I waited, did you?" Andrew asked, genuinely worried.

Caius looked at him in surprise and then laughed. "No. One of the benefits of sleeping for sixty years is your investments continue to work while you don't."

"You're into investing?" That was even more alarming.

Andrew's father was into investing. He was shocked to think that Caius and his father had something in common.

"When you've lived as long as I have, you find that two things are essential." Caius held up a finger. "Always have some money saved for when you can't find work or a peasant mob runs you out of town at the last minute." He raised a second finger. "And make sure you have an amazing lawyer so no one can take your money away when they think you're dead."

Andrew thought Caius was kidding about the peasant mob, but he couldn't be sure. "How old are you?"

"That's a rather personal question, and one I don't care to answer. Besides, the math would offend me, and I'd rather not know it. You don't want to make me feel *old*, do you?"

"I don't think you could ever feel old."

Caius gave him one of his approving smiles. It made Andrew feel warm despite his lingering worries.

They spent the rest of the morning visiting every name brand shop in town. By eleven o'clock, Andrew was famished and threatened to leave Caius's bags on the sidewalk unless they found something to eat.

"You *wouldn't!*" Caius exclaimed in horror.

"I would."

Caius considered for a few moments but wisely decided not to challenge Andrew's threat. "Where shall we eat?"

Andrew took him to his favorite breakfast place, The Eatery. The restaurant was only open for breakfast and lunch, and managed to be packed full even during weekdays. The owners had purchased the old house from a bankruptcy auction and turned it into a thriving business with seating both inside and on the wraparound porch. It was a bit crowded, and the acoustics weren't the best, but the food more than made up for it.

Caius looked skeptical as they were led to a table.

"Trust me," Andrew said. "I'm not going to let your first meal in sixty years be a bust."

Caius's countenance didn't change as they took their seats and looked over the menu. "I'm sorry to see that diner menus haven't changed much in the last six decades," he said. "In fact, I think they've gotten worse."

"Wait until I take you to a real diner. Some of those can make your eyes cross."

Caius raised an eyebrow at him. "And that motivates me to visit one, how?"

Andrew sighed. "Trust me, okay? If you end up hating it, I'll take you somewhere else."

Caius didn't say anything and went back to reading his menu. Andrew didn't bother trying to appease him. The food would do that once it arrived.

"Caius," he began. "Everything that's happened until now...that's all been real?"

"Everything meaning all that you've experienced since the night you slept at my house?" Caius asked, his eyes still on the plastic sheet of food offerings.

Andrew nodded.

"Yes," Caius said, finally setting the menu aside. "Everything has been real. You visited me in dreams and woke me from a spell, and now we're really here at a quaint yet acoustically unfortunate diner about to have brunch."

Andrew took a moment to let that sink in. He had a feeling it would take longer than one meal to get used to the idea, but he was doing his best. "What happens now?"

Caius took a deep breath. "Now I sort through the red

tape of returning to the real world and decide what to do with The Cut Sleeve."

"The Cut Sleeve? Oh, you mean Ghost House." Andrew vaguely remembered the name from his Google search.

"You have a terrible habit of referring to my home by that moniker," Caius said.

"That's what everyone calls it."

"Well, don't. It is very unflattering."

"And The Cut Sleeve? How is that any better?"

"You've never heard of the 'passion of the cut sleeve?' No, I suppose not. Chinese history isn't a requirement for your studies, and I'm sure this wouldn't be a part of it even if the subject was mandatory." Caius paused as their waitress approached their table. Once they had ordered and she had left, he continued. "During the Han Dynasty, Emperor Ai had a lover named Dong Xian." His accent when he spoke the names sounded accurate to Andrew's ignorant ears. "One afternoon when they had fallen asleep together, Emperor Ai had to get out of bed. He cut off his sleeve rather than wake his sleeping lover. Hence the phrase 'passion of the cut sleeve'."

"And you named your business after that?"

"Can you think of a better way to advertise a gay establishment without being obvious about it?"

Andrew was sure there were other ways, but he realized that wasn't Caius's point. "You really are a romantic, aren't you?"

"*Absolutely*."

Brunch had been much better than Caius had expected, and he'd spent the rest of the morning happily dragging

Andrew around town. Andrew was very accommodating, and Caius made a point to reward him for his patience when they met for dinner later that night.

It was two o'clock when he arrived home. Andrew had left for a hockey game, and Caius had called a taxi to help him schlep his bags and boxes to the house. Caius was amused by the driver's surprise when he stated their destination. The man kept looking at him warily in the rearview mirror as he drove and continued to do so as he carried Caius's packages to the front door. Caius waved cheerfully as the taxi drove away, but once he was alone, his smile faded.

Caius hated The Cut Sleeve. It was difficult not to when he'd been trapped inside it for over half a century. He would have loved to burn it to the ground and never look back, but after spending the day exploring, he'd realized that was not an option.

Caius had lived a long time. He'd always understood that, no matter what, the world was constantly changing. He'd changed along with it as the years went by, riding the waves of invention and innovation, bad fashion choices, and questionable artistic movements. Except this time, he hadn't been a part of that growth. He'd been stuck in a glass jar, unable to affect the world or be affected by it.

So much of the town was the same, yet everything was different. The bank had been where he'd remembered it, but it was so much bigger than it used to be, with polished marble floors and technology on every surface. Computers had barely been more than a concept in the early 1950s. Now they ran everything.

Earlier in the day, he and Andrew had passed an electronics store, and he'd seen an array of televisions for sale in the window. They were so *big*, yet much flatter than he remembered. And the *colors*! Some of them were more vibrant than real life!

The thought of exploring all of these new inventions was exciting, but it was also jarring. Caius felt very out of place. Despite his dislike for the building that had been his prison for sixty years, it was the one place he was familiar with. Until he became accustomed to this new time, he couldn't afford to let it go. It would have to be redone, of course, but that was part of the fun. He'd consider it practice in modernizing himself to fit his surroundings.

With that thought in mind, he unlocked the door and let himself inside. He was in the middle of moving his packages and shopping bags into the foyer when a shadow fell across the stoop.

"Ro—"

"Uh uh," the Snake interrupted, holding up a hand. "I left that name behind long ago. You called me the Snake in your dreams. I find it fitting for you to continue to do so in the real world."

That was fine with Caius. The figure standing before him was no longer the lover he'd known years ago. Back then he had been handsome and charming, with wavy blond hair and a chiseled jaw. Now his chin came to a point, and his hair had thinned to almost nothing. At a glance, the Snake was a complete stranger.

"Congratulations," the Snake said. "I was wondering if you'd ever find a prince charming to wake you."

"I'm surprised you weren't keeping potential candidates from me," Caius retorted.

"Oh, I did for the first few decades. What fun would it have been for you to break the curse after only ten years?"

"And yet Andrew made it through. That must gall you."

The Snake's lips curved into a sneer. "Just because you

have woken up, doesn't mean you will live happily ever after. You had a prince charming once, and that didn't work out so well. Who's to say Andrew will be any different?"

Caius glared at him. "Andrew *is* different. He would not have been able to break the curse otherwise."

"The curse had nothing to do with Andrew. His access was all based on your feelings for him, and let's face it. You've never had the best of luck with men."

"You know nothing about my feelings."

The Snake gave him a pitying look. Caius hated the sight of it. He turned and stormed inside, slamming the door behind him.

Alone again, his anger faded, but the echo of his ex-lover's words stayed with him. The Snake was right. Caius did like Andrew. It was those feelings and his desire to keep seeing Andrew that had allowed the student to return to the dream every night, but there was more to it than that. Andrew had believed in Caius. He had gone so far as to search an abandoned building for Caius's body and woken him. Caius had to believe that meant there was more to Andrew than a cute face, a fit body, and an adorable blush. He'd seen signs of it in the way Andrew had treated him in the dream. He had to be right this time. He had to be.

Caius pushed the thoughts away and set about putting his home back in order. He threw himself into the work as a means to distract himself from his musings. With a touch of magic, he had the place cleaned of dust in no time. Then he brought up the lights and got the phone working. The change from abandoned derelict to livable space lightened his spirits once more. He was feeling immensely better by the time he lifted the receiver to call his lawyer, making a mental note to buy a phone from this decade when he had a chance.

His lawyer's office picked up before the second ring, and a professional female voice answered his call.

"Hello, I am a client of Mr. Montgomery's. I would like to make an appointment to see him." Caius hoped the man wasn't dead. That was one of the downfalls of being asleep for so long. Everyone else in the world aged without you.

"And your name is?"

Oh dear, what name had he used back then? "Alexander Sterling."

"Please hold, Mr. Sterling." There was a click before classical music filled the speaker. Before he could place the piece, the music was gone and a new voice spoke to him.

"This is Richard Montgomery speaking."

His lawyer sounded as ancient as he had to be—in his nineties, at least—but he was alive. That was what mattered.

"You're not dead yet!" Caius exclaimed. "Oh good. Listen, Monty, I'd like to return to the land of the living, possibly as my own grandson perhaps? I assume you've set aside paperwork for this sort of thing. I did say it would be a possibility when I hired you. What do you need to do to get the ball rolling? And you've kept my investments in order while I've been away, yes?"

There was a long pause on the other end of the line before his lawyer said, "You sound like you haven't aged a day since we last spoke."

"Yes, well, that's the thing about curses and magic. It messes with the natural order of things. Though I don't see how this should come as a surprise. I did tell you I was a lot older than I looked when we met. What made you think I would suddenly start to age now?"

"You told me that while I was drunk," Montgomery pointed out. "At your insistence, I might add. I was fresh out of college, and the amount of money you thrust in my face would make anyone call a crazy person eccentric just to be hired."

"Yes, but I didn't lie, and now you know I didn't. You should be honored I was so honest with you."

Montgomery groaned. "I'm too old for this."

"Think of it as one last adventure before you retire. You did prep the paperwork, didn't you?" A note of worry crept into Caius's voice, but he squashed it. No use panicking. He would handle whatever obstacles came his way. He'd done it before.

"Yes, I did. I don't know why, but I did."

Caius released the breath he'd been holding. He hadn't noticed how tense his shoulders had become until they dropped in relief. He'd have to brush up on his charms and enchantments to prevent moments like this in the future. Life was less stressful when things went his way without a hitch.

As if following Caius's train of thought, Monty said, "You're going to have to find another way to do this in the future. With the improvements in technology, it is getting harder to create false identities. This is widely outside my area of expertise. I did the best I could, but unless you know a hacker or have connections to the black market, I think you're going to be out of luck in the future."

Caius took the warning under advisement. "I under-stand," he said. Monty was too old to count on for much longer anyway. Caius would have to see about making new connections. He was starting from scratch, and he didn't think Andrew, his only solid link to the real world, would be of much use for these kinds of things.

"If your apparent age hasn't changed since I last saw you, then I agree that being your grandson would be best. I will begin the process of transferring ownership of The Cut Sleeve and your investments today. Do you know what you want to do with the building?"

Burn it down? "I still plan to live here for a while," Caius said. "I'd prefer to keep the basic structure intact, but a renovation is in order. We can discuss the details when we meet. I'm sure you have lots of paperwork for me to sign."

"Yes, and I will have updated statements of your current investments for you as well as other necessities."

"Oh, I'm so glad you're still alive, Monty. I don't know what I would have done without you. You're not still going to court defending justice for the masses, are you?"

"No, I'm working with wills and real estate mostly. I've been behind the desk for years, and I was planning on retiring soon."

"I've returned just in time then," Caius said. He sounded cheerful, but unease slithered down his spine. The world had become much smaller than it used to be. It was harder to disappear without a trace if necessary. If the Snake had wanted to keep him trapped in the curse for a hundred years or more, Caius didn't know what he would have done once he'd woken.

"I can have the initial paperwork ready by tomorrow afternoon," Monty said, interrupting his thoughts.

"Wonderful. I will see you then." Caius hung up.

Shaking off the anxiety of useless "what ifs," Caius turned his attention to something much more pressing and fun. What was he going to do with The Cut Sleeve? He wondered if he could keep the name for whatever he turned it into. Obviously, he couldn't reopen it as a bordello, although he had seen a gentleman's club when walking with Andrew earlier. The look of the place had made it apparent that the word "gentleman" did not apply. Caius wouldn't like running a business like that, but he did like the idea of managing something social.

He would also need to redecorate. He was tired of geometric shapes and functional styling. He wanted something warmer but flashy. Maybe he'd get electric lights for the bar! He could get performers into his establishment too. It would give him an excuse to keep the piano for more than his personal enjoyment. And the hookah lounge, were those in fashion anymore?

He needed to do research. He needed access to that thing called "Google," but first, he'd do things the old-fashioned way: he'd make a list. There was so much to do! Better to write it all down before he got too carried away. With a glance around the room, he realized the first things he would need to shop for: paper and a pen. He quickly changed into one of the outfits he'd purchased that morning and headed out.

Now that Andrew was away from Caius, he was having a hard time believing the events of the morning. Had he really woken someone from a sixty-year sleep, or had it just been another dream? Perhaps he'd snapped and was hallucinating.

That was a frightening thought.

He glanced over at Jason who was chatting with some of the other members of the hockey club. Andrew was tempted to ask him for advice, but he wasn't sure where to start.

"Hey, Jason, do you believe in magic? Like, if Harry Potter were real type magic?"

Yeah, that would go over well.

"You okay?" Jason asked.

"Yeah. Lost in thought is all."

"I noticed you didn't come home last night. Can I assume that everything worked out for the best?"

Andrew didn't know what to assume. He'd gotten what he'd wanted. Caius was in the real world, and a relationship was now a possibility. The realization struck him dumb for a moment. Tonight's date would not be in a dream. The more he thought about it the more excited he became.

"I'm still working on the details," he said, "but so far so good."

"Think you can introduce Charlie and me one of these days?"

Jason sounded happy for him. Andrew hated to make that feeling go away. "Yeah, but not yet. Things are...a little complicated right now." He felt like he should say something else, so he added, "Soon, all right?"

"Okay."

Andrew knew Jason wouldn't let the subject drop forever, but he wanted to enjoy having Caius in the real world for a bit before he had to share him with anyone. Plus, if he was going to introduce Caius to his friends, it would mean finally coming out to them. He wasn't ready for that yet.

That night when Andrew arrived to pick up Caius for dinner, he was surprised to see a light on over Ghost House's front door. Before he could knock, the door flew open, and Caius greeted him with a beaming smile. He was wearing a pair of skintight jeans and a sweater, and he looked *good*.

"I see you got the electricity going," Andrew said, hoping Caius had missed how blatantly he'd been checking him out. The glint in Caius's green eyes told Andrew that he'd been caught.

"I did more than that," Caius bragged. "Come in and see."

Andrew followed him inside, then froze as he took in the main room. The chandelier was lit, its iron polished and the crystal sparkling. The rest of the furniture had been cleaned as well. If not for some worn spots on the cushions, Andrew would have thought Caius had purchased everything new.

"I even tuned the piano," Caius said.

"How?" Andrew couldn't imagine Caius scrubbing the place clean.

Caius held up a hand and wiggled his fingers. "It's not something I'd like to make a habit of, but until I hire someone to clean for me, I'll have to make do."

Of course. Caius could do magic. He didn't need to scrub something to clean it.

A delicious smell wafted by Andrew's nose, and he sniffed the air. "Are you cooking?"

Caius lifted his chin proudly. "That's one of my talents that does not need a magic touch. I have a table set for us in the bar and a bottle of wine to share."

This really was a date. Speechless, Andrew followed Caius into the bar where there was a table set for two. Caius disappeared into the kitchen while Andrew took a seat. He appreciated not having to sit on those weird cylinder chairs, but he still didn't understand why there had been a difference in Ghost House's interior between the dream and reality.

Caius returned carrying two steaming bowls. He set them down before seating himself across from Andrew. "All this furniture has to go," he said as he lifted his spoon.

"It's completely dated, and I'm tired of looking at old things."

"What are you planning on doing with this place? You can't make it into a brothel again."

"No, that ship has sailed," Caius agreed.

"Have you figured out what you want to do?"

"Oh yes." Caius's eyes sparkled with excitement. "I've decided to open The Cut Sleeve Inn and Tavern. It's not a *drastic* change from the bordello, but I do love owning a social place where people can gather and gossip. And I'm hoping it won't be too big a ripple in the neighborhood pond. I'd rather not ruffle too many feathers with the word 'change.'"

Ghost House already had a kitchen, bar, and bedrooms upstairs. Turning the place into an inn sounded like a logical choice, but Andrew wasn't sure how lucrative the business would be. Ghost House was too far from the university to be a regular hangout, and it wasn't like the town had any major tourist attractions. Unless Caius made the inn into one.

"You should use the notoriety of Ghost House to draw people in," he suggested. "It's a well-known story, and the rumor of a haunted house could be a good lure."

Caius pursed his lips as he considered the idea. Then he gave Andrew a smile that made Andrew feel warm all over.

"I love it," Caius said.

"Are you planning on doing the renovations yourself?" Andrew asked. If Caius could accomplish what he had today in a couple of hours, he'd have the place transformed in no time.

"I'd love to," Caius admitted. "It would save me plenty of time and money, but that is unfortunately out of the question. I need to have the place redone, both inside and out. How would it look if the building were transfigured overnight?"

He had a point. "You could do the interior."

Caius shook his head. "People will be coming in and out of here, and it will be apparent that I only arrived in town recently. I can't have the interior redone and everyone wondering how that happened while they work on the outside. The same is true for if I wait. Why wouldn't I have the place done up all at the same time? Besides, this is tedious work and I hate using my magic for tedious things."

"When do you plan to start?"

"I'm meeting with my lawyer tomorrow, and I want to begin preparations immediately."

Setting aside his questions about how Caius had a lawyer when he'd been asleep for sixty years, Andrew thought Caius was rushing things a bit and said so.

Caius shrugged. "When I want to do something, what is the point of waiting?"

"I'm not surprised you're the impulsive type," Andrew said, "but this..."

Caius set his spoon down carefully and leaned forward. He looked...serious. Even the moments where he'd been straightforward hadn't felt so solemn. "I have savings enough to live on, but I cannot afford to be idle," Caius said. "Like the rest of the world, I need a job and a way to support myself. Given the fact that I am much older than I look and have mysteriously arrived in town, it is safer for me to become a functioning part of the community as soon as possible. Otherwise, questions may be asked."

"I don't think people would naturally assume the truth," Andrew pointed out.

"No, but you'd be surprised at how much people

distrust a stranger in their midst. I cannot afford to take chances. I'd rather allay their suspicions before they have a chance to raise them. It is one of the things you learn when you've lived as long as I have. You need to blend in."

"You don't strike me as the type of person who likes to blend in with the crowd," Andrew said.

"Blending in doesn't mean always being quiet or boring and never causing trouble. You can be the eccentric neighbor, or the loudmouth, or just an ordinary person, but whoever you are needs to be a puzzle piece that fits into the bigger picture. I built a bordello at a time period when people needed an escape. It was a risk, and even though I didn't advertise in the local paper, everyone knew what my place really was, but at the time, its existence made sense. Mine was the town secret, the place you never talked about, but that was the role I played. That was how I fit in."

"How do you plan to explain who you are now?"

"I am the grandson of the previous owner, and I inherited the property from the grandfather I never knew."

"So the rumors of the murder and disappearances are as much of a mystery to you as to everyone else."

"Exactly."

"What did happen here that night?" Andrew asked.

Like a mist wrapping around him, Caius's cheerful mood returned, and Andrew knew he wouldn't be getting a straight answer. "No one was murdered," he said as he lifted his spoon. "I can say that much for sure."

"That was the night you were cursed, wasn't it?"

"That's a silly question," Caius said. "Of course it was."

"The Snake is the one that cursed you. He practically said as much last night."

"And?" There was a touch of annoyance in Caius's voice.

"What is the connection between you two?" Andrew asked.

"He was once my lover," Caius said flatly.

A sudden jolt of pain shot through Andrew's chest. He hadn't expected that. "Did you curse him?"

Caius slammed his spoon down with a loud clank. "Is this a date or an interrogation?"

Crap. "I'm sorry," Andrew said, putting a hand out to placate him. "I didn't mean to press. I'm still trying to get used to this whole fairy tale as reality thing."

Caius was still fuming as he looked at Andrew. His lips were pressed into a thin line, and Andrew wondered if he would walk out.

"It's our first real date," he said. "Let's not ruin it."

It took a few moments before the muscles in Caius's face relaxed. "I made *andouillette* for dinner. I hope you like sausage."

Relieved, Andrew said, "I do. I'm looking forward to it. The soup you made is excellent."

Caius beamed, and the tension of the moment evaporated. "That's because it is one of my special recipes. I have learned a lot over the years. Did you know I once apprenticed to a famous French *patissier*? My *poire belle Helene* is to *die* for. I make everything from scratch."

"Did you make that tonight?"

"Oh no, my dear." Caius's eyes shone with a wicked glint. "That is a third date dessert, and only if you're *very* lucky."

NINE

—◆·◆—

The rest of their dinner had gone smoothly. Caius had been happy with the results of his cooking, and from the look of his clean plate, Andrew had enjoyed it as well. Caius suggested they take dessert in the parlor. He brought out a cup of the cinnamon tea Andrew liked and a chocolate cake designed to melt in one's mouth. He was sure the treat would go over just as well as the rest of the food had.

It did, though Andrew only had room for a small slice. Caius didn't mind. They ended up cuddling on the couch together with Caius resting his head against Andrew's shoulder. Caius enjoyed the position for a while, but once their teacups were empty and the pot had gone cold, he said, "You told me once that you would not have sex with me in a dream."

"Yes."

"We're not in a dream now."

Andrew smiled. "Take me to your room, Caius."

Caius wasn't one for being ordered about, but he supposed this was an acceptable time to make an exception.

He stood and held a hand out to Andrew. Andrew took it, and Caius led the way up the stairs to the third floor.

"I always knew this hallway felt short," Andrew said as they walked down the hall to Caius's bedroom. "This was a blank wall hidden by magic. It must have been how no one found you."

"You found me."

The look Andrew gave him made Caius's heart skip a beat. "Yes, I did."

Caius turned away before the palpitations could continue and opened the door to his room. "Won't you come in?"

He'd opened the curtains that divided his sleeping space from his sitting area so one could easily see the bed from the doorway. He wasn't sure why the sight of it made him nervous. He'd had many lovers before. There was nothing different about the act they were about to perform than what he'd done in the past.

Except it was. He could feel it in the brush of Andrew's fingers against his neck, and the kiss that followed the touch. A shiver ran through Caius, and his eyes drifted closed. He could sense Andrew walking around in front of him, and he tilted his chin up. The kiss was slow and sweet. He slid his hands up Andrew's arms and around his neck to pull him closer. Warm, strong arms wrapped around his waist.

The kiss broke as Andrew bent at the knees. Suddenly, he was being lifted and carried toward the bed. Caius laughed. "How can you carry me?" he cried. He knew Andrew was strong, but Caius wasn't a featherweight.

"If you wiggle around too much, I won't be able to."

Caius patiently waited while his prince carried him to the side of the bed and set him back on his feet. "Do I have you all night?" he asked.

"Yes."

"Good." Caius didn't want to rush. Every time Andrew looked at him, he felt precious. He wouldn't waste a single moment of that.

Andrew resumed kissing him, and every place his lips touched Caius's skin tingled. He assisted when Andrew lifted his sweater up and off. He insisted, and Andrew's shirt made the same journey to the floor.

"Hockey's a good sport for you."

Andrew chuckled. "Is that so?"

Caius nodded as he caressed the planes of Andrew's solid chest. "Absolutely."

"You know most of the sport involves skating. That's not an exercise that works out your chest."

Caius's interest had been piqued. "Oh? Is there another part of you I should be inspecting?"

"If you'd like."

"I would." Oh yes, he would. Caius reached around Andrew and slid his hands up Andrew's shoulder blades and down his back. He reached further and *oh my god.* "You are not allowed to wear anything but skintight pants from this moment forward. How dare you hide this from me."

"I haven't been hiding anything."

Caius fondled Andrew's rear end a bit longer, squeezing and massaging the luscious muscles. "We need to put this artwork on display, Andrew. I would like to spend a good amount of time admiring it."

"So would I."

They both froze. From where he stood, Caius could not see anyone else in the room, but that didn't mean anything. He should have known after bumping into Rowan—the Snake—earlier that the ghost would still be around. He probably couldn't leave the premises.

"Perhaps we should postpone for another night?" Andrew asked.

Regrettably, Caius agreed. He was not one for audiences in the bedroom, particularly when the voyeur was his ex. They collected their shirts and headed back downstairs.

"I hope you enjoyed this evening, despite our unwanted guest."

Andrew pulled Caius close and planted a kiss on his lips that clearly stated the incident had not diminished his interest in the slightest. "Have a good night, Caius."

"Goodnight," Caius said breathlessly. He watched until Andrew was out of sight around the corner before closing the door. Overall, it had been a wonderful first date.

Caius was practically floating the following morning. When his lawyer arrived for their meeting, he opened the door with a cheerful "Monty!" and a beaming smile. Given the situation of Caius becoming his own grandson, they had decided it would be best if Caius stayed away from his attorney's office and potentially prying eyes.

Richard Montgomery had aged considerably since Caius had last seen him. Even as a young man, his hairline had been threatening to leave him. Now it had flat out run away. His face, once so handsome, was lined with wrinkles, and his skin hung soft and loose on his bones.

"I am so relieved to see you still creaking around," Caius said as he gestured for Monty to enter. "I would have sent you a fruit basket, but I wasn't sure what you could eat besides prunes."

His lawyer shot him a pointed look before taking a seat on the couch. Caius was relieved to see the spark in Montgomery's eyes. *There* was the man he had originally hired just out of law school! Back then, Monty had been fresh and ready to tackle the world, not yet ruined by long work hours and the injustice of reality. Caius had hoped he hadn't lost his spirit over the years.

"So," he said, clapping his hands together. "What do you have for me? A ton of paperwork to sign? Never fear," he reached into his pocket, pulled out a ballpoint and clicked it. "I have a pen."

Monty didn't jump on board with Caius's enthusiasm, but he'd always been straitlaced about being professional. Boring though the idea may be, Caius did appreciate it in a lawyer. It was a necessary evil.

"Not all of your investments are where we'd like them to be," Monty began, "but they are sufficient to get you started and to cover your expenses for the renovation." He pulled a folder out of his briefcase and slid it over the coffee table to Caius. "Please review and sign the documents in here. They finalize your new identity and the inheritance that comes with it. I've taken the liberty of inventing your parents' names, but your given name is the one that you chose. I have also opened a new bank account for you at the local branch. You won't be needing a passport any time soon, will you?"

Caius shook his head as he scanned the paperwork, filling in signatures and initials where indicated. "I'll be basing myself here for a while. I'd like to get the business started and reestablish myself in the world before I start traveling again. Hopefully, that won't be a problem for a long time."

"I hope not," Monty said. "Like I said on the phone, with modern technology and digital records, it is getting harder to separate you from your past. An errant photo in a

Google search and people may start asking questions. Is there any coffee?"

"Oh! Yes, I put the pot up. It should be ready by now. If you'll excuse me."

Caius hurried into the back to get his guest some refreshments. He scolded himself for not being a good host. Sixty years of sleep was no excuse for rudeness.

"By the way," he said when he returned, "I heard that my books were donated to the university library. I take it many of my belongings have been stolen while I've been away?"

Monty didn't reply. He looked deep in thought as Caius reached the couch where he sat.

"Monty?" he called, worried that the old man was going senile.

With a start, the lawyer's attention snapped back to the present. "What? Oh. What were you saying?"

Caius's looked at him for a moment longer. He hoped that Monty wasn't losing his marbles. Caius couldn't afford to have him do that before all of the paperwork was settled. "I was asking if there has been much theft of my things while I've been gone."

"Due to the rumors of a murder, the premises were cordoned off as a crime scene, but with no body, the case was left unsolved." Monty accepted his cup and took a tentative sip. The coffee was black with a touch of sugar. Monty nodded in approval, and Caius was glad he had remembered correctly.

"Once the case was laid aside, they assumed the property would go into bankruptcy and it and its contents would be auctioned off. There was quite a stir when they discovered that the taxes were being paid on it even though no one had come forth to claim the place."

"That doesn't explain the missing paintings and silver."

"Thieves most likely. Students have come here for years playing haunted house."

"You couldn't have put everything into storage?"

"Storage would have cost more and brought up unnecessary questions. How would I have the authority to pack up the place if we hadn't been in touch? Besides, I had no idea where you had gone nor when you would be returning."

Caius thought there was more to the story. Perhaps the curse had kept Monty away. If the house had been cleaned out, his body would have been discovered upstairs even with magic hiding the door.

"And the books? Those would not have been stolen." They had been in his bedroom.

"Donated. A few of the neighbors were clamoring to have the building torn down, no matter who owned it. I figured a charitable donation in addition to paying the taxes would smooth over the ruffled feathers."

"You couldn't have taken the furniture instead?"

"It wouldn't have made as good an impression."

Caius took a deep, slow breath. He was trying very hard not to be angry. Of all the possessions he'd owned, the books had been some of his favorites. He never would have parted with them if it had been his choice.

"I need contact information for reputable construction companies. I also need a good electrician and a plumber."

"I thought you might," Monty said. He reached into his suit jacket and produced a handful of business cards and a flat, rectangular object. "I took the liberty of purchasing you a cell phone and signing you up for a basic plan."

A cell phone. Caius had heard of them, but this was the first time he'd held or even seen one. He turned it over in his hands. It was matte black on one side, with a rubbery texture. The other side was smooth and also black.

"How do I use it?"

Monty showed him how to turn it on and make phone calls. "If you want to know more advanced techniques, find someone at the university to teach you. For now, this should be sufficient."

Yes, Caius could get work started with this, and he had just the university student to give him further instruction.

"Wait a week before you start scheduling renovation estimates. I need some time to get these papers filed."

"Thank you, Monty. As always, you've been a gem."

Monty rolled his eyes, and it reminded Caius of the day they'd met. It had been in the coffee shop next to the university just after Monty had graduated. Caius had tried to flirt with him then and many times afterward. Monty's eye rolls had become a familiar sight during that time.

"That's all I have for you today," Monty said. He finished his coffee, collected the signed paperwork from Caius, and rose. "I'll give you a call next Monday with an update."

Caius walked him to the door. Just before stepping over the threshold, Monty turned to him. "Next time, I would prefer it if you gave me a warning before you disappeared," he said.

Caius's disappearance had not been by choice, but he nodded anyway. It was nice to know that Monty cared.

He saw the lawyer off and closed the door behind him. Now that things were officially under way, a bubble of excitement filled his chest. He hummed cheerfully as he dialed the number on the top business card Monty had given him.

· · ·

Like Caius, Andrew had woken in a good mood, but it was short lived once his phone rang. Although things had gone well when he'd visited his parents, he couldn't help the habitual sense of dread when he saw the word "Home" on his cell phone screen. Bracing himself, he pressed talk and set the phone to his ear.

"I've set up a summer internship for you at Anderson and Associates."

"What? No hello?"

"The opportunity will give you experience as well as an outside perspective for when you come to work for me," his father continued, oblivious to—or more likely ignoring—his sarcastic remark.

"Dad," Andrew said, pinching the bridge of his nose with two fingers. "I told you that I would look into it myself."

"Well, you haven't been," his father said bluntly. Andrew didn't want to know how his father knew that. It would only frustrate him more.

Besides the frustration, Andrew also felt disappointment. A part of him had thought things might change between them after his visit. He'd had some really good conversations with his dad when they'd discussed the company for Andrew's final project. Andrew had hoped it would be the beginning of better communication between them in general. He'd even toyed with the idea of finally telling his father what he wanted—or rather, what he didn't want—to do with his life, but it seemed that had been too much to hope for.

"I know you are working hard on that project, Andrew, but this is also important," his father continued. "College will be over before you know it. Classes can only teach you so much. You need real-world experience, especially if you want to run a company one day."

So now he was running the company and not just working at it? "Can we talk about this another time?" Sometime when he hadn't been assaulted by the announcement and could think of a way to get out of it that his father would actually listen to?

His father sighed. It was a familiar enough sound for Andrew to feel the full weight of his disappointment through the phone. "Fine," he said finally. "But you can't put this off forever." Andrew knew that all too well.

"Thanks, Dad."

"Goodbye, son."

Andrew didn't feel any better once he'd hung up. Even if he didn't want to take over the company, he still wanted his father's approval. He hated how he always ended up pushing it away. He needed a diversion. Something to make the murky feeling go away. Jason would normally be his first choice, but now that he was fully awake, he realized he was alone in their room. Jason was probably out with Marie. They sometimes liked to have breakfast in places where they could watch the sunrise. Andrew wasn't fond of waking up that early, but when he considered the idea as a date with Caius, he could understand the appeal.

Caius would also be a great distraction, but he was busy working on arrangements for Ghost House's future. Andrew couldn't just drop by. Or maybe he could. Even if Caius was busy, he still had to eat. Grinning, he grabbed his wallet and keys and headed out the door.

He stopped by his favorite bar, The Bucket and Barrel, on the way. The place served a great burger. Although he couldn't imagine Caius eating burgers—or anything that required using his hands instead of utensils—it was the easiest lunch on short notice, and it was cheap. Unlike Caius, Andrew wasn't rolling in dough that had been multiplying for decades.

The bag was still warm when he knocked on the door. Caius looked pleased to see him and ushered him inside.

"I didn't know how much work you had to do today," Andrew said as he entered, "so I brought you some lunch."

"How sweet!" Caius exclaimed. "Though I am suspicious of the grease stain forming on that paper bag you're holding," he added, eying the package warily.

"Did I steer you wrong with The Eatery?"

"No..." Caius admitted reluctantly.

"Then trust me on this. Though I recommend grabbing some plates, and the beers should chill before we drink them."

Caius fetched plates, napkins, and a bucket of ice for the beers, and they set up their lunch in the parlor.

"Goodness! I haven't had a hamburger in *years!*" Caius dove in, taking a giant bite of the sandwich. He moaned in pleasure as he chewed. The sound was something usually reserved for a bedroom. "This is delicious!"

"I'm surprised you've eaten one before. Somehow I always picture you eating at tables where there are more utensils than food."

Caius laughed. "My dear, I have dined at the *finest* of restaurants, and I have been poorer than the poorest of men. You'll find I have experienced most of what life has to offer, though I am always pleased when there is even more to discover."

"And what have you discovered so far, now that you're awake?"

Caius pondered the question. "For one thing,

hamburgers have only gotten better with time," he said before taking another pleasure-filled bite.

Caius never ceased to surprise Andrew. Something warm filled his chest as he watched Caius eat, and he couldn't help thinking that he'd like to keep having times like these in the future.

"Oh! I forgot a bottle opener." Caius put his hamburger down and rose. "I'll be right back."

Andrew nodded and watched him go. Then he remembered his own burger and bit into it. Yeah, he was glad he'd brought these. The Bucket knew how to make a burger, unlike those fast food joints all around town. He imagined Caius's reaction if he'd tried one of those and laughed as he pictured it.

"Aren't you forgetting something?" a voice hissed in his ear.

Andrew choked on his food and whirled around, but no one was there. He coughed as a stray piece of meat threatened to go down the wrong pipe and carefully swallowed, his eyes watering as he searched the room. If he wasn't mistaken, the voice had sounded like the Snake's. Just like the one from last night.

"I've been meaning to ask you," Caius said as he entered the room. Catching sight of Andrew, he asked, "Is something wrong?"

Andrew shook his head. "Ate too fast. I'm fine." There was no reason to worry Caius. He wasn't going to let the Snake ruin their time together if he could help it.

Caius didn't look convinced, but he let it slide. He sat and reached over to pop open two of the beer bottles. "So, as I was saying, I've been meaning to ask you if hookah smoking is in fashion."

"Hookah smoking?" Andrew asked as he accepted one of the bottles.

"Yes, like the pipe you saw behind my curtain. I was wondering if I should offer it when I reopen."

"I'm not sure. I've never come across it except for here, but that doesn't mean it's not popular. Though the law prohibits smoking in public places unless it's in a designated area. You'll have to look into that before you decide."

"I'll make note of that and ask Monty about it when I speak to him on Monday."

"Monty?"

"My lawyer."

"Oh."

The thought of the lounge behind the curtain reminded Andrew of the "woman" he'd met in his dream. He'd forgotten all about the ghosts after Caius had awoken. "Caius," he said. He took a swig of beer before continuing, feeling braver with the liquid courage. "The people I met the night I woke you. Did you really curse them all?"

"I'm assuming you mean the boys who had worked here in the dream."

"They didn't all look like boys the night I woke you."

"Yes, they were all cursed by me."

Andrew was surprised by Caius's blunt delivery. He had expected one of his usual whimsical replies, the kind that avoided answering anything.

It must have shown on his face, because Caius said, "I have no reason to lie."

Memories of the blind man and the mute boy came back to him, and he couldn't help asking, "Why?"

"I don't need to justify my actions to you," Caius said. "They're in the past, long before you were even born."

"You told me once that you cursed to punish, but I..."

He still couldn't get past the idea that Caius could be so cruel. "Did you really turn someone into a woman so they'd be treated badly?"

Caius laughed. "Oh yes, and with *pleasure*."

Andrew's eyes widened in horror, and he instinctively leaned away from Caius. What sort of a monster had he woken? Had the Snake been right all along?

"Given your reaction," Caius continued, "I take it the dream did not tell you that he and his friends were the type of men to violate women without a thought. I simply gave him a taste of his own medicine."

"And the rest?"

"Similar. I won't pretend that none of them were inspired by personal grudges, but they all had a reason."

"Like the toad?"

"It was a fitting description for him," Caius said. "I do wonder if anyone kissed him to break the spell. They would have been very disappointed unless he'd learned to change his ways by then."

"What about the blind man?" Andrew asked.

"What blind man?"

"There was a blind man in the hall. He said his sight had been taken from him because he'd displeased you."

Caius's brow creased in confusion. "What did he look like?"

"I don't know. It was dark when I met him."

Caius was silent.

The sight of him thinking so seriously made the hairs on the back of Andrew's neck stand up. "Is something wrong?"

"I'm not sure."

That was worrying. Andrew tried to remember the blind ghost, but couldn't think of any more details to offer. When the lights had returned, the Snake had been there with him and the ghost had been gone. Maybe the Snake had tricked him into believing there was a blind ghost? If so, why?

As he thought back to that night, Andrew remembered the man on the stairwell who'd been so afraid to look at his own portrait. "You never cursed that boy," he said. "The one with the painting."

Caius looked confused for a moment before he smiled warmly. "No, I never cursed him. I only told him I did."

"So he wouldn't think he was ugly?"

Caius nodded.

"And the blind man?"

The furrow returned to Caius's brow. "I never used blindness as a curse," he said, "but I do know a man who became blind."

"Who?"

Caius hesitated, and when he looked at Andrew, his usual chipper mask was in place. "Let's save the stories for another time, shall we? What are you doing tomorrow?"

Caius sat on the couch replaying their conversation in his mind for a long time after Andrew had left. Like he'd told Andrew, of all the curses he'd performed, none of them had ever been blindness, but he'd known a man who'd become blind. Caius's feelings about the incident had been mixed at the time, due to his relationship with a man named Rowan.

During the Roaring Twenties, Caius had met a beautiful blond man one night at a party. Like a scene in a film, they had spotted each other from across the room. Caught up in the music and laughter all around him, Caius had indulged in some not-so-innocent flirting. There had been something magnetic about the stranger that had provoked

Caius to take the chance in believing the man shared his proclivities. They began to see each other quite often, and it wasn't long before Caius had fallen completely. Rowan was handsome, charming, and full of interesting stories of the places he had been.

Rowan was also a sorcerer. His power was not as strong as Caius's, but it ran like a natural extension of his being. His talent was charisma. He was a master of charms, and even if he didn't know how to manipulate his power as intricately as Caius, he knew how to employ it to get what he wanted. Caius understood that temptation.

Yet even with the danger of trusting another sorcerer, Caius had wanted to believe in love. He had hoped that he'd finally found a man who would stand by him. Unfortunately, the past tended to repeat itself, and just like before, Caius was proven wrong. He'd caught Rowan cheating on him, and in his anger, he'd cursed his lover to become a snake.

Not long after that, the man who Rowan had been cheating with was thrown from a horse into a nasty thorn bush and blinded.

"Is that what this is all about?" he asked. The empty room was quiet, but he waited, knowing it wouldn't be for long.

Finally, the Snake answered. "I have no idea what you're talking about." Caius could sense him standing behind the couch, but he didn't turn to look.

"The blind man," Caius said. "He's the one you cheated on me with, isn't he?"

"Blind man?" the Snake asked, but the innocence in his voice was falling flat.

In a rage, Caius stood and whirled around. "You

trapped me in a dream for sixty years," he snapped. "I deserve to know why!"

The Snake's mouth curved into a sneer. "You know why. You know exactly what you did."

"Yes," Caius agreed. "I turned you into a snake for cheating on me. Did that really warrant a sleeping curse? And how did you manage it anyway? Curses were never your forte. You didn't have the power to build one this complex."

"I had help."

That much was obvious. Caius let his own expression turn wicked and taunting. "Not for much longer," he said. "You don't have the strength to hold the curse anymore. I'm sure being dead doesn't help."

The Snake leaned forward, bringing his face in close to Caius's. "I'm still strong enough to hurt you."

"Oh?" Caius asked, his voice dripping with sarcasm. "How do you figure that? From where I'm standing, you're already fading. Or did you think I wouldn't notice that your feet are soft around the edges just because you're hiding them behind the couch?"

He felt immense satisfaction when the Snake vanished without another word.

TEN

———◆·◆———

Caius had seemed interested when Andrew had told him about the hockey club, so Andrew had offered him an invitation to the game on Sunday. He hadn't expected Caius to actually show up, but there he was in the stands. He stood out among the sports jerseys and university sweatshirts in a fur-edged lavender jacket. Andrew shouldn't have been surprised when others noticed him.

"Who's that?" Jason asked, nodding toward Caius. "I haven't seen him before."

"Do you memorize everyone who comes to our games?" Andrew asked. "Keeping tabs on your fans?"

"At least I have fans," Jason said, gesturing to where Marie sat in the front row.

"That's *a* fan. And she's your girlfriend, so it doesn't count. She has to be here whether she wants to be or not."

"Are you saying she's only here out of a sense of duty to me?"

"Yup."

Jason attempted a glare, but it was a losing battle. "I'll

take it. I'd rather have Marie than no fans at all." He looked pointedly at Andrew.

"My popularity is like a cult classic," Andrew said. "Underrated by those not in the know."

Jason laughed, but his smile faded as he said, "Get your *girl* to come." Something in his tone felt like a challenge, but Andrew didn't know why that would be. *He couldn't know, could he?* Before he could figure out what was up, a whistle blew. The game was about to begin.

It had been a long time since Caius had attended a sporting event, and he'd never seen a hockey game before. For the first fifteen minutes, he'd had no idea what was going on. Then he'd asked the sweaty gentleman next to him to explain the rules. Among the rain of pretzel pieces flying out of the man's mouth, Caius managed to catch the pertinent details. From that point on, it was a matter of admiring Andrew in his uniform and cheering when necessary. Unfortunately, hockey had nothing on baseball when it came to uniforms, but he had a good time overall.

After the game, Caius waited for Andrew in the lobby, hoping to congratulate him on his team's win. It wasn't long before the players stampeded out of the locker room sharing congratulations and patting each other on the back. When Andrew finally appeared, Caius was fascinated by the sheer joy on his face. Andrew's cheeks were flushed, his hair damp with sweat, and his grin couldn't have been wider.

Apparently, it could, because it brightened even further when he caught sight of Caius. Caius's heart skipped a beat at that look, and he couldn't help but smile in return.

As his teammates thundered by, Andrew moved closer to Caius. "You came," he said.

"I told you I would."

Andrew was looking at him like Caius was the most wonderful thing he'd ever seen. It was almost too much for Caius to take. "You'll miss your bus."

"Yeah," Andrew said, but he didn't move to leave.

"Meet me at the house later? I'll make you a celebratory dinner."

"Okay." Andrew hesitated a moment longer, and Caius wondered if he was going to be kissed. In *public*. The moment passed, and Andrew headed out to the shuttle bus. As he exited, Caius spotted one of Andrew's teammates watching him. The young man looked at Caius curiously before following Andrew out the door. Caius wondered if this was the best friend Andrew had referred to when they had first met. He was handsome. Andrew had good taste. No wonder Andrew had been in love with the boy for so long. Perhaps he was in love with him still. Caius didn't care for that thought. At all.

"I thought you didn't know that guy," Jason said as he and Andrew dropped into their seats on the bus.

"What guy?" Andrew asked. He was still reeling over the fact that Caius had come to the game. Between that and their win, the excitement had almost driven him to kiss Caius in front of everyone. *Not* the way he wanted to come out to the world.

He forced himself to focus his attention on Jason. He'd see Caius later.

"The guy in the purple jacket," Jason clarified. "I thought you didn't know him."

Shit. "I didn't say I didn't know him." That much was true.

"Who is he?"

"Just someone I know." That sounded lame. "I told him about the game, and he decided to come see it."

"He didn't look like a student. Where'd you meet him?"

"What's with the third degree?" Andrew flinched at his tone. "I'm sorry. I didn't mean that."

"Whatever, man," Jason said, turning away from him in a huff.

Andrew wondered if an apology would help or if it would just seem reactionary.

"You know," Jason said, looking at him again, "you're welcome to have a life of your own, but you could at least tell me about it. I thought we were friends, man. I thought we could tell each other anything."

At that moment, Andrew wanted to. He wanted to lay all his cards on the table, spill all the secrets he'd been carrying, but the words stuck in his throat. His silence went on for too long. With a disappointed sigh, Jason gave up waiting and looked out the window. They rode the rest of the way back to campus in silence.

Andrew's fight with Jason put a damper on his high that stayed with him until he went to Caius's for dinner. His mood must have shown on his face, because as soon as he arrived at the house, Caius asked, "What's wrong?"

Andrew hesitated to answer. He remembered how Caius had kicked him out of the dreams because of his friendship with Jason. He was hesitant to find out how Caius would react if he brought him up now. "Jason's mad at me. He thinks I'm keeping secrets from him."

"Are you?"

"...Yes."

Caius looked at him pointedly before stepping aside to let him into the house. "Come in and sit down. I'll get us some wine, and you can tell me your excuses."

This was going better than he'd expected. "My excuses?"

"For the secrets you're keeping. I'm sure you have your reasons. If I'm going to defend your choice, I'll have to know what they are."

"When did you become so reasonable?"

Caius turned to him. "What do you mean when? I've always been reasonable."

"Says the sorcerer who's cursed a dozen people and kicked me out of his dream on the assumption that I was in love with my best friend." He winced. He probably shouldn't have brought either of those things up.

"You are in love with your best friend," Caius pointed out. "As long as you show me that you're devoted to me, I will not fault you for it."

"That's reassuring," Andrew said, his tone only partially sarcastic.

"Sit down before you put your foot in your mouth any further and tell me what happened."

Andrew sat. "It was after we left the game, when we got on the bus. He was asking about you, and I didn't know how to answer, and he got upset."

"Understandable. I'm sure it's difficult to explain how we met. It has never been a good idea to spread the knowledge of magic far and wide. Most people are reluctant to believe in it. Telling them the truth often causes more trouble than it's worth. That is one of the reasons sorcerers keep their identities secret."

"You told me."

"While we were in a magic spell," Caius pointed out.

"One I never thought I would leave, or I probably wouldn't have told you."

"Why not?"

"People who know about a sorcerer react with either fear or greed. Both are dangerous motives for betrayal. That is why we keep not only our identities secret but our particular talents."

"You must know other sorcerers though. You're not the only one, are you?"

"No, I'm not, but ordinary people are not the only ones who can betray us. Our own kind can be worse. This is why we don't tell anyone who we are. Secrecy is ingrained into us all."

Andrew was quiet for a moment. Then he asked, "Do you regret telling me?"

"So far, no," Caius said. "And I hope I never will."

Andrew would make sure he didn't give Caius any cause for regret.

Apparently feeling the serious portion of their conversation had gone on long enough, Caius's expression lightened with a smile, and he changed the topic with his usual chipper flair. "You're going to have to fix this situation with Jason. I can't meet your friends if you're having a tiff with one of them."

"You want to meet my friends?" Andrew asked, surprised.

"Of course! I would introduce you to mine if I had any left. Unfortunately, the only acquaintance I can get in touch with lately is unfit for civilized company, not to mention dead. And you've already met him."

Introducing Caius to his friends meant coming out. Andrew still didn't feel ready to do that yet. At least he had a legitimate excuse to put it off for now. "I'll have to work on making up with Jason then."

"Don't make up with him too well," Caius cautioned. "If he suddenly decides he wants to be more than friends, you better tell him you're unable to accept. I *do not* share."

"I am well aware of that." Andrew gestured to the wine bottle. "I thought you were going to feed me. I was promised a home-cooked meal in celebration of my team's win."

"And you shall have it as soon as—" A distant alarm sounded from the direction of the bar. "Dinner will be out in a few minutes." Caius rose. "Pour for us in the meantime?"

"Mind if I come with you? I've never seen a bar kitchen before."

"It's not that exciting, but if you insist." Caius led the way, turning off the alarm once they were inside. He opened the oven and pulled out a ham, setting it to cool on the stove while he took some vegetables out of the fridge to make a quick salad. He was focused on his task, but the warmth of another body behind him made him pause his chopping.

"I've never found cooking to be sexy before," Andrew commented.

A shiver ran through Caius's body at the close proximity of Andrew's voice and heat. He thought of food as a sensual experience, sometimes even sexual, but the process of making it had not been a turn on. Until now. "Oh?"

Andrew wrapped his arms around Caius's waist and closed the gap between them. "Perhaps it's the cook who turns me on."

"I would hope so," Caius said. "If it's the lettuce, we are going to have to discuss your sexual interests."

Andrew chuckled and kissed Caius's neck. Caius closed his eyes as he savored the touch. "I'm going to slice my hand if you keep that up. You're terribly distracting."

"Then put down the knife."

"What about dinner?"

"Put down the knife, Caius."

Caius set the utensil on the cutting board and turned in Andrew's arms. His lips were immediately met by Andrew's. Sliding his arms up over Andrew's shoulders and around his neck, he succumbed to the sweet pleasure of being devoured. They were both panting when they came up for air.

"If my ham has turned cold because of you, I will be very cross."

"I highly doubt that."

Andrew was right. "We should eat. I did promise to feed you, and I wouldn't want to break my word." Reluctantly they separated, and Caius turned to finish preparing the salad. "Why don't you keep yourself busy by setting the table?" he suggested. "The plates are in that cabinet by the door and the silverware is in the drawer beneath it."

It wasn't long before they were seated and eating. The ham had cooled more than Caius liked, but with the way Andrew was looking at him across the dinner table, he didn't care.

"How is your schoolwork going?" Caius asked in an attempt to distract himself from thoughts of what he'd like to do to Andrew once they were finished eating. He was almost sorry he asked when a cloud shadowed Andrew's expression once more.

"Okay, I guess. I have this big project that I'm working

on for my operations management class. I'm doing it on my father's company. He owns a management consulting firm."

"You don't look thrilled about it." Not that Caius had cared for schoolwork when he had been in school, but this looked to be more than boredom for Andrew.

Andrew sighed. "I'm not. Did I tell you my dad wants me to work for his company after I graduate? He has this idea that I'll work my way up the company and maybe even take over for him in the future."

"Sounds like a plan for a secure future," Caius hedged. His first lover's parents had planned their son's future out for him too. It hadn't ended well for Caius.

"I don't want that future. I like the idea of helping people, but I don't want to do it on such a large scale. It feels...impersonal."

"Then why do your project on a business you don't want to be in?"

"I couldn't think of any other options."

Andrew needed to be more motivated. Caius could understand not wanting to pursue something he wasn't interested in, but he had never had a problem finding something to be interested in. "What about a small business that is just starting? In fact, it hasn't even opened yet, but the owner would be more than willing to give you all the information you'd need on the process and future plans."

Andrew gave him a small smile for trying, but it apparently wasn't enough of a push. "I already turned in my proposal stating that I would do the project on my dad's company."

"It couldn't hurt to ask. Make another proposal and present it to him. Explain that this is an opportunity to see a business grow from the ground up. I'm sure your professor would be thrilled by your initiative, and if he doesn't like the idea, you didn't lose anything for asking."

Andrew was quiet as he considered the idea. Caius let him simmer as he poured them more wine.

"I suppose it couldn't hurt to ask," Andrew said finally. "Besides, it would be a lot more fun working with you on Ghost House than it would be writing about my father's company."

"I do believe I told you not to call my home by that moniker."

"Old habits are hard to break."

"I still think you should make it up to me for using it."

"I'd be happy to, but you'll have to wait until tomorrow. It's getting late, and Monday's my early class."

Caius had a meeting with a contractor in the morning, but that didn't keep him from being disappointed. "One of these days I would like a date that doesn't end until the sun comes up."

Andrew leaned forward and kissed Caius sweetly. "Tomorrow. We can stay up till dawn and eat breakfast while watching the sunrise."

Caius liked the sound of that. "I will hold you to that. Rest up then. You'll need plenty of energy for me tomorrow."

"Yes, sir," Andrew said with a smile and another kiss. This one merged into another and another. Fifteen minutes later, lips swollen and smiling dreamily, Andrew left The Cut Sleeve. Caius, in a similar state, stood in the doorway and watched until he was out of sight.

—◆◆—

ELEVEN

While Monty was busy working on bypassing probate with something called a transfer-on-death deed—Caius had no idea what that meant, but Monty assured him it made things run more smoothly—Caius was getting a head start on The Cut Sleeve's renovations by getting a few estimates from local contractors. He had remembered Monty's request to postpone contractor meetings, but Caius was impatient to start. His first appointment arrived early Monday morning ready to get to work. Caius appreciated the man's focus. He gave an informative tour of the building, filling the workman, whose name was Bill, in on his vision for the project. Bill asked questions and offered recommendations regarding design, potential material, and budget. Caius welcomed the input. They ended the tour in the parlor where they sat to discuss the plans in more detail.

Unwilling to be a bad host, Caius asked, "Would you care for something to drink? Coffee? Water?"

"Water would be great. Thank you."

Caius fetched two glasses of ice water from the kitchen

and returned to find the receiving room empty. Confused, he left the drinks on the table and went in search of Bill. The man was nowhere to be found.

Caius was completely bewildered. Where could the man have gone? He went to the front door to check for Bill's truck, but it had vanished as well. He tried calling Bill's phone, but it went immediately to voicemail. He left a concerned message, followed by a more stern one an hour later when the contractor failed to reappear or return his call. Frustrated, he hung up the phone and left the house. It was a brisk day, perfect for letting off steam with a walk. He headed for the university. Andrew was just the sort of diversion he needed, and it wouldn't hurt to return the surprise lunch favor.

When he arrived on campus, he had no idea where to go, nor did he know where Andrew would be at that hour. He asked a passerby for directions to the business building, which he learned was named Boyle Hall, figuring the location of Andrew's major would be the perfect place to start.

Boyle Hall was suitable for learning, he supposed. It had an open lobby with a few benches centered in the middle of the room. He assumed the setup was meant to be a place for people to loiter while waiting between classes, but the seating was far from comfortable. Wooden benches without even a hint of cushioning were not welcoming to one's posterior. Still, the place was meant for learning, not comfort, and the multitude of doors and hallways branching off from the entrance hall spoke of plenty of classrooms that fulfilled the location's purpose. It also meant finding Andrew in here would be like finding a needle in a haystack.

"Excuse me," he called to a woman who looked to be no

taller than his elbow. "Would you happen to know an Andrew Hollenbeck?"

"Yes, he's in my Intro to Statistics class."

"Do you know if he has class now?"

She shook her head. "Class ended about fifteen minutes ago. I saw him head out with someone. Don't know where they were off to."

That was disappointing. Andrew could be anywhere. Caius glanced at the clock on the wall. It was just twelve o'clock. Perhaps Andrew and his friend—who Caius assumed was Jason—had gone for lunch.

"Can you point me in the direction of the cafeteria?"

"Sure, follow the path back toward the main road and it will be right across the street."

"Thank you."

The wind had picked up, and Caius reached into his pocket to pull out his gloves. Instead, his fingers encountered rubbery plastic. He was still becoming accustomed to the concept of cell phones. He pulled it out, planning to call Andrew, but stopped when a glass case on the wall caught his eye. He remembered Andrew mentioning the set of Shakespeare plays he'd found that reminded him of Caius's. Caius stepped forward to take a closer look. They appeared to be pristine, but Caius knew there was a fold on page twenty-two of the *Taming of the Shrew* and that the spine on the *Merchant of Venice* was slightly warped. There was no doubt in his mind. These were his books.

A rush of anger heated his body, making him clench the device he still held in his hand. Monty had had no right to donate them. They had been a gift from—

Caius froze. His eyes widened as the picture became clearer. His heart began to race as a new fury took hold of him.

"That *asshole!*" he screamed. Then, to the group of startled onlookers, he added, "My apologies," but he wasn't sorry. He was *furious*. Jaw clenched, he stormed out of Boyle Hall. His breath came in short huffs out his nose like a dragon getting ready to spew fire as he marched home, his plan to treat Andrew to lunch forgotten.

Jason hadn't been the one to pick up Andrew when he got out of class. He was still giving Andrew the silent treatment. Instead, it was Charlie who caught him as he was leaving class and walked with him to The Grill for lunch. The Grill was a decent hamburger place in the Student Union, although it was better known as a hot spot for watching sports games on the big screen TVs bolted to the restaurant's walls. On game nights the place was packed, but for lunch, you could still carry on a conversation while you ate.

"Wait till you hear the news!" Charlie announced, his hands moving as animatedly as his face.

Trepidation over another of Charlie's schemes distracted Andrew from his disappointment that Jason was still avoiding him. Andrew hated that his friend was angry with him, but he wasn't ready to explain his and Caius's relationship yet. Even if he was willing to tell Jason that they were sort of dating, he couldn't tell him that they'd initially met in a dream. Jason was right. He was keeping secrets, but he didn't know what else to do with the information.

Charlie was oblivious to the tension when they met up with Jason at The Grill. He'd been grinning the whole walk over, and the smile only brightened now that he had a bigger audience.

"Guess what I heard," he said as they took their seats.

"What?" Jason asked. Andrew noted how his friend's attention was solely on Charlie. Andrew's exclusion was loud and clear.

"Someone's planning to reopen Ghost House."

Andrew dropped a fry in surprise. He'd known Caius was working on reopening the place, but he'd just started. Andrew hadn't thought the news would spread so quickly.

"Seriously?" Jason asked. "They can't expect to keep it as it was."

"No, they want to turn it into a bar or something. My father's a contractor, and he was called to come in and give an estimate on the work that needs to be done."

That explained how Charlie had gotten his news. Andrew felt some relief at that, but only a little.

"Who's going to open it?" Jason asked. Andrew knew the answer to that, but he kept his mouth shut.

Charlie shrugged. "Some guy. I think he's a relative of the one who ran the place before it closed." Charlie's enthusiasm brightened a few notches as he added, "Maybe he knows what happened that night. We should drop by to meet him and see if he'll tell us."

"I don't think so." The words were out of Andrew's mouth before he could stop them. Charlie and Jason both turned to look at him.

"Why not?" Jason asked, his voice sharper than usual.

Andrew scrambled for something legitimate to say. "If he knew what had happened, don't you think he would have told the police or someone already?"

Charlie shrugged. "We could still ask."

Andrew didn't want to ask, he already knew.

"I'm game for going," Jason said. "Maybe he'll let us see the place in daylight."

Charlie turned to Andrew expectantly. Andrew hesitated. He didn't want to show up at Ghost House and have
Jason and Charlie find out that he knew Caius and hadn't
told them. He considered turning Charlie down with disin-
terest as an excuse, but one glance at Jason's face and he
knew it wouldn't fly. "Okay," he said reluctantly.

"Great!" Charlie exclaimed. "Hurry up and finish
eating so we can go."

Anger had fueled Caius all the way home where he
wrenched open his front door, planted himself in the
middle of the foyer, and yelled, "Get your wretched, wrig-
gling self out here!"

A slow, mocking laugh answered him, but no one
appeared.

"Rowan! I said get out here!"

Quick as a gale, the Snake's sharp, pointed face was
inches from his own. "I *told* you never to call me that again."

Caius was not intimidated. "You. You're the one who
made Monty donate those books. You couldn't bear to let
me keep them since you'd given them to me."

"*I* don't think you deserve anything at all," the Snake
replied, "but especially not those. They were a precious
commodity and should only be given to worthy lovers."

"I'm not the one who cheated," Caius spat.

"Oh poo. It was a simple indiscretion. There was no
need to ruin lives for it."

"Like you wouldn't have done the same if it had been
me who'd cheated."

The Snake's eyes narrowed. "I wouldn't have injured an
innocent man just to satisfy my own heartbreak."

Caius laughed. "Yes, you would. You'd hurt Andrew to hurt me the first chance you got."

The Snake smiled, and Caius immediately regretted bringing Andrew into the conversation.

"You hurt me and mine, it's only fair I return the favor."

"I never did anything to yours, only you," Caius said.

The Snake sneered. "*Don't* lie to me. I know *exactly* what you did to him."

"Get out," Caius snapped. "Get out before I—"

"What?" the Snake asked mockingly. "What can you do to me that you haven't already done?"

The fury inside Caius smoothed into something darker. The air around him became charged as he reached for power, like the onset of a lightning storm. He leaned forward, pinning the Snake with his gaze. "If you hurt one hair on Andrew's head, I will rip you into pieces so tiny that not even time will be able to find you."

The Snake vanished.

It had been a long time since Caius had threatened someone. It was nice to know that in all those years he hadn't lost his touch.

Andrew had spent the half hour walk to Ghost House trying to figure out how to explain Caius once everyone inevitably met. His solution had been to pray that Caius wouldn't be home.

Unfortunately, he was. Before they could knock, Caius had opened the door. He'd seemed puzzled to see them at first, but when he'd noticed Andrew, he'd smiled. Despite his reservations, Caius's presence loosened the knot in Andrew's chest.

"Hey, I know you," Jason said. "You're the guy who spoke with Andrew after the game on Sunday."

Andrew felt the blood drain from his face.

Caius's cheerfulness wilted slightly. There was something aloof about it now, like the kind of look people gave acquaintances when asking how they were when they didn't actually want to know. "You're the teammate I saw waiting for him," he said, extending a hand toward Jason. "Caius. It is a pleasure to meet you."

"I'm Jason," Jason said, shaking his hand, "and this is Charlie. How do you know Andrew?"

"I told you," Andrew interrupted before Caius could say anything, "we're acquaintances, nothing more."

Caius slowly turned his gaze to Andrew. Andrew felt it like a knife plunging into his chest. He surreptitiously felt his hips and stomach to make sure he was still human.

"Yes," Caius said, his voice as cold as his stare, "we're acquaintances and nothing more." He looked back at Jason, charming once again. "How can I help you?"

"We heard you were reopening Ghost House," Charlie said. "Is it true?"

"I'm working on it."

"Are you related to the guy who used to own it? Do you know what happened to him?" Charlie's enthusiasm left no room for tact.

Caius's tone turned chilly. "I'm afraid not. If you'll excuse me, I have things to attend to."

Without waiting for them to reply, he stepped back and closed the door. Andrew was suddenly overcome with a need to throw himself at it and beg Caius to let him in so he could explain, but he couldn't do that in front of Charlie and Jason. He was so distracted that he missed Charlie's question.

"What?"

"I said, you know that guy? Why didn't you tell us you knew the person who was opening Ghost House?"

"I—"

"Andrew likes to keep secrets," Jason interrupted. "Didn't you know?" He brushed by Andrew and started down the road toward campus.

"What's going on with you two?" Charlie asked.

Andrew sighed. "I don't know." Except he did. He just didn't have the energy to explain.

"Whatever, man. Let's go. This was a bust."

Andrew hesitated. He knew he should tell Jason and Charlie to go off without him so he could apologize to Caius, but he didn't know what to say. It was pretty obvious what he'd done. He'd come back later, once he could sneak off without either of his friends asking questions. With one last look at the closed front door, he turned and followed.

Caius was still fuming later that night when Andrew knocked on his door. He knew it was Andrew even before he went to open it. He knew exactly what the little twerp had come for too. He was going to apologize to Caius for lying in front of his friends and explain how he couldn't have their relationship known. Caius knew this scene well. He'd been a participant in it before, in the same role as he was now, and he hated it. He considered not answering and letting Andrew stew on the front stoop until he finally went away but decided that it would be more satisfying to yell at Andrew's face.

Jaw clenched, eyes narrowed, he yanked open the front door and said, "Shouldn't you be with your *friends*? What could you possibly need here at the home of a simple *acquaintance*?"

Andrew shrank before him, obviously at a loss. "I'm sorry I said that."

"Are you? I think you knew exactly what you were doing. I think you're a manipulative little shit who prefers to cower in fear rather than be himself. I, for one, would never date a man so spineless, and I have no intention of being anyone's dirty little secret. You can go now; your work here is done. Do me a favor and never darken my doorstep again."

With that, he slammed the door in Andrew's face.

He waited through the moments of silence while Andrew no doubt recovered from his shock and decided to leave. He listened to Andrew's fading footsteps with disappointment. Perhaps if Andrew had tried to fight for him, banged on the door, or yelled for Caius to listen, he might have been inclined to forgive him, but he didn't. He silently gave up and walked away.

Caius deserved better than that. He deserved a knight in shining armor, or a prince to stand beside him. He was better off pushing Andrew away than settling for less.

With a sigh, he pressed his forehead against the wood of the door. He didn't feel any better.

Why was it every time he took a chance on love he was betrayed?

"Sounds like he's a carbon copy of your first boyfriend," the Snake taunted from behind him. "Too afraid to come out to family and friends, so he'll choose them over you time and again. What irony that the boy to break your spell is just like the one who started things off."

"Oh go away, will you?"

There was no reply, and when Caius finally turned around, the Snake was nowhere to be seen.

Andrew was grateful for the walk back to campus. His eyes burned the entire way, but no one was around to say if he cried or not. He bought a bottle of Canadian Mist from a local liquor store and was well into the bottle when he stumbled into his dorm room.

Jason was at his desk and didn't look too pleased to see Andrew in the state he was in. The sight of his friend and the fact they were not talking only made Andrew feel worse. The burn behind his eyes turned into the threat of real tears.

"Shit," he said, turning away so Jason wouldn't see them.

"What the hell is *wrong* with you?"

Andrew couldn't answer. If he said something, he might start crying. What *was* wrong with him?

"Seriously," Jason said, his voice softer, concerned. "What's wrong?"

Andrew felt a hand on his shoulder. He closed his eyes and let his emotions wash over him. He slumped into his desk chair and said, "I fucked up." He let out a shaky breath. "Big time."

"Is this about that guy? You're dating him, aren't you?"

Andrew whirled, his heart racing with sudden panic. "What?"

"When I saw the way you smiled at him, I thought that was the reason you'd been hiding your 'girlfriend' from us. Besides, you kind of let it slip a few days ago. You used the word 'him' instead of 'her.'"

Andrew felt like he couldn't breathe. He wasn't ready

for this, but when he looked at Jason's face, he wondered what the big deal was. He'd always known Jason would be okay with it. Why had he hidden it for so long?

"Why didn't you say anything?" he finally asked.

"I thought I should wait until you decided to tell me, but that plan wasn't working out so well."

"Yeah," Andrew admitted sheepishly. "I'm sorry I've been a dick about it. I just...old habits are hard to break, I guess?"

Jason nodded. "Is that the only thing you've been keeping from me?"

"That and I knew about Ghost House before Charlie did."

Jason laughed. "You should probably keep that part a secret. He'll be so disappointed if he finds out."

Andrew agreed. It felt good to be talking with Jason again. He'd missed his best friend. "I really am sorry, Jase."

"It's okay. Really. Just don't do it again, all right?"

Andrew nodded. "Okay."

"Can I meet him? Like, for real this time?"

"About that..." Andrew's mood deflated again. "He was really upset with what I said today. He..." The pain threatened to overwhelm him again. "He broke up with me."

"You were a douche," Jason pointed out.

"Thanks," Andrew said, but his sarcasm lacked its usual bite. "I know I was. I went there tonight to apologize, and it blew up in my face."

"Sounds like you'll need more than an apology. Give him a day or two to cool off and use the time to think about how you can make it up to him. Being honest about your relationship is a good first step. Speaking of which, are you going to come out to your parents?"

"I haven't even told Charlie! Let me get past that hurdle first."

"Charlie already knows."

Andrew gaped at him. "What do you mean he knows?"

"I told you, you slipped, remember? It was in front of the two of us."

"How did he take it?" Andrew asked warily.

"It was a bit of a shock for him, I'll admit, but he's okay with it. I wouldn't suggest talking to him about your love life in detail, but it's not like he'd end your friendship over it or anything."

Andrew was surprised by how relieved he felt to hear that. He didn't care if he couldn't swoon over guys in front of Charlie. That wasn't something he did anyway. And maybe now he wouldn't have to put up with Charlie playing matchmaker anymore. That was a plus.

"Thanks, Jason."

"For what?"

"For being a better friend than I deserve."

Jason laughed. "Oh, I've always been that. As long as you're aware of it, that's fine."

Andrew glared at him but failed to hold the expression for long. "Asshole."

Jason winked, and Andrew knew everything was going to be okay, at least with him and his friends. Caius on the other hand... He didn't think kissing Caius's feet would be enough this time. Like Jason had said, he'd have to find a way to make it up to him, and knowing Caius, it was going to take something huge.

TWELVE

——◆◆——

B ill may have been the first contractor to disappear on Caius, but he had not been the last. It took until his fifth appointment for Caius to realize that each of the workers had vanished after he'd left them alone. He could only assume that this was how Rowan was planning on making trouble for him. He felt like an idiot for not noticing sooner, but he blamed his distraction on Andrew. From that point on, he didn't let any of the contractors out of his sight.

By Thursday, he had decided which company he wanted to work with and sorted his budget for the renovations. All he had to do now was wait for news from Monty that the paperwork had been finalized.

By Friday, with no word from his lawyer, Caius was going stir crazy. He almost wished he were back in the dream. There had always been something to *do* or someone to talk to there.

Besides the boredom, Caius was frustrated by the lack of contact from Andrew. He'd been angry the night Andrew had visited him—and reasonably so—but that didn't mean

Andrew couldn't have tried again. Was Caius worth so little to him?

No. That was not the way he should be thinking. He was better off without Andrew. If the boy didn't want to put in the effort to be with Caius, and especially if he couldn't be honest about it, then he wasn't worth Caius's time.

If only it wasn't so lonely without Andrew around.

"Problem?"

Caius rolled his eyes and didn't bother to turn toward the sound of the Snake's voice. "Go away."

"But you look so forlorn," the ghost taunted. "I thought you'd like some company."

Caius ignored him.

"It was amusing how you guarded those workers against my influence," Rowan continued. "Have you considered what you're going to do once work begins?"

What was that supposed to mean? And then it dawned on him. When the renovations began, there would be multiple people working all over the house. He would have no way to keep an eye on them all. He wouldn't be able to stop the Snake from scaring people away.

Before he could consider the implications further, he was startled by the sound of his cell phone ringing. A silhouetted figure and Monty's name appeared on the screen. Caius tapped the little green circle necessary to answer it. Touchscreen technology was both fascinating and weird.

"Hello?"

"You're all set," Monty's voice came through the almost invisible speaker. "Everything has been finalized. You can start the renovations."

"That's great."

"I can hear you jumping for joy from over here," Monty said. His sarcasm was not lost on Caius.

Caius shook himself and injected some cheer into his voice. "Forgive me, Monty dear, I was distracted. This is *wonderful* news. If you'll excuse me, I'd like to begin making phone calls right away."

"Of course."

Caius hung up but didn't call anyone. He looked around and was reminded once again of why he hated this place. The curse had kept him locked up in the 1920s. Caius had assumed it was because that was when he'd both met and cursed Rowan. Here in the real world, the decor was as it had been in the fifties when he had been cursed. Although it had looked different in the dream, the memories remained.

He'd never expected Rowan to curse him. His ex hadn't had the power to do something that big, nor had curses been his talent. It was one of the reasons why Caius hadn't seen the Snake's retaliation coming. Taken by surprise, Caius hadn't been able to defend himself. There were so many failures tied up in this house. Caius didn't want to be reminded of them anymore.

When he'd been with Andrew, the pain had lessened. He'd been making new memories and with the renovation, he would transform The Cut Sleeve of the past into something new, something he could enjoy again. Now Andrew was gone, and although the curse was broken, he was still being haunted by his past. He'd originally hoped to have work begin early next week, but was there even a point in trying to change things?

After his talk with Jason, things had been much better

between them, but Andrew was still in a funk. He hadn't made up with Caius yet. The thought of knocking on Caius's door and being thrown away again twisted his guts. In his head, he went through so many possibilities of what he could say, how he could apologize, but even in his head rejection was inevitable. He had no idea how to get Caius to forgive him.

He was so lost in his misery that he completely forgot his mother's birthday until his father called Friday night to make sure he was still coming up for the weekend. Was there any way he wasn't fucking up lately? Maybe the trip could distract him from his thoughts of Caius. He could at least pretend it would.

Jason agreed to go with him. His gift to Andrew's mother was to bring Marie for the celebration, so early Saturday morning, the three of them piled into Jason's car and headed off for Andrew's parents' house.

They were only an hour into the drive when Jason asked, "Have you made up with him yet?"

Andrew had been staring out the window, watching the houses scroll past. It took a moment to pull his attention back inside the car. "What?"

"With your boyfriend. Have you made up with him yet?"

Andrew was sure the answer was obvious. "No."

"Have you tried?"

"I don't know how," Andrew admitted. "I need to do something big. Something that will make an impression and show him that I'm sorry. Telling him isn't enough."

"You know," Jason said, "big doesn't have to mean complicated. You don't have to skywrite a proposal to make it special."

"I'm not proposing to him."

"It's the same principle, Andrew. You don't have to skywrite your apology. Just make it something where he'll get the message that you were listening."

Andrew was quiet as he considered this. He felt like an idiot when the idea finally came to him. "Hey, Jase, do you have any plans for after the game tomorrow?"

"Marie and I were going to hang out."

Andrew leaned forward to address Marie in the passenger seat. "Do you mind if I borrow him? It shouldn't take more than an hour."

"Sure." Marie shrugged.

Jason looked wary. "What do you have in mind?"

"Don't worry. We won't be skywriting anything."

"I didn't think that was an option."

"Well, my dad does have those frequent flyer miles..."

Jason rolled his eyes. "Just let me know if I'll need to set up bail money."

"Okay."

After coming up with an idea to get Caius to forgive him, Andrew thought of nothing else for the rest of the ride to his parents' house. An urgency similar to the one he'd felt the night he'd woken Caius gripped him, but there was nothing he could do about it until tomorrow when they were back on campus.

He did his best to curb his feelings for his mother's sake. She was thrilled to see them when she opened the door. She was particularly welcoming to Marie, grinning broadly at her and complimenting her shoes. The two women went off to chat while Andrew and Jason brought in their bags from the car.

"You're cooking on your birthday?" Andrew asked, following the smell of delicious food into the kitchen.

"Why not? I like to cook, and I love it even more when I have guests to feed."

Andrew wondered if Caius felt the same way about cooking.

"Marie, Jason, will you two set the table please?"

Alarm bells rang in Andrew's head at his mother's obvious ploy to get him alone. Once the others were gone, she asked, "What is it?"

"What is what?"

"Something is troubling you. Is this about that girl Jason mentioned? The one he hasn't met?"

"He's met— They've met. Sort of."

"I don't like the sound of this, Andrew." Her tone was a warning.

"We broke up," Andrew announced. "I did something stupid, and...I was dumped for it." That was the second time he'd almost slipped up and said "him" or "he." The reminder of his secret drove the knife into his chest even deeper. No wonder Caius had broken up with him.

"Oh honey, I'm so sorry." She pulled him into a hug. He hadn't known he wanted one until her arms were wrapped around him. She was too short to lean into, so he dropped his head onto her shoulder and let her presence comfort him. "I've never seen you like this," his mother said. "You must really like her."

"I do." Andrew's voice was thick.

"Have you apologized?"

He nodded.

"And she didn't forgive you?"

"I'm going to try again when we get back to campus."

"That's good," she said, patting his back. "I'm sure all

she needs is a little time. She'll come round." She took hold of his upper arms and stepped back to look at him. "And then I want to meet her. Anyone who is worthy of you should be good enough to meet your mother." She smiled and patted his cheek. "I just want to see you happy, baby. If she can do that, I'm sure I will love her."

"Yes, Mom." Despite that he was still hiding that Caius was a guy, Andrew did want to introduce him to her. She'd like him.

Although Andrew, Jason, and Marie tried their best to make lunch a celebratory event, Andrew's mother steered the conversation like she always did. She wanted to know everything Andrew and Jason had been up to since she'd seen them last, and she wanted a full update from Marie. With her matter-of-fact nature, it wasn't fully an inquisition, but Andrew was relieved whenever the spotlight wasn't on him. In the end, it ended up being a regular family meal just like any other.

"How is that project of yours coming along?" his father asked during one of the rare lulls in the conversation.

The question reminded Andrew of Caius's offer to let him do the report on Ghost House. He hadn't put together that second proposal before they'd broken up. Now it was too late to even try. "Fine," he said. "I got a lot of information when I visited, and Melody has been really helpful through email. I should have it put together by the end of next week." He needed to have the rough draft put together by then if he was going to have any hope of finishing it on time.

"Let me know if you need any more help."

"I will." It was nice having his dad on his side for a change. Though he should have known the peace of the moment wouldn't last.

"I read an article in your school's paper that said someone was planning on renovating that abandoned building off South Main," his father said. Andrew's dad kept up with campus news, partially because Andrew went there and partially because it was his alma mater. The fact that his dad had attended the school was one of the reasons Andrew went there as well.

"You mean Ghost House?" Andrew asked. How had the paper heard about the renovations? Had Charlie talked to someone else about them?

His father scowled. "They should have torn that place down years ago."

"What's so wrong with it?" Andrew asked. "It's not like it's a derelict."

"Too many wild rumors," his father said. "It promotes delinquency."

"It's an urban legend, Dad. No one actually cares what happened. It's all for fun."

"Breaking and entering is fun? Don't think I don't know what the university kids do at that place." He turned a sharp eye on Andrew. "Have *you* gone in there?"

Instead of lying, Andrew avoided the question. "I heard they want to turn it into an inn."

"Like a bed and breakfast?" his mother asked.

Andrew nodded. "Being a haunted house would make it an interesting place to stay on vacation, don't you think?"

"Only idiots believe in ghosts," his father interjected.

Andrew believed in ghosts, but only because he'd met them. "Then there are a lot of stupid people in the world, Dad. Why not let Caius make some money off them?"

"Who's Caius?"

Shit.

"He's the guy renovating Ghost House," Jason cut in.

"We met him the other day. Charlie's dad was called about the renovations, and we stopped by to see what was up."

"Is that the kid who wore underwear on his head that time he came to our summer barbecue?"

"Yes."

His father's sigh spoke volumes about his disapproval of Andrew's friends. Seeing as he wouldn't like anyone Andrew got along with unless they were the next CEO of Google or something else beneficial to his future career, Andrew chose to ignore it.

"Where was the article?" Andrew asked. He wondered if Caius had seen it.

"I found it online yesterday."

It shouldn't be too hard to find then. He made a point to print out a copy before heading to Caius's on Sunday. Even if Caius didn't forgive him, Andrew was sure he'd love to see the article.

After lunch, Marie and Jason excused themselves to visit Jason's parents, and Andrew let his mother take him out shopping as his gift to her. The next morning, they left early so Andrew and Jason could make it back to campus in time for their weekly game. Andrew was itching to see Caius and apologize. The added delay of the game drove him crazy. He tried to curb his nerves, but he couldn't focus on anything else. He didn't realize that he'd begun vibrating until Jason put a hand on his knees to stop him.

"You're going to drill a hole through the bus floor if you keep this up," he said.

"I can't help it."

"I know. Just a little longer, okay? If you look like you're on something, coach is gonna bench you."

And that would only make things worse, because then he'd have nothing to do while his thoughts were racing. Andrew forced himself to concentrate, letting the game drive his pending visit to Caius's from his mind, if only for a little while.

As they piled into the bus after the game, his nerves came back with a vengeance. "What if it's not enough?" he asked Jason. "What if he doesn't forgive me?"

"From what you've said, he's not completely heartless. If he sees that you're sincere, he'll forgive you."

Andrew hoped so. He was still clinging to that hope as they walked up the front steps to Ghost House an hour later. Steeling himself, he raised a hand to knock, but the door flew open before his knuckles could touch the wood. Suddenly, Caius was standing before him, and Andrew's mind had gone completely blank.

Caius raised an eyebrow. "Can I help you?" he asked coolly.

Andrew swallowed. "I was hoping we could come in and talk."

"I'm on my way out."

Andrew hesitated, his doubts surfacing once again. A sharp jab to his lower back brought him back to the present. He took a deep breath and looked Caius squarely in the eye. "I wanted to introduce you to someone," he said. He moved aside so Caius could see Jason standing behind him. "Caius, this is my best friend, Jason. Jason, this is my," he paused before uttering the unfamiliar word, "boyfriend, Caius." With a glance at Caius, he added, "At least, I hope that part is true."

Caius was silent for what felt like an eternity. Finally he sighed, a hint of exasperation in the sound. "I *suppose* I could give you another chance," he said.

An overwhelming joy filled Andrew's chest until he thought he was going to burst from it.

"Would you like to come in?" Caius asked.

"I'm late for a date with my girlfriend, actually," Jason said, "but maybe we can all meet for dinner?"

"That sounds like a lovely idea," Caius said. "Drop by the house around seven. I'll cook something."

Jason nodded. "Sounds great. See you then." With a pat on Andrew's shoulder, he headed off.

Caius turned to Andrew. "And you?"

Now that Jason was gone, Andrew wondered if he had truly been forgiven. "Would you mind if I came in?"

"I think that would be in your best interest," Caius said. "You have to finish making your apology before they show up for dinner, after all."

Andrew looked at him in surprise. "What do you have in mind?"

Caius's gave him a wicked smile. "I'm sure I'll think of something."

Andrew couldn't help smiling in return. "I have something that may be a good start." He held up the page he'd printed from the school's newspaper site. It was a small article, little more than a blurb, and he wasn't sure what Caius would think of the title "A Relic to be Reincarnated." Still, it focused on Ghost House, and the attention could only mean good publicity for the future of the inn.

Unfortunately, he was wrong. At the sight of the article, the light went out of Caius's eyes, and he looked...sad. "Ah, yes," Caius said. "I've seen that article. The reporter who wrote it wants to interview me for a more in-depth piece."

"That's fantastic," Andrew said. "Why don't you sound excited?"

Caius hesitated. "I'm not sure there's going to be a renovation."

"What? What do you mean?" When Caius had first thought of the idea, it had seemed like nothing would stop him. What had changed?

Caius gestured for Andrew to come inside and sit down. He was surprised when Caius did not immediately launch into a ramble of explanations. In fact, he looked like he was at a loss for words. The thought was baffling.

"What's wrong?"

Caius was slow to respond. "Maybe waking me wasn't such a good idea after all."

Andrew felt a chill run down his spine. "What are you talking about?"

"In the dream, I was able to do things. I may have been stuck in the same place, but I had people to talk to, guests to entertain, and there was always an influx of newcomers to keep things interesting. I don't have any of that here."

The chill turned into a stab that twisted in Andrew's chest. "What are you talking about? Once you renovate this place, you'll have more guests than you'll know what to do with." And what about him? If Caius were still in the dream, he wouldn't have Andrew.

"I can't do the renovations," Caius said.

"Why not?" Had he run out of money? Andrew didn't think Caius had been spending frivolously beyond that initial shopping spree.

"He won't let me."

That was unexpected. "He?" Andrew asked, but as soon as the word was out of his mouth, he knew. "The Snake."

Caius nodded. "He's still here, planning to ruin my life

even after the curse has been broken. Turns out Ghost House is haunted after all," he added wryly.

Caius hated that name. He must have been really upset to use it. "How can he stop you? If he's just a ghost, he can't really do anything, can he?"

"That's just it. He's a ghost. Who better to scare people away than a phantom?"

Andrew didn't know what to say.

"He's already done it," Caius continued. "He scared away a bunch of the contractors I called for estimates on the job. Who's to stop him when the work crews get here? It's not like we can keep him away. This is where he haunts, and I can't keep an eye on all of the workers at the same time."

It wasn't fair. Caius's curse had been broken. It wasn't right for the Snake to continue punishing him after he'd woken up. "There has to be some way around this," Andrew said. "You can't let him do this, Caius. Not after all this time. You can't."

Sadness and defeat dampened the sparkle in Caius's eyes. "Let's talk about something else, please."

Andrew's heart ached. He wanted to help, but he didn't know how. A kiss wouldn't solve the problem this time. "What do you want to talk about instead?"

"You never told me what you plan to do after you graduate," Caius prompted.

Thinking about that was almost as painful as seeing Caius look so dejected. "That's because I don't know what I'm going to do. I told you that my dad wants me to take over his company, but I'd rather slit my throat. The problem is, I don't know what to do instead."

"Have you spoken to your father about this?"

Andrew shook his head. "My dad isn't exactly the listening type."

"You're going to have to tell him eventually."

"That's what Jason says every time my dad calls."

"Doesn't make it any less true. I assume this also means that you are not 'out' to your parents?"

Andrew's stomach sank. "Yeah."

Caius nodded.

"Caius, I'll—" He stopped when Caius raised a hand to interrupt him.

"I'm not angry," he said. "I expected as much given how hard it was for you to come out to your friends." He turned a sharp look on Andrew. "But I will *not* be kept as a secret."

"I understand," Andrew said, "but if I'm going to come out to my dad, you have to do the renovations."

Caius's brow furrowed. "I don't see the connection."

"You can't let the Snake win. You broke the curse. You're allowed to be happy."

"*You* broke the curse," Caius pointed out.

Andrew rolled his eyes. "Either way, the curse was broken. Are you really going to let him continue to make you miserable? Are you really going to let him win?"

Caius sighed. "You don't understand. I hate it here. I've been trapped here for so long. Why should I stay?"

"I'm here."

Caius's expression softened in agreement, but the sadness in his eyes remained. "There are so many bad memories here," Caius said. Too many for Andrew to compete with apparently.

"Aren't there good ones as well?"

Caius hesitated, but finally said, "Yes."

"Tell me about one?"

Caius took another deep breath. "You remember the boy with the painting?"

"Yes."

"When he first came to The Cut Sleeve, he'd just turned eighteen. He was skittish, as if at any moment someone would point out that he didn't belong there. It's a familiar look for first-timers, particularly the younger ones. I sent him one of my gentlest boys, and it wasn't long before he'd calmed and they both went upstairs."

"I assume he came down smiling?" Andrew asked.

"Of course," Caius said, though the claim lacked his usual exuberance. "My boys were the best."

"How did he come to be the boy in the painting?"

"I was sure his first visit had been his first time with a man, so a return visit was not guaranteed, but a month later, he came back. His previous lover was otherwise occupied, but I introduced him to another who could be just as sweet. They chatted for a while and went upstairs together. After that, he became a regular visitor. He didn't come too often, once a month or so, but he became familiar with a few of my gentlemen and had his favorites.

"Now, I am never one to turn away good business, but there was something about him that nagged at me. No matter how bright his smile when he left, he always arrived looking despondent. He was young and beautiful, and he should have had the world at his feet. So why did it feel as if my house were a place of refuge for him in a world that had turned dreary?"

As he spoke, the sadness that had plagued Caius at the beginning of the story lightened. Andrew felt like he was sitting for Story Time, and he eagerly wanted to know what happened next. "What did you do?"

Caius gave him one of his sly, teasing smiles. "If you

want to learn anything about someone, the best place is pillow talk. People are most relaxed with a lover and are willing to share more secrets than they would when their clothes are on."

"Please don't tell me your prostitutes doubled as spies."

"Not as such, but they were a good source of information in a case like this. I spoke to the boys who'd had the most contact with our guest, and they revealed to me that our patron's heart had been captured by another boy his age. He had been charmed for a while before this other boy turned on him and broke his heart. It seemed the vile wretch was the type who liked to make others feel bad about themselves to make himself feel better."

That sounded like someone Caius would want to curse. Andrew's theory was proven right when Caius said, "No one knew who this other boy was—our innocent refused to speak his name—and so I could not punish him. Even if I had, it wouldn't have solved the real problem. Our boy had taken his love interest's words to heart and believed himself to be ugly and unworthy of love. I wanted to prove otherwise, so I devised a plan to do so. I must admit, I took some inspiration from one of my favorite authors when I came up with this plan."

"I thought the idea sounded vaguely familiar."

"You've read it?"

Andrew shook his head. "They made a movie out of it."

"Really?"

"I'm not sure how it stands up to the book, but I'd be happy to watch it with you."

"I will hold you to that, but first I must finish my story."

"Please do."

"The next time the boy visited, I took him aside for a chat. It didn't take long for him to open up to me. He'd come to feel safe at The Cut Sleeve. During the conversation, I mentioned that I had once acquired a beautiful golden frame. I told him it came from some exotic location, I don't remember which, and it was said to have magical powers. The frame would make any person whose portrait hung in it beautiful."

"And he believed you?"

"Not at first, but he wanted what I said to be true, so it wasn't difficult to nudge him toward the possibility. I told him it wouldn't hurt to give it a try. If it didn't work, he wouldn't be any worse off. Once he'd agreed, I hired a local artist who could do a proper oil portrait. I needed someone who could create an adequate likeness, or my plan would not have worked.

"Now, one thing you must know is that sitting for a portrait takes time and skill. It also takes a measure of confidence. A painting is a reflection of the model, just like a mirror. If you see flaws in yourself when you look in the mirror, can you imagine those flaws being permanently applied to a canvas? Our young man saw many flaws in himself. The hours he sat for that painting must have been pure torture for him."

"Then why make him do it?" Andrew asked.

"That was part of the process. Without those feelings, the end result would not have been the same."

Andrew still didn't like the idea of making the boy sit for all that time feeling bad about himself, but Caius was already continuing with his story. "It took three days for the painting to be finished. It was a perfect likeness, and it was beautiful."

"Yes, I saw it in the dream."

"When the boy saw it, he stared in speechless awe, a high compliment for the artist. I sent the painter to play with one of my boys—the compensation we had agreed upon for the painting. Once we were alone, the boy found his voice. 'That's not me,' he said. Instead of insisting on what was obvious to an onlooker, I replied 'it could be.' I reminded him about the magic frame but cautioned him on the price of its use. Once the painting was inside the frame, he would not be able to look upon it again. If he did, the truth of him would be revealed. His desire to look like the boy in the painting overtook his doubts, and he agreed to the terms. When he left The Cut Sleeve, he was glowing happier than I had ever seen him."

"What happened to him?"

"I don't know. He never returned, but I like to think he found the confidence to stand up to his oppressor. I hope he found someone who appreciated him for who he was and made him feel beautiful without a painting."

"It could have gone the other way though. Dorian Grey turned into a terrible person when given eternal beauty."

"Yes, gifts like that are dangerous. They tend to bring out parts of our nature that may otherwise have been hidden."

"Then why did you take the chance?"

"That boy was gentle and sweet. He treated my boys well, and they were quite fond of him. I like to think that the version they saw of him was the real one, and in giving him the gift of confidence, he could be that person all the time."

"What about the price for the spell? Was that real?"

"Yes. I may not have cursed him, but I did put a spell on him. As you said, my gift could backfire, but as long as he remained the boy we knew him as, the reflection he saw in the mirror would be the same as he'd seen in the painting. If my hopes were misplaced, he'd see the monster he thought he was. The one he had become."

"Sounds like curses weren't your only talent," Andrew said.

"Are you saying you approve of what I did?"

"I don't know, but you were more like a fairy godmother than a villain in that story."

"I suppose I can take that as a compliment."

Andrew snorted, but his amusement faded as he remembered the point of Caius telling him that story. "Do you really hate it here? Aren't there more good memories that you want to keep here?"

"My opinion doesn't matter. Either way, Rowan is still a problem."

"We'll figure out a way around that."

"How?"

Andrew shrugged. "I don't know," he admitted, "but I'm sure we can think of something. Why don't you start with that article?"

Caius was silent for a long moment, but Andrew waited him out. "*All right*," he finally said. "I'll do the article. Hopefully, it won't be a bunch of false promises."

"It won't be," Andrew promised. "I believe in you."

Caius's eyebrows rose. "Oh really?"

"After all we've been through, isn't that obvious?"

Slowly, Caius smiled. The expression was small, but it was warm, and it was genuine.

THIRTEEN

Caius loved throwing dinner parties, but he was struggling with this one. He wanted to make a good impression on Andrew's friends. There were five places to be set, and he only had bar furniture to work with. He refused to have a dinner party in the parlor, and that seating would be even worse. He'd created a menu he hoped would appeal to university students without being "pub food" as some of them liked to call it, and made sure there was beer in the fridge in addition to the wine he'd planned on serving. By the time the doorbell rang, his stomach was aflutter with nerves.

"Come in, please." He took their coats and directed them to a table of hors d'oeuvres. After disposing of the outerwear in the old hookah lounge, he returned to his host duties.

"Who do I not know?" he asked when Andrew failed to begin introductions.

"This is my friend Charlie," Andrew said, pointing to a tall man with dark hair. He looked older than Andrew and Jason and had a cheeky air about him. Caius remembered him from the day they'd stopped by the house, the day he'd fought with Andrew. "And this is Marie," Andrew continued, gesturing to the only girl in the group. She was pretty, with warm brown skin and caramel colored eyes that were suitably framed by wire-rimmed glasses. Although she appeared to have a quiet demeanor, her curls were wild and untamed. Caius decided that was what he liked best about her.

"Is it true you're the grandson of the original owner of this place?" Charlie asked. He'd asked a similar question the last time he was there.

Instead of answering, Caius turned to Marie. "Please tell me you're dating Jason and not The Inquisitor."

Marie laughed softly. Amusement brightened up her face in a way that was truly lovely. Caius could see why Jason was attracted to her. "Yes," she said.

"Hey, I'm only asking," Charlie protested. "You're the only one who might know what happened here the night everyone disappeared."

Caius looked at him with a theatrically wide-eyed, innocent expression. "And what makes you think I'll tell you what I know?"

Charlie groaned. "That's not fair, man. You gotta share the news."

"Yes, it's not fair," Caius said, "but it's *fun*."

Jason laughed. "He's got you there, man. The more you complain, the less he's going to tell you."

Charlie didn't like that one bit. He turned to Andrew instead. "He must have told you something. You're dating, right? He had to have told you."

Andrew chuckled. "If you think he's not as secretive with me, you are mistaken. Caius is a mystery."

Caius could have been offended by that, but he decided to be flattered instead. He liked the idea of being a mystery.

"Please make yourselves comfortable," he said. "Would you like anything to drink while I check on dinner?"

After hearing their requests, he left them to the appetizers and headed into the kitchen. He was wary of leaving them alone, but he didn't think the Snake would risk trying to scare the group. With Charlie's enthusiasm, Caius had a feeling an attempt like that would backfire.

"So how did the two of you meet?" Jason asked once Caius had returned. "Andrew was vague on the details."

Andrew looked at Caius, his eyes wide and pleading. Caius continued to serve the drinks, resisting a smile. The poor boy was on the verge of panic.

"We met at a party," he said.

Charlie whirled on Andrew. "You went to a party without us?"

Andrew was still floundering for a reply, but Caius was kind enough to come to his rescue. "It was accidental, I assure you. In fact, he didn't look like he was having any fun, so I kicked him out."

"You were *kicked out* of a party without us?"

Apparently, there was no winning with Charlie, so Caius focused his attention on Jason. He *was* the one who'd asked. "After that, we kept running into each other. I suppose it was fate, really."

"Do you believe in fate?" Marie asked.

"No," he said, "but I wouldn't be surprised if it believed in me." He winked.

Caius thrived on being the center of attention, that much

was clear. He was like an orchestra conductor, keeping each person entertained with ease. He saved Andrew from awkward moments, frustrated Charlie with his evasions, and charmed Jason and Marie with his exuberance. For as long as Andrew had known her, he hadn't ever seen Marie laugh as much as she had tonight. All the while, Caius's eyes sparkled with joy and amusement. Any sign of his earlier sadness or self-doubt had completely evaporated. He was practically glowing. Andrew found it difficult to look away from him.

His chest swelled with happiness as he watched his boyfriend interact with his friends. If he had known how wonderful it would be to have a moment like this, he would have spoken up sooner. He felt silly for being so afraid. Out of the corner of his eye, he saw Jason look his way. When he looked back, his friend smiled knowingly. Life didn't get any better than this.

Jason, Charlie, and Marie didn't stay long after dinner, and Andrew had to admit he was relieved. Caius was still beaming with happiness, and he wanted some of that exuberance to be directed his way while they were alone.

"You know what would make me really happy?" Caius asked as they cleared the dishes together.

"What?" What could possibly make things better than this?

"For you to finally fulfill your promise to me."

It took a moment for Andrew to remember which promise Caius was referring to. "That's a bit difficult with a ghost haunting the place. Exhibitionism is not one of my kinks."

"You have others?" Caius asked, a mix of tease and curiosity in his voice.

"Maybe," Andrew teased in return.

"Ooh, you are getting better at this." Caius stepped

closer, sliding a hand over Andrew's hip. Heat shot through Andrew's body, and he didn't think it had anything to do with magic, only Caius's touch. "Maybe I'm not the only one who is a mystery."

"You're the mystery, Caius," Andrew said, pulling him closer so their bodies touched. "I like the challenge of figuring you out."

"And how do you plan to conquer this hurdle?" Caius purred.

Instead of answering, Andrew brought their mouths together. Caius's lips were soft and parted easily. Andrew delved into his warm mouth, savoring the flavors left by dinner and the underlying taste of Caius. As their tongues danced, the air around them turned cloying. The luscious flavors of his boyfriend turned vile and sickening. Andrew choked and broke the kiss.

"Oh, don't mind me. I was enjoying the show."

Andrew looked around. He couldn't see the Snake, but the smell was a strong reminder of why they could not be alone in the house. "That's it," he said. "Tomorrow night I'm kicking Jason out of our dorm room. He can go sleep with Marie. You and I are going to have some time to ourselves without anyone, dead or alive, to stop us."

"My hero." Caius smiled, though he kept working his tongue as if to get rid of a bad taste in his mouth. "Let's finish cleaning up here and then I'll walk you home."

"You don't have to take me all the way to campus."

"I will not have this be our last kiss of the night."

A long walk alone with no one dead to interrupt them. Andrew smiled. "I'd love it if you walked me home."

It was a quiet night. There was only a sliver of moon, but

the sky was clear and the stars shone brightly. It was the perfect evening for a stroll with one's lover, and Caius planned to enjoy it.

"I've been thinking," Andrew said.

"That's not a good sign," Caius couldn't help responding. He had a feeling he wasn't going to like this topic, whatever it was.

"You once told me that you cursed people as a punishment, that they were meant to learn something from it."

"Yes."

"What have you learned from being cursed?"

That was unexpected. "This wasn't my curse. The rules aren't the same."

"Are you sure? There has to be a reason why the Snake cursed you."

"He was angry with me. I turned him into a snake."

"Is that really all there was to it?"

"What do you think I was supposed to learn from this curse? You obviously have something particular in mind."

Andrew was quiet for a while. Caius would have been content to drop the topic, but then Andrew spoke again. "Do you ever wonder what happened to the people you cursed?"

Ah, so Andrew was still hung up on that. "Does it really matter?"

"Yes."

Andrew's straightforward answer startled Caius. Why? Why was it so important that he think of the past? But he knew the answer, just as he knew the answer to Andrew's question. Caius wasn't as heartless as he pretended to be. He had been hurt more than once. Many of the times he'd performed a curse was due to a broken heart, Rowan among them. He didn't like to look back and think of that pain.

"Yes," Caius replied finally. "Not all of them, mind you, but...some."

He wondered if they had broken the curses he'd put upon them. He wondered if they'd been able to find happiness, but even those thoughts were painful. No matter the outcome of the curse, Caius was never the one to bring his lover happiness. The thought was lonely and unfair. He didn't want to think about it.

Shaking off the threatening melancholy, he said, "It doesn't matter. Among the many things my powers are capable of, time travel is not one of them. So it has no bearing on the here and now."

"Actually, I think it has everything to do with the here and now. You may not be able to do anything about the past, but there is always the future."

"Are you sure it's my future you're thinking about, or yours?" Did Andrew fear Caius cursing him if they broke up? They'd parted twice already, and he hadn't done it. Caius couldn't imagine Andrew hurting him so badly as to push him to resort to curses. Then again, he hadn't expected his previous lovers to do so either.

"I'm not thinking of me, Caius. I'm thinking of you. Whether you realize it or not, these curses are a burden on you. I don't want you weighing yourself down more than you already have."

"You want me to hang up my sorcerer hat and stop cursing people?"

Andrew smiled. "I may have seen magic, but miracles are another thing altogether."

"Ouch. Is that what they call 'shade' nowadays?"

Andrew laughed. "I would never tell you to stop being yourself, Caius. Just...I don't like the thought of you being the villain."

"Is that how you see me?"

"No." When Andrew stopped to look at him, it was clear he spoke the truth. Caius melted before the tenderness in Andrew's eyes. "I don't see you as a villain at all."

Caius stepped forward and kissed Andrew gently. "Good," he said. It was all he could manage to express how much Andrew's words had meant to him. He didn't want to be the villain, and it warmed him to know that someone, Andrew especially, didn't see him as such.

Andrew's plan to kick Jason out of the dorm room didn't go as well as he would have liked. Turned out Marie's roommate had caught something nasty. Instead of Jason staying the night at Marie's dorm, Jason asked Andrew if he wouldn't mind Marie staying with them for a few nights until Marie's roommate was no longer a carrier of whatever plague was in her system. Andrew felt bad saying no, but he didn't relish the idea of breaking the news to Caius. Caius took it with the usual grumpiness and pouting Andrew had expected, but in the end, he'd understood.

Caius was also still hesitant about the renovations, but he wasn't as melancholy as he had been when they'd spoken about it. He even sounded excited when he'd told Andrew that he'd scheduled an interview with a reporter from the university's newspaper. Andrew was happy for him and looked forward to reading the article.

Wednesday morning the in-depth article hit the stands. Andrew was anxious, but he didn't have time to grab a paper before he headed to class. He shifted restlessly while he waited for his morning classes to end so he could get back to his dorm and look the article up online.

Jason was in their room when he returned. Andrew

immediately launched into an interrogation. "Well? Did you read it? How was it? Think it'll get some attention for Ghost House?"

Jason didn't share his enthusiasm. He slowly rose from his desk chair with an expression on his face that was akin to a doctor about to let a family know that his patient had died on the operating table.

"What? Is it really that bad?"

"I think you'd better sit down."

Jason's serious tone curbed Andrew's excitement. He sat.

"What is it?" he asked, not sure he wanted to know.

Jason set his laptop down on Andrew's desk. His browser was open to the school's newspaper website. At the top of the page was the article title *HISTORY MAKES HISTORY*. What was it with this newspaper's shitty titles? The subheading was even worse, and as Andrew read it, the air left his lungs in a rush.

LGBT Friendly Locale Opening Soon

What? Andrew felt dizzy and was glad he was sitting down. "What are they talking about?"

"Read the article."

Andrew swallowed and did as he was told.

The Cut Sleeve, known to locals as Ghost House, has a scandalous history. The building ran as a brothel from the 1880's until 1955 when it was unexpectedly closed.

That wasn't so bad, but then Andrew saw the next line.

Although this much is common knowledge, many do not know that the bordello exclusively catered to gay clientele, a brave stance for its time.

"Are you okay?" Jason asked. Andrew hadn't realized that he'd stopped breathing. He took a deep inhale and continued reading.

I am happy to announce that The Cut Sleeve seeks to remain an LGBT friendly location when it reopens its doors as 'The Cut Sleeve Inn and Tavern.' Although it will no longer be exclusive, it will retain its position as a safe space for those in the LGBT community.

The article went on, but Andrew couldn't read anymore. What the hell was Caius doing? Granted, that was a wonderful stance to take, but that was not at all how Andrew had been expecting an article about Ghost House to go. Hadn't he suggested playing on the haunted theme to attract patrons? Where was this "safe space" stuff coming from?

"Keep reading," Jason said.

Andrew couldn't imagine there was anything more in the article to get flustered over, but then he saw what Jason had been waiting for him to read.

Caius Sterling, the owner of the establishment, is an openly gay man. His relationship with local university student Andrew Hollenbeck has inspired him to create a welcoming environment for his boyfriend's and future generations.

"What the fuck?" Andrew exclaimed. Caius had just outed him. In a *newspaper*. "How could he do this to me?"

The sound of his phone ringing interrupted his tirade. One glance at the caller ID and he felt the blood drain from his face. A lump formed in his throat as his building anger took a sharp turn toward panic. "Oh shit," he said. "My dad's seen this, I just know it."

"You don't know that," Jason objected.

"Yes, I do. And even if he hasn't, he's going to. Oh my god, what do I do?"

"For one thing, you can let go of the laptop before you break it," Jason said calmly.

Andrew looked at the plastic device in his hand. His knuckles were white around it. He pried his fingers loose and set it back on the desk. "What am I going to do, Jason?"

"Talk to him."

"My father will kill me."

"I meant Caius."

Andrew glanced back at the screen. The words "LGBT friendly" stared back at him. Without another word, he grabbed his jacket and keys and headed out the door.

Caius answered with his usual sparkling smile, but for once, Andrew was immune to it. He pushed past his boyfriend into the sitting room and whirled on him.

"How could you do this to me?"

"Do what?"

Andrew rolled his eyes. "Out me for the whole world to see when you know damn well I wasn't ready for it."

"What are you talking about?"

"The article, Caius. The *article!*"

"I haven't read it yet."

Caius's calm only made Andrew's blood boil. "How do you expect me to believe that?"

"It's been a very busy morning. I was just about to sit down for lunch and read the paper when you showed up."

"Then read it now," Andrew demanded.

For a moment, it looked as if Caius would argue, but he turned and picked up a newspaper that was lying on the coffee table. Andrew watched as a furrow appeared between his brows. It deepened as he read. When his green eyes widened, Andrew knew he had reached the part where they were both mentioned by name.

"This is *not* what I had in mind," Caius said.

"Well, that's a relief," Andrew retorted.

Caius's mouth tightened in annoyance. "I can understand why you're angry, but I did not mention any of this when I was being interviewed."

"You didn't say we were dating?"

"No. My personal life is personal. I spoke about my plans for the renovation and nothing more."

"According to this," Andrew gestured to the paper in Caius's hand, "our being gay is part of your renovations."

"You know that isn't true."

"Do I?"

Caius's lips were pressed tight, and Andrew could practically see the steam coming out of his nose as he huffed, but Caius didn't say anything. Instead, he turned back to the paper and reread the article.

"Perhaps this isn't so bad after all," he said. "It's not like our relationship would have been secret forever, and as a gay couple, it could make similarly inclined visitors feel more welcome."

"I'm so glad you can make this into a marketing ploy," Andrew retorted. "I'll remember that when my father is ripping my balls off."

Caius flinched. "Has your father seen the article?"

"Most likely."

Caius tilted his head thoughtfully. "Maybe it's better this way."

"Excuse me?"

"You were going to tell him eventually, and you said he was a difficult man to talk to. This article has broken the ice."

Andrew closed his eyes and concentrated on taking deep breaths. Otherwise, he was likely to wrap his hands around Caius's throat. "How is that better?" he asked when he could speak again. "This article took away my choice of when and how to tell him. How could that possibly be better?"

"You weren't choosing, Andrew," Caius said. "You've let your father dictate the course of your life. He chose your major. He's choosing your future career. I wouldn't be surprised if he tried to choose your future wife. You've had plenty of opportunities to tell him what you want, and every time you've let them pass you by. And it's not only with him. You only came out to Jason because he did it for you. How is this any different?"

So that was what Caius thought of him. Maybe his talk about being okay with Andrew being in the closet to his parents on Sunday had been a lie. Maybe he'd planned to force Andrew out of the closet when he agreed to do the interview.

"How did they find out, Caius?"

"I told you," Caius said in that annoyingly reasonable tone of his. "I didn't say anything."

"Bullshit," Andrew snarled. "There's no one else who could have said anything. The only people who know about us are my friends, and you're the only one who talked to the reporter." He shook his head. "You had no right. You had no right to do this to me. You always do things your way and never consider the consequences for other people. It's just like your curses. You punished people because you felt like they deserved it, but you never took responsibility for your actions. You've hurt people, Caius. You do it all the time, and now you've done it to me." He stopped, his anger overwhelming him. "I can't be here," he said, bolting for the front door. He threw it open and ran out. He didn't bother looking back.

. . .

Caius didn't think the news article fiasco was as bad as Andrew was making it out to be, but he should have known that Andrew needed a delicate hand in these matters. The only way Andrew would have ever come out to his parents was if he'd been pushed to do it, but he hadn't had to say it so bluntly. He would make a point to apologize later. In the meantime, he needed to figure out how this article had come about. He hadn't lied to Andrew. He hadn't said anything about being gay or that The Cut Sleeve would be gay-friendly to the reporter. Granted, everything she'd written had been true, but that wasn't the point. Who had put the idea into her head in the first place? Caius could only think of one person.

"You did this," he said to the empty room.

The Snake didn't respond.

Caius was sure Rowan was listening. He wouldn't have suddenly vanished, especially when he could now gloat over Andrew's anger. Caius considered the possibilities and could only think of one conclusion. "You showed yourself to her," he said. "How else would you be able to give her all of this information? A disembodied voice would have scared her like the contractors."

The Snake still did not respond.

Caius's brow creased in concern. "Did you really use up that much of your power?" He laughed. "Are you now unable to show yourself even to me?"

"I can still show you," the Snake hissed in his ear. Caius turned to look at him and blinked in surprise. He had expected Rowan to have faded from his efforts, but he hadn't thought it would be so much. The ghost was fully see through. Vague lines and pale colors made up his being, and his legs faded into nothing at the knees.

"Was it worth it?" Caius asked.

"He seemed pretty angry to me," the Snake said. "He's finally learned that you ruin the lives of others, especially the ones closest to you. I wouldn't be surprised if he never came back."

Caius shook his head. "Andrew isn't like that. He was angry, but he won't be angry forever. You're not going to win."

"We shall see," the Snake said before fading away.

"Yes, we will," Caius agreed.

It was a brisk evening, and the cool air helped to soothe Andrew. He still couldn't believe what Caius had done, but he slowed his pace and let his anger dissipate. He had more important things to worry about, like the inevitable confrontation with his dad. The thought alone made him feel sick. Thank god Jason would be around. Maybe he could help Andrew come up with a plan to minimize the damage. Once he was in his dorm, he'd talk to Jason and then call his father back.

His father, yet again, had other plans for him. The man was waiting for him in his room when Andrew got back. He was red-faced and talking angrily into his phone. Before Andrew could sneak away, his father saw him. He jabbed a finger in Andrew's direction and pointed sharply to Andrew's desk chair. Heart in his throat, Andrew slowly moved into the room. Before he sat, he spotted Jason sitting on his own bed. His jaw dropped in surprise. Any sane man would have run from his father's temper. He was touched once again by how awesome a friend he had in Jason. He caught Jason's eye and mouthed a silent thank you to him. Jason nodded in return.

His father hung up. "What is this?" he demanded, shaking a copy of the school's newspaper in Andrew's face.

"A newspaper?" He knew he was playing with fire, but he was already in it. Did it matter how badly he was burned?

The color in his father's face darkened, and Andrew worried he might give himself a heart attack. "This isn't funny, Andrew! This article could ruin your career! I have already spent the morning saving your internship and threatening to sue the paper if the article isn't retracted. How could they publish such a thing? Does this Caius or that reporter have something against you? No, how could they? It's not like you've ever taken a stand on anything."

The echo of Caius's words made Andrew wince. "What is that supposed to mean?"

"What do you think, Andrew? I've told you time and again that you need to be more proactive or you will not get anywhere, and what do you do? You hang out with your friends and play ice hockey. I'm working to give you a future. Please try not to fuck it up before you even graduate."

Andrew was speechless. He couldn't tell if he was hurt or angry. He concluded that he must be in shock. He'd made his father angry plenty of times, and had felt guilty for disappointing him. But did his dad really think so little of him?

Andrew tried to think of something to say but couldn't. Then, without any thought at all, he said, "I don't want your future."

He father laughed. "You don't know what you want."

Anger finally seeped through the numbness in Andrew's brain. "How do you know?" he asked. "From the moment I could walk, you've been marching me in the direction you've picked for me. You've never asked me what I want. Do you even care?"

His father looked baffled. "Of course I care. I wouldn't push you so hard if I didn't."

"That's not the same, Dad."

"Oh?" His father crossed his arms and looked at him expectantly. "And what is it you want?"

For the first time, it seemed like his father would actually listen. He would probably reject whatever Andrew said, but he would at least hear him out. Unfortunately, Andrew didn't know what to say. "I don't know."

His father nodded, as if that was what he had expected to hear. "And this is why I push you. By the time you decide what you want to do with your life, it will already be over."

"Mr. Hollenbeck, I think—" Jason began.

"What is going on here?" Andrew's mother's voice cut through the room. "I leave to get one bottle of water and you all look like the world is going to end." She turned to Andrew. "How do you not have water in your room? Young man, you know how important hydration is, and if you needed me to get it for you, you know I would have. And that goes for you too, Jason," she added sharply. "Now, what is the problem here?"

Just like in the past, his mother's presence eased the tension between Andrew and his father. Andrew had never been more grateful for it in his life. Taking courage from his relief, he stood and faced her.

"Mom," he said. "I'm gay."

—◆•◆—

FOURTEEN

"Hmm," Andrew's mother said.

Before she could say any more, his father pushed his way between them. "You are *not*—"

"Now, Howard," his mom said with a hand on his father's arm. "Just give us a moment." When his father looked like he would argue, she said, "Why don't you wait outside? I'll be there in a minute."

There was a long stretch of tense silence before his father turned and walked out.

"Wow," Jason said.

Andrew's mother shook a finger in his direction, and he immediately followed his comment with an apology. Then she turned to Andrew. "You were saying?"

He had to say it again? "I'm gay."

"Yes, you've said that part. Anything else?"

More? What more could there be? Then he remembered the contents of the article. He bit his lip, wondering if he would now face his mother's wrath but for a completely different reason than he'd expected. "I have a boyfriend."

"Mmm hmm," his mother said. "I assume this is the person all the drama was about when you visited?"

"Yes, ma'am."

"And I'm also assuming your attempt to reconcile has gone well?"

"Yes, ma'am." He wouldn't risk telling her he'd just had another fight with Caius. For all her lack of blustering, there was something about his mother that made her scarier than his father at times.

"Then I expect to see him at dinner tonight. No excuses."

"Yes, ma'am."

She nodded. "Now, I'm going to straighten out this nonsense with your father. I should be able to calm him down in time for dinner. Shall we say Luigi's at six o'clock?"

"We have practice," Andrew said.

"Seven then. I expect to see you there too, Jason. Bring Marie." With that, she made her exit.

Andrew dropped back into his desk chair like a string cut from a balloon. "Did that just happen?"

"Yes."

Andrew turned to look at Jason. "I can never pay you back for this."

Jason rolled his eyes. "What kind of a friend would I be if I left you alone? Don't worry about it, man."

"Thank you."

Jason nodded.

Andrew was quiet for a few minutes. "I just came out to my parents."

"Yes, you did. You also told your dad that you didn't want to take over the business. Sort of. You might have to revisit that conversation."

"I'm sure it will all be revisited." Andrew wasn't looking forward to that.

"Do you think she knew?"

"Knew what?"

"That you were gay."

She knew about his heartbreak in eighth grade. How much she knew about it Andrew wasn't sure. "Maybe," he said. "I'm just glad she took it in stride."

"She was more upset about not meeting Caius yet," Jason said. "Oh my god, I just imagined what that meeting is going to be like. I can't wait for dinner tonight."

Andrew laughed. He knew exactly what Jason was picturing, but his amusement faded when he remembered what he'd done. "Shit. Caius."

"You didn't break up with him again, did you?"

"No, but I said some things I shouldn't have." Andrew rubbed the back of his neck. "He's probably pissed at me."

"Don't take a week to apologize this time. I can't handle you being that miserable."

Andrew didn't want to go through that again either. He grabbed his coat. "I don't think I'm going to make practice today."

"I'll let coach know."

He threw open their door and jerked to a stop when he saw Caius standing in the doorway.

"What are you doing here?" he asked.

"I decided that this time it was my turn to apologize. Hello, Jason."

"Hi, Caius."

"May I come in?"

Andrew stepped back to let him in and closed the door behind him. He chucked his coat on top of his closet and followed Caius into the room.

"How did you find us? I never told you what dorm we were in."

Caius gave an irritated sigh. "Don't remind me. I went to each residence building and had to convince the person at the sign in desk that I wasn't a suspicious person so they would tell me if you lived there or not. Thank goodness I look so young."

"Even if they told you that, they don't let off-campus visitors in without being signed in by a resident."

"Must be my charming personality," Caius said with a wink. Andrew had a feeling "charming" meant "magical." "But that is not the reason I am here. I would like to apologize to you, and as I am a bit rusty in that practice—I can't remember the last time I've given an apology, honestly—I would prefer it if you sat quietly and listened."

Andrew shook his head. "You don't have to apologize. I know it wasn't you who told those things to the reporter. You wouldn't do that. I was just too shocked to think straight."

"I know, and you can apologize for your brashness later. Like I said, it is my turn now." Caius gestured to the desk chair and Andrew sat.

"I should leave you two alone," Jason said. "I have to get to practice anyway. I'll see you later for dinner, Andrew."

Caius waited while Jason grabbed his bag and left. Then he turned to Andrew. "I may not have been the one to tell your secret to the reporter, but it is my fault it happened," he said. "Rowan overheard us talking the other night, and he spun the story for her."

Rowan... "You mean the Snake?" Andrew asked.

Caius nodded. "I'm surprised he's been able to do so much, especially after the curse was broken. He was never very powerful when he was alive."

Andrew was confused. "If he's dead, how can he still have power?"

"Emotion, my dear Andrew. Emotion drives ghosts, and the Snake had enough hatred for me to power a curse for sixty years. Manifesting in front of one reporter is simple by comparison."

It made sense. "Why does he hate you so much?"

"I turned him into a snake when I caught him cheating on me. It severely depleted his dating pool."

"Caius," Andrew said warningly. "This is serious."

"I *am* serious. Don't you think a snake is a fitting punishment for a cheater?"

Andrew ignored the question. "And there is nothing else you can think of?"

"For most people, becoming a snake is a fairly big deal. Although..." he trailed off thoughtfully. "You mentioned something about a blind man once."

"Yeah. He was one of the ghosts the night I woke you."

Caius tilted his head, lost in thought.

"What is it?"

"The man Rowan cheated on me with became blind not long after I cursed Rowan."

"So?"

"Perhaps that's why he's so angry with me."

"If you didn't make him blind, why would it be your fault?"

"Rowan must believe I did. He's a ghost of anger and revenge. Logic and reason need not apply."

Well, that sucked. "So apologize."

Caius gave him a startled laugh. "*Excuse me?*"

"Apologize," Andrew repeated. "Whether you did all the things he blames you for or not, he's not completely off the mark. You turned the man into a snake. And I wouldn't be surprised if you just vanished after doing so. He might not have all the details correct, but you ruined his life and abandoned him. Don't you think you should apologize for that?"

Caius sputtered. "And what about me?" he demanded. "Don't *I* get an apology for being stuck in a dream for sixty years?"

This time it was Andrew's turn to remain reasonably calm. "You hurt him first. It's only right you start the apologies."

Caius glared at him, but Andrew was unmoved.

"I'm sorry about the article," Caius said flatly. "Now if you'll excuse me." He turned to leave.

"My mother invited you to dinner tonight," Andrew said. "We're meeting them at Luigi's."

Caius paused, but he didn't turn around. "You've spoken to them about me?"

"A little."

Caius finally turned to face him. "How could I *possibly* make a good impression at Luigi's? Bring them to The Cut Sleeve. I'll cook something magnificent."

"On such short notice? We scheduled dinner for seven."

"Do you have so little faith in me?"

Andrew smiled. "I'll let them know the change in plans."

Caius gave a sharp nod. "I'll be ready by seven."

As Andrew watched the door close behind him, he hoped dinner with his parents would go as well as this conversation had.

Caius paced his sitting room, torn between two emotions. He was still baffled that Andrew would even *suggest* he apologize to Rowan, but he was even more excited about the prospect of meeting Andrew's parents. He couldn't remember if any of his past lovers had introduced him to their families. He'd known his first love's parents very well, but that was because they had grown up together. This was different. This time he would be introduced as a boyfriend.

"You look happy."

Caius turned toward the Snake's voice, but it took him a moment to find him. Rowan had faded even more since he'd gone to Andrew's dorm.

"I am happy," Caius said. "Your plan to ruin the relationship between me and Andrew has failed. In fact, I would say your plan inadvertently made things even better," he added smugly.

The nasty taunt he had been expecting didn't come. In fact, from what he could see of Rowan, he looked exhausted.

"If you don't let go of this you're going to fade away and be stuck as a ghost forever," Caius said. "That can't be what you planned."

"No, it isn't," the Snake admitted.

Caius looked at him more closely. In addition to the lack of color, his face looked less sharp than it had been. He could almost see his old lover in the face of the ghost before him.

"Why did you curse me?" Caius asked. "The truth this time."

The Snake laughed. It was a quiet huff of breath but no longer had the reptile hiss it had before. "You ruined my life," he said. "You've ruined so many lives. You'd told me about the people you cursed, but I never realized what it must have been like for them until you'd done it to me."

"And that is why you trapped me with visions of my past."

Rowan nodded.

"How did you do it? You never had the control to create something this intricate."

Rowan laughed again. "I was jealous of you; did you know that? Charm came so easily to me, but you...you could do so much more. It wasn't until I'd died that I was finally able to accomplish something new."

"Death wouldn't have changed your being," Caius said. "Curses were still beyond you."

"Yes. For a while, I could do nothing but stew in my hatred for you, but it was what made me stronger. Finally, I formulated a plan. Do you remember the books I gave you? The ones I had given away?"

Yes, Caius remembered those books. It still stung that he wouldn't be able to get them back.

"The man who sold them to me dealt in many things, including antiques and what he liked to call "mysterious relics." To the discerning eye, that meant magical tools. When I was strong enough, I found him and convinced him of what I needed. I promised he could have anything he found of worth in The Cut Sleeve in exchange for a way to channel my power into a curse. He gave me a witch's talisman through which I could focus my power. He buried it beneath the grounds of the bordello, and I used it to curse you for the last sixty years."

"It must have bound you to the house as well," Caius said. "No wonder you were always in the dream with me."

"Yes, it trapped me too, but it didn't matter if I could see my vengeance play out. As long as my hatred burned, the curse was fed and continued."

Rowan's hatred wouldn't burn for much longer. Caius's

ex had faded to the point that Caius had to strain to see him if he wasn't moving. There was nothing to the Snake's being now but sadness, and it cooled the anger Caius had been carrying.

"I didn't curse him, you know," he said. "He fell from a startled horse into a thorn bush and was blinded."

"I know. I was the reason his horse startled."

Caius gasped, the pieces of the puzzle suddenly falling into place.

"He married eventually," Rowan continued. "Even with the scars on his face, he managed to land a beautiful woman and produce beautiful children. I always wondered if he ever thought about me."

Caius had wondered the same thing about his first love. Had he broken the curse? If so, did he end up married to the woman his parents chose for him, or had he found love in the arms of another man? Had he ever thought of Caius and the time they'd shared, or had he only cursed Caius's name?

"I'm sorry," he said. He reached toward Rowan with his magic, saturating the ghost with color and form. The twisted features of the Snake's face softened, and his old lover stood before him once more. He hadn't realized how much he'd missed that face. "I don't want you to fade away," he said. "I don't want you to be stuck as a ghost forever." A tear gathered in his eye, and it became harder to speak. "Please, Rowan, forgive me."

The ghost regarded him sadly. He stepped forward and caressed Caius's cheek. His touch was insubstantial and feather light. "I suppose I've punished you enough," he said. "Do things right this time, okay?"

Caius nodded. "I will."

Rowan leaned forward and brought their lips together. The kiss was solid, and Caius knew his ex was using the last of his power to say goodbye. When Rowan stepped back, he flashed Caius a familiar cheeky grin.

"Now it's you who cheated," he said with a wink. Then he was gone.

"Jackass," Caius said. No answer came from the empty room and it never would again. He let his tears fall with this thought, but he was smiling as he cried.

The absence of the Snake was a mixed blessing for Caius. He no longer feared interference from the ghost in his renovation of The Cut Sleeve. He knew nothing would upset dinner with Andrew's parents—and that had to be *perfect*. He had a new sense of freedom now that the curse was well and truly broken, but there was a weight Rowan had left behind. Caius didn't regret any of the curses he performed in his past, but as he got ready for dinner, he found himself thinking about those he had spelled. What had happened to them? Some he did not care to know the result. Those that had been truly cruel deserved their punishment, even if they had never learned from it. It was the others he wondered about. Had his dear beast learned his lesson and followed his heart? Had the mute learned to watch his tongue and treat those beneath him better? Had the boy who thought he was ugly ever see the beauty Caius had known was there all along?

Was there a way he could find out what happened to them? Perhaps with today's internet, it would be possible. That thought made him smile and a bubble of hope filled his chest. He would ask Andrew to help him, which meant he would have to tell Andrew what had transpired with Rowan that afternoon. He had planned to tell him anyway, even though this would put his boyfriend in a position to say

I told you so. Caius didn't plan to let him have the upper hand often. Might as well treat him this one time.

Feeling much better, he set to making dinner with gusto. He created a menu that, although it lacked the sophistication he would have preferred when trying to make a good first impression on his boyfriend's parents, would at least show off his talents and create a warm and homey atmosphere. He worked a little magic on his table setting. He could *not* have Andrew's parents sitting in a *bar*. He hid the bar behind a curtain and stuffed the highboy tables into one of the upstairs bedrooms. He couldn't do anything about the booths, but he created a dining table in the center of the room with proper seating and covered it with a lovely tablecloth he found in the back of the kitchen pantry. He'd had to "clean" a few stains from the fabric, but it shone fresh and white once it lay on the table. He abstained from using candlesticks. This was a family setting, not a romantic dinner, but he took out his fine china and crystal glasses. He might have been short on time but that was no excuse for being a shoddy host.

He was still cooking when his doorbell rang at six. He gasped in a sudden panic. Andrew had said seven, hadn't he? He quickly wiped his hands on a towel and rushed to the front door. Pulling a winning smile from somewhere, he flung the door wide to greet his guests.

"Oh, it's only you."

"Only me?" Andrew asked. "I'm suddenly feeling unwanted."

"Not to worry, my dear," Caius said, pulling Andrew inside by his shirt front and shutting the door behind him. "It would take more than an early arrival for my prince to lose favor with me. Come. You can help me cook."

"Uh, Caius. I don't cook very well."

"Then you'll stand in the kitchen and look pretty while I finish up." Caius didn't wait for a response and headed back to the kitchen. He couldn't risk letting the meat dry out or the vegetables to overcook.

"I thought you would be arriving with your parents," Caius said. He was stirring one pot while tapping spices into another. Like with the last dinner party, the man was like an orchestra conductor, and Andrew was fascinated by him.

Andrew hadn't wanted to risk getting trapped in a conversation before he'd had a chance to arrive and gain witnesses. "They'll meet us here, as will Jason and Marie."

"So I have you all to myself for an hour?"

"Yes."

Caius grinned. "If only I didn't have to cook," he teased.

"Haven't we established that fooling around here isn't going to work?"

"First off, what I plan to do with you when I have you alone in a bedroom will be much more than 'fooling around.'" Caius may have been scolding him, but Andrew felt a rush of heat run through him. He couldn't wait to find out exactly what Caius had in mind once they were alone. "Secondly," Caius continued, "that won't be a problem anymore."

It took a moment for the words to sink in, and even after they had, Andrew was still confused. "What do you mean?"

Caius paused in his ministrations and turned to look at Andrew. "I apologized to him."

Again, understanding did not immediately dawn in Andrew's mind. When it did, his eyes widened in surprise. "Really?"

Caius nodded. "You were right. I never took responsibility for my actions. I ended up hurting someone more than I anticipated, and it came back to haunt me."

"What did he say?"

Caius hesitated before answering. "He forgave me," he finally said, his voice tight.

Andrew stepped forward and wrapped his arms around Caius's shoulders. Caius leaned into him and closed his eyes.

"I'm sorry," Andrew said softly, running his fingers through Caius's hair.

"What are you apologizing for?"

Andrew couldn't imagine what it had been like, but he could tell Caius was sad. "He was once your lover. Even if you hated each other for a while, it must have been hard to say goodbye."

Caius nodded. "He told me to do it right this time."

"I think you should follow that advice."

Caius smiled. "He kissed me."

The thought horrified Andrew. "Ew."

Now Caius laughed. "He didn't look like that at the time. He looked the way I remembered him."

Well, that was a relief of sorts, though Andrew still didn't like the idea of Caius kissing someone else. "You don't plan on making that a habit, do you?"

"Kissing my dead lovers?"

"Kissing other people in general."

"No." Caius tilted his head back in what was clearly an invitation.

Andrew took it, pressing their lips together briefly. "Good."

The sound of a timer beeping broke their tender moment. Caius pushed away abruptly. "My roast!" He rushed about the kitchen with more fervor than before.

Andrew stepped back to give him room and to make sure he didn't get run over.

When the flurry of activity calmed once more, he said, "So there's no one to interrupt us anymore when we want to be alone, huh?"

"No one of the phantom variety."

"Now I'm wishing we didn't have to do dinner with my family."

Caius grinned. "Think of the anticipation as foreplay."

"Just what I want to do when talking to my dad about how I'm gay and I don't want to work with him in the future."

"It'll be a reward for your bravery."

"Let's hope I have the courage."

Caius breezed by, planting a kiss on Andrew's forehead on the way. "You do. You've faced ghosts and sorcerers. I'm sure your father will be a small challenge in comparison."

"You haven't met him yet."

"If I've learned anything, it's that we tend to turn the simplest actions into grand feats when they do not have to be. When you finally came out to Jason, was it as bad as you thought it would be?"

"No."

"Perhaps this won't be either."

He didn't think it would go as well as his talk with Jason, but maybe Caius had a point. "Does this mean you'll apologize for things more often?"

Caius scoffed. "How dare you assume I'll need to."

"Oh yeah. It's magic that's real, not miracles."

Caius swatted him with a pot holder. "Help me plate these. Your parents will be here soon."

. . .

Caius was setting the last bowl on the table when the door-bell rang. He and Andrew went to answer it together. Outside, Marie and Jason stood with two people whom Caius assumed were Andrew's parents. "Please, come in." He ushered his guests into the foyer. "May I take your coats?" Andrew helped him collect the outerwear. Caius sent Andrew to put the garments in the small lounge by the stairs. He still hadn't decided if it would remain a hookah lounge or not.

"Jason, Marie, it is a pleasure to see you again," Caius said, then turned to the unknown pair. "And I take it you are Mr. and Mrs. Hollenbeck?"

The couple was older than he'd imagined, mid-fifties he guessed. Andrew's mother was a short, plump woman with a sweet face and freckles. Andrew had gotten his unruly hair from her, as evidenced by the curls escaping the chignon she'd gathered it into. Andrew's father, on the other hand, had too stern an expression for a face that was still handsome. Caius was happy to see that hair loss was not something that ran in Andrew's family. Mr. Hollenbeck was a silver fox. If Caius was lucky, one day Andrew would be one too.

Mrs. Hollenbeck smiled, and Caius was delighted to see dimples appear on her cheeks. "And you must be Caius. I haven't heard nearly enough about you."

Caius heard Andrew groan behind him, but he ignored it in favor of turning on one of his best beaming smiles. "We'll have to remedy that immediately." He linked her arm through his and led her into the parlor where he had set a bottle of wine to chill and some hors d'oeuvres on one of the coffee tables. "What would you like to know?"

"Why are you taking advantage of my son?" Mr. Hollenbeck interjected.

"I assure you, I have not taken advantage of him." Yet.

Andrew must have read the unspoken word in Caius's mind. A faint tint colored his cheeks. Caius would have to see if he could make Andrew blush fully when they were alone.

"How old are you anyway?" Mr. Hollenbeck continued. "You don't look old enough to run a business."

"I acquired The Cut Sleeve as an inheritance, and I would assume from what Andrew has told me that you are the perfect example of someone who has run a successful business while young." He didn't know how old Andrew's father had been when he began his business, but the flattery appeased him, if only slightly.

"Enough about business," Mrs. Hollenbeck ordered. "I want to know how you and my son met."

Caius was going to love this woman, he could tell. "It's not a romantic story, unfortunately. Andrew accidentally crashed a party I was throwing. I didn't know what a gentleman he was at the time, so I must admit that I threw him out almost on his ear."

"Andrew!" Andrew's mother exclaimed. "I didn't know you were the partying type."

"I'm not, Ma. Like Caius said, I ended up there on accident. I never meant to...crash the party."

"Our second meeting went much better," Caius said. "He found me having tea and reading one of my favorite books."

"Oh, I love tea," Andrew's mother said. "I usually have to beg Andrew to have some with me."

Caius leaned forward to whisper conspiratorially. "I'll share with you some of mine. He loves the cinnamon. He won't be able to resist your next invitation."

"Are you really trying to arrange tea times for me and my mother?" Andrew asked.

Jason laughed. "You're going to have to introduce us all to this magical tea of yours, Caius."

"It's nothing of the sort," Caius protested. He turned a mischievous smile on Andrew. "I keep my magical talents for other things."

Mr. Hollenbeck sputtered, and Caius looked at him innocently. He hadn't meant anything scandalous at all by that comment. How rude of the man to assume so.

"Shall we adjourn to dinner?"

The bar had been completely transformed, though Andrew didn't know if the changes were magical or part of Caius's future renovation. Either way, it looked like a restaurant and dinner looked delicious. Marie commented as much as they took their seats around the table.

"Smells delicious too," Jason added.

Caius was preening from the compliments. "Help yourself."

For a while, the sounds of people savoring food were the only conversation. Caius had outdone himself, especially with so little time to prepare. Andrew looked to his mother for her approval. She had a critical tongue when it came to cooking, but she was humming with pleasure like the rest of them. The only one who wasn't was his father. Although his dad had been surprised by the food and was obviously enjoying it, Andrew felt like he was pointedly not looking in his son's direction. The only words he'd spoken were from the short interrogation he'd shot Caius's way. The silent treatment hurt, though Andrew didn't think it would last.

His mother, on the other hand, was a conversation pro.

After tasting every dish, she began asking Caius about his cooking skills. She was surprised to learn that he'd studied professionally.

"I may have to get some recipes from you," she said.

"I will happily share, though nothing beats a mother's home cooking. I look forward to tasting your cuisine sometime."

"If you can get my son to visit more often, I will cook you anything you'd like."

Caius laughed. "Challenge accepted."

Even Jason and Marie joined in the conversation. The only silent parties were Andrew and his dad. It felt like their end of the table had been shadowed and secluded from the rest.

"Dad," Andrew said softly. "Are you ever going to look at me?"

His father sighed and slowly looked up from his plate. There was something in his expression that tore at Andrew's heart. It was worse than disappointment. Was his father...hurt?

They stared at each other until his father finally asked, "Do you really intend to risk your future on a trifling romance?"

"It's not a trifling romance," Andrew said, willing his father to understand. "And even if it was, it doesn't change the fact that I'm gay. I always have been."

"That's not the point."

"It is the point, Dad. I don't want a job where I have to hide who I am. I've done that enough. I'm not doing it anymore."

"That doesn't mean you need to go broadcasting it."

Andrew tried hard not to roll his eyes at that statement. "I'm not planning on doing that either. My private life is my business, but if there's a company party, Caius is going to be my date." Andrew liked the thought of taking Caius to a work function. Caius would stand out in the crowd yet work it flawlessly like he did everything else. Andrew smiled as he pictured it. He may not know what kind of company he wanted to work for, but he realized that wherever he went he wanted Caius with him.

"Your mother said there would be no changing your mind about this," his father griped. "I'll have to have a talk with the board."

And here was the part where he really had to be brave. Andrew glanced at Caius and found his boyfriend looking back at him. Caius gave a small nod of encouragement.

"Dad, I already told you, I don't want to work for Hollenbeck Consulting."

"You have another career in mind?" When Andrew hesitated, his father said, "If you're not going into business, then what am I spending all of this money on your college education for?"

"I do want to go into business," Andrew said. "I just don't want to work for your company. I don't know where I want to work yet, but I don't think working for a big corporation really fits me for a career."

His father gaped at him. "You want to go into business?"

Andrew shrugged. "It's not what I would have chosen, but I've learned a lot and some of it's interesting. Helping Caius brainstorm for the inn has been fun too. Maybe I'll end up running a company one day like you, but it'll have to be for something I'm interested in or I'll never have the motivation to make it work."

"You've thought about this."

Andrew hadn't realized how much he had, but what

he'd told his father was true. "I never told you because I'm still not sure what I want to do, what type of business I want to go into. I thought I'd need to know that before I could convince you that I wasn't just being lazy."

His father nodded thoughtfully. "It's difficult to run a business, especially from scratch. It's going to be a loss for the first five years at least, and even then it could still fail." He turned a solemn gaze on Andrew. "But if you're serious about this, and you take an internship like I told you to, then I'll help you."

Andrew's lips parted in surprise. "Really?"

His father nodded.

Andrew cringed. "Do I have to intern with Anderson and Associates?"

"If you find something else, and I feel it will give you sufficient experience, then you can intern elsewhere." He put up a hand. "But you will not be interning at The Cut Sleeve. Don't even think of suggesting it."

Andrew hadn't been. He wouldn't mind helping Caius out, but he didn't think interning with his boyfriend was a good idea. He held a hand out to his father. "It's a deal," he said.

His father gripped his hand solidly and gave a sharp nod. Though it didn't show in his expression, Andrew felt that his father was proud of him. He smiled, happiness bubbling up inside him. His father had listened and had agreed to help him. He felt like he'd been given something he'd always wanted, but even as he was overjoyed with the success, it felt fragile and small. He hoped it was a baby step to a better relationship with his dad overall.

"Now that that's settled," Caius said, "would anyone care for dessert?"

. . .

Later that night, when the guests were leaving, Andrew pulled his mother aside. There was a question he'd wanted to ask her all night, but he hadn't wanted to do it in front of everyone else.

"You knew, didn't you?" he asked once they were alone. "You knew who I was crushing on in eighth grade."

His mother smiled. "From the day you met, your face would shine like the sun whenever you two played. Then one day, you came home and it was like the sun had been stolen from your sky."

"Why didn't you say anything?"

"I did, honey. Don't you remember?"

Andrew didn't like to think about that day and the jealousy he'd felt seeing Jason with his new girlfriend. Now he tried to remember what had come after the jealousy, when he'd gotten home and locked himself in his room. "You knocked on my bedroom door and brought me milk and cookies," he said.

His mother nodded. "You told me not to treat you like a child, but you ate them anyway."

"I still don't remember you saying anything to me about my being gay."

"I didn't have to. I asked you what was wrong and if you'd had a fight with Jason. You told me no and that everything was fine."

"And that was it?"

"And then we sat and ate cookies together, and you told me about your day until the phone rang. Somehow you knew it was Jason on the line. You brightened up immediately and ran off to answer it."

"Why didn't you say anything after that?"

"I wasn't sure how much you were aware of. Then as time passed and you figured it out, I thought you would tell me if you felt you needed to." She patted his cheek, then pinched it hard like he hated. "It's never mattered to me whether you're gay or not, Andrew. I just want you to be happy."

"I am happy, Mom," he said, rubbing his throbbing cheek.

"I know. I do believe this one is a keeper. Make sure you bring him to Thanksgiving dinner. I'd like him to taste my sweet potato pie."

"I'm sure he'd love that."

With a hug and a kiss, she headed out to the car where his dad was waiting. He watched them drive off, then headed back inside to find Caius.

The rest of the dinner had gone smoothly. Although Mr. Hollenbeck hadn't fully warmed to Caius's charms, he had been civil. Caius wasn't worried. He'd won over Andrew's mother with promises of recipes and baked goods. It was only a matter of time before he found the way into Mr. Hollenbeck's heart, and he didn't mind putting in the effort. It was a small price to pay for the pleasure of Andrew's company.

The guests had all gone back to their respective homes and only he and Andrew remained at The Cut Sleeve. They had cleared the table and settled into the parlor with steaming cups of tea. Caius was seated with his feet tucked under him. He leaned against Andrew's side, and Andrew slid an arm around his shoulder. He sighed, contented. This was the perfect wrap up to a pleasant evening.

"You were right," Andrew said.

Caius was ready to be annoyed by the broken peace of the moment, but those words were acceptable at any time when they were directed at himself. "Oh? I usually am, but, please, tell me how I did it this time."

He was sure Andrew rolled his eyes at the comment but didn't bother to look. "I wasn't taking action on my own. I was too caught up with agonizing over the things I wanted to do that I just waited around until someone pushed me to do them."

"You were very brave tonight. I think it went well."

He felt Andrew's nod against his head. "I'm going to try to do that more often in the future."

"I'll be happy to let you know when you're not speaking up," Caius offered.

"As long as you don't use a newspaper article to do it."

Caius grinned. "And I'm sure we'll have plenty of fights about responsibility in the future as well." He was willing to admit that he wasn't perfect, if only indirectly.

Andrew shifted to smile down at him. "You can bet on it."

Caius tilted his head up to be kissed. Andrew obliged but didn't linger. He caressed the side of Caius's face. "Let's go upstairs."

Caius was off the couch in a flash. Finally! The wait was over! He turned to Andrew, ready to pull his boyfriend along, but Andrew hadn't moved. The expression on his face was one Caius had never seen before. "Andrew? Are you all right?"

"I love you, Caius."

Caius was stunned. In all the years he'd lived, and with all the lovers he'd had, he couldn't remember one of them telling him that they loved him. He blinked rapidly when tears threatened to overwhelm him. His heart felt like it was in his throat. He launched himself back onto the couch, throwing himself into Andrew's arms and kissing him like some overjoyed heroine from a story. Andrew laughed when Caius let him up for air, and they sat for a moment, foreheads pressed together, enjoying their proximity.

"Just in case it wasn't clear," Caius said, "I love you too."

Andrew smiled. "Maybe there is such a thing as happily ever after. Think we can find it?"

"I'm willing to find out," Caius said. "And I do believe our search will begin in my bedroom."

Andrew laughed. "Point taken."

Caius slid off Andrew's lap and helped his boyfriend to his feet. Hand in hand, they walked upstairs and down the hall to Caius's room. Caius kept the lights low, wanting a romantic atmosphere for their first time together.

"This is far from my first time," he said, "but it feels like the first time for real."

"You've been living in a dream for far too long." Andrew stepped forward, closing the space between them and kissed the side of Caius's neck.

Caius shivered. "You have to make up for sixty years of celibacy."

"No pressure, huh?" Andrew asked as he kissed the other side of Caius's neck.

Caius would have replied, but Andrew's mouth closed over his, and the only thing to escape was a groan.

When their lips parted, Andrew whispered, "Caius..."

There was a hesitancy in his voice that demanded Caius's attention. The light was bright enough for Caius to see a faint coloring on Andrew's cheeks, and the awkward way his gaze skittered to and from Caius's face made it clear he had something important to say but was too embarrassed to say it. Caius had an idea of what that thing could be. Could he really be so lucky to not only find someone who loved him, but who was truly his alone, untouched by another?

He cupped Andrew's face and leaned forward to kiss him sweetly. "Not to worry, my dear. I'm an excellent teacher."

Andrew's blush deepened, but he smiled. "You mean you're good at telling people what you want."

Caius winked at him. "Right now I want you to kiss me. You are quite good at that already."

Andrew obliged, and as their tongues tangled, Caius could feel the tension in his muscles relaxing. Good. He didn't want Andrew so nervous he wouldn't enjoy himself. Caius, on the other hand, was relishing the moment. He pressed against Andrew, delighting in the play of firm muscle and the feel of a man's body next to his. It had been way too long.

When he could stand it no longer, he ordered, "Skin. I need skin."

Andrew apparently had no problem with that idea. His lips never left Caius's except for when his shirt was lifted up and over his head. Caius didn't know where it ended up, and he didn't care. He was too busy running his hands all over his boyfriend's body. The contrast between Andrew's smooth back and the hair sprinkled over his chest sent zings of sensation through Caius's fingertips. Caius felt as if his skin was on high alert, drinking in each sensation to make up for the touch it had been missing all these years. And it wasn't just his skin that wanted more. He wanted to taste what he touched. He wanted to experience Andrew with every sense he had. He mouthed a line down Andrew's neck to his collarbone and chest. Nuzzling the curls on his pecs, he flicked out his tongue to sample the flavor of

Andrew's skin. The sharp tang of dried sweat pinged his taste buds, and he lapped again for more.

"Caius, you're going to kill me."

"Oh no, my dear," Caius murmured against Andrew's shoulder. "What good would that do me?"

Andrew's hips rocked, pressing a firm invitation into Caius's thigh. And what an invitation it was! Not too long, but from what Caius could tell, Andrew's member was thick like Caius liked. His mouth watered with the thought of becoming intimately acquainted with it.

"I want to taste you, Andrew."

Andrew groaned.

"Has anyone ever done that before?"

To Caius's disappointment, Andrew nodded. Fair enough. He was in college. He must have experimented at one time or another. But after tonight, whatever scamp had had his paws on Andrew would be forgotten. Caius would make sure of that.

"I'm going to blow your mind," he said.

Whether it was to prove this statement or to punish Andrew for having let another man touch him, Caius wasn't sure. Perhaps it was a mix of both that propelled him to take one of Andrew's nipples into his mouth and suck hard on it. He flicked the small nub repeatedly with his tongue and nipped at it with his teeth. Andrew made a chorus of delightful sounds which prompted him to continue the torture until Andrew was begging him to stop. He did for a moment. Then he resumed on the other nipple.

"Caius!" Andrew yelled. "Please! I...I need..."

"What?" Caius asked, lapping sweetly at the abused nipples. "What do you need, Andrew?"

The power he felt hearing Andrew's desperation was a heady thing. Caius liked to take the lead in bed but knowing it was Andrew he led made it all the sweeter. Andrew, the boy who'd trusted him, believed in him. His prince, his savior, his precious love. It was a terrifying thought, taking a chance on love again. It was so easy to get one's heart broken once it was given to another. Yet Caius knew he could give his to Andrew. He kissed the nipple, then slowly lowered himself until his knees hit the carpet beneath them.

"Is this what you need?"

Andrew's answer was a groan.

Caius made quick work of Andrew's button and zipper, seeking the prize that lay beneath it. The smell of sex reached his nose as he pushed the denim out of the way, and he inhaled deeply. He'd missed that scent. Musk, sweat, and man. Precum had made part of Andrew's briefs sheer, letting him see the thick red head of Andrew's erection through the fabric. It was beautiful, and he ached to taste it. He licked the wet spot, savoring the salty flavor soaking through the cotton.

"Caius..." Andrew groaned again, his legs twitching.

Perhaps standing wasn't such a good idea for this. "Lie down on the bed for me."

He helped Andrew remove his pants and get on the bed. Caius wondered if Andrew's nervousness from before would return, and if so, when it might appear. For now, he didn't see any trace of it. Andrew lay back among the pillows, his erection straining his underwear. The pure desire Caius saw in Andrew's gaze was an aphrodisiac more powerful than anything he'd experienced before. No one had ever looked at him like that, a mix of lust and need that was for more than just sex. It was for *Caius*.

Caius froze, shaken by that look. It brought an ache to his chest that rivaled the one in his groin. "Andrew," he said breathlessly.

Andrew seemed to understand. "I love you, Caius."

Yes. Caius nodded, unable to voice the same words, but he felt them like an overwhelming force filling his heart. Needing to make this connection physical, he joined Andrew on the bed. They embraced, and Caius found he could breathe again. Their mouths met, and Caius put all the feelings he could not find words for into his kiss. With each touch of his mouth on Andrew's, he said "I love you." With his kiss to Andrew's shoulder, he said, "You're precious." He trailed compliments with his tongue down Andrew's body. "You're beautiful. You're amazing. You're mine. I love you." He settled between Andrew's legs, placing a last kiss to Andrew's cock.

"Caius..."

Caius looked up into Andrew's eyes. The pressure in his chest had finally been relieved, and he found his voice. "I love you too, Andrew."

He pulled Andrew's underwear down, using the elastic waistband to frame Andrew's package like a platter served up just for him. The first stroke of his tongue was rewarded with a moan that made him shiver. Andrew was so beautifully responsive to touch. It wasn't just his promise to Andrew that made him want to blow his mind. He loved hearing the pleasure in Andrew's voice. He wanted to give his lover as much pleasure as he could take, and Caius had plenty to give.

Blow jobs were one of the many skills Caius had acquired over the years. He loved giving them, and he loved receiving them. His extensive years of "study" had imparted him with plenty of knowledge to work with. He employed that knowledge now for Andrew's benefit. He licked and sucked, teased and pleasured until Andrew's sweet moans turned into gasps and cries. On a whim of curiosity, Caius stroked the cleft of Andrew's ass, wondering if there would be an invitation there for later. Perhaps if he hadn't been lost in the building ecstasy, Andrew might have resisted, but the insistent rocking of his hips when Caius pressed a fingertip to his hole told Caius that that was a region to be explored in full one day. Caius looked forward to doing so.

Andrew's thighs trembled with mounting pleasure, and Caius knew the end wasn't too far off. He applied himself to Andrew's erection with fervor and was rewarded with louder cries for his efforts. He drew out as many as he could before the tipping point became inevitable and then plunged Andrew deep into his mouth for an orgasm that spilled down his throat like a waterfall. Caius drank every drop, then kissed his lover's cock before drawing off completely.

Andrew was panting heavily, and it took him a few moments to recover. Caius took that as a good sign. When Andrew finally found his voice, he said, "That was incredible."

"I'm glad you liked it." Caius resisted asking if it was better than his previous experience. He didn't think it was possible for it not to be, but he'd rather not be proven wrong.

Feeling rather overdressed for the occasion, he stripped down to his underwear before crawling back up the bed to lay down beside Andrew. His own erection called for attention, but he could wait for Andrew to recover before they took care of it.

As if reading Caius's mind, Andrew asked, "That isn't all we're doing, is it?"

Caius smiled at the concern in Andrew's voice. "Not to worry, my dear. That was only round one."

. . .

"Good." Andrew's head was spinning from the best orgasm he'd ever had in his life, but there was a lot more he wanted to do with Caius before the night was over. He was almost disappointed he'd had that frantic blow job at that one party. Compared to what Caius had just done, it only counted as a blow job on a technicality. He could only imagine what other things would feel like when Caius did them.

As the overwhelming pleasure of his orgasm faded, the unease he'd managed to set aside returned. He wanted to have sex with Caius. He wanted to try it all, and although he was nervous, he knew Caius would make it worthwhile. That wasn't what made worry settle in his gut. It was all well and good to lie back and let Caius lead, but would he be good enough when he was the one taking charge? Who knew how many years of experience Caius had behind him? Not to mention he had owned a bordello and had known a ton of prostitutes who'd had sex for a living. How was Andrew supposed to compete with that?

To distract himself from his nerves, Andrew brushed a hand over Caius's thigh. His skin was smooth. Had he shaved? Did he use magic for that? Caius's muscles twitched beneath his fingers.

"Do you mind?" Andrew asked.

"You can touch me wherever you like," Caius said.

Given free rein to do as he pleased, Andrew moved his hand higher, cupping the firm curve of Caius's ass. It was still encased in cotton, and he wondered if it was as hairless as his legs. Not yet ready to find out, he stroked upward, following the planes of Caius's back, up his long body to his shoulders.

"That feels nice," Caius murmured.

It was soothing Andrew as well. Feeling a little bolder,

he shifted closer and kissed Caius's shoulder. He trailed his mouth along the path his fingers had taken, only this time he moved down. When he hit the hollow where Caius's back met his butt, Andrew licked a line just above his waistband. Caius's skin had a sheen of sweat that tasted sharp on his tongue.

Caius moaned. "Do that again."

Andrew did, and Caius's hips rocked in response. Curious to see how else he could make him react, he took hold of Caius's underwear and drew it down. Caius's ass was plump and perfect, and as smooth as his legs. Andrew couldn't resist massaging it. He licked his lips, wanting to taste it, but was still nervous. He'd seen plenty of rimming in porn videos, but he wondered what it would be like in reality. Only one way to find out.

He licked Caius's lower back again. This time he moved a little lower, dipping the tip of his tongue into Caius's crease. Caius's moan was louder this time, and it encouraged Andrew to go farther. Needing better access, he pulled Caius's underwear all the way off.

"Spread your legs a little wider for me?"

Caius did as requested, and Andrew lay down between them. He kneaded Caius's ass cheeks before separating them and taking his first look at Caius's hole. It was just as perfect as the rest of him. *Here we go.* Andrew stuck out his tongue and licked a line from the base of Caius's balls to the top of his ass. The moan that greeted this was longer and louder than any of the others. The sound reverberated through Andrew's body and down to his cock. Holy shit, that was good. He did it again, and Caius melted into the mattress, tilting his ass up to give Andrew better access.

"More," Caius groaned. "Do it more."

Feeling more confident, Andrew did. Caius was a very

vocal lover when it came to rimming. Any doubt Andrew had about being good enough for him vanished as each caress of his tongue drew sounds of pleasure from Caius. It wasn't long before Andrew was hard again. Wanting to go even further, he tried pressing his tongue inside Caius's body. The ring of muscle was tight at first but loosened as he continued to massage it.

"Oh..." Caius moaned. Andrew hadn't thought it possible, but his lover sank even further into the mattress. "Don't stop," Caius begged. "Don't stop."

Andrew wouldn't dream of it. He thrust his tongue deep inside Caius, and Caius's moans turned into growls. He began to press his ass back against Andrew's face, trying to get Andrew's tongue deeper inside him. Could this get any hotter? Andrew moaned and humped against the bed. He could feel a wet spot growing under his cock, and he ached to come again.

"Oh my god... ohmygod," Caius cried.

Andrew's tongue was beginning to cramp from so much exercise, but he didn't want to stop. He wanted to make Caius groan like that forever. Why had he waited so long to have sex? This was amazing! But even as he had that thought, he knew the answer. It was only this amazing because he was with Caius.

"Take me."

Andrew was too absorbed in his task to register what Caius had said at first.

"Andrew, please," Caius begged. "Fuck me. Now."

Holy crap. Andrew pulled his tongue out of Caius's ass to both of their reluctant groans. His tongue was tingling, and his jaw ached, but he didn't care about that. Caius wanted him to fuck him. Where were the damn condoms when he needed one?

"What are you waiting for?" Caius demanded.

Andrew was in as much of a hurry. "Condoms."

"I'm a fucking sorcerer, Andrew. I'll kill any disease that deigns to get near us."

Andrew still hesitated.

"Fine." Caius pushed up from the mattress, but instead of moving to a night table or the bathroom, he turned and pushed Andrew back down onto the bed. The next thing Andrew knew, Caius was straddling him with one hand wrapped around Andrew's dick as he lined it up to his ass. Andrew would have protested, but when he looked to see what Caius was doing, he saw a condom on his shaft.

"What the—?"

"Sorcerer, remember? Making a condom is child's play in comparison to a curse."

Andrew's awe of the magical condom was short lived as Caius lowered himself and his cock pressed inside him. This time it was Andrew's turn to be vocal. "Fuck..." he groaned out as tight heat enveloped the head of his erection. The sensation slowly moved down until his dick was fully encased in it. "Caius..."

He didn't remember closing his eyes. He opened them to find Caius looking down at him, smiling. "Think you can handle it if I move?"

Yes. No. "Please."

Caius began to rock up and down, and the shifting friction around his cock sent sparks through Andrew's body. The wet heat of Caius's mouth hadn't been like this. But even as the physical sensations mounted, something was missing. Andrew looked up at Caius, and he knew what it was.

"Kiss me."

Caius leaned forward, bringing their mouths together,

and it felt like a circle completing. They belonged together. Andrew could feel it in his bones.

He pushed up so he was sitting with Caius on his lap. He wrapped his arms tight around his lover, and they continued to make out as Caius moved. Eventually, a need for oxygen drove their lips apart, but even then, Andrew could feel that connection as he gazed into Caius's sparkling green eyes.

"Is this magic?" he asked.

"Yes, but none of mine." Caius caressed the side of Andrew's face. "I think I'm under your spell this time."

Andrew drew him back down for another kiss. He moved his hips in counterpoint to Caius, and soon their movements became frantic as pleasure built between them.

"Touch me," Caius pleaded.

Close to the edge, Andrew took hold of Caius's cock and worked him fast. He wanted them to come together if possible.

"So close..." he panted.

"Yes."

They clung to each other as they climbed higher and higher until, with a groan, Caius shuddered and came, his seed spilling between them. The clench of Caius's orgasm around Andrew's cock was enough to send him over the edge, and he thrust deep as he came. Spent, they collapsed back onto the bed, Caius still wrapped around Andrew like a limpet.

They lay panting for a while, neither in a hurry to separate. Even after they had both caught their breath, Andrew didn't do anything more than his fingers lazily through Caius's hair.

"Was it worth the wait?" he asked. A trace of his earlier

nervousness returned when Caius didn't immediately answer.

"Yes." Caius raised his head to look at Andrew, and Andrew realized they weren't talking about sex. "You were worth waiting for."

The air left Andrew's lungs in a rush. He didn't know what to say to that, so he pulled Caius down for a sweet, lingering kiss instead. "I love you."

Caius smiled. "And that's the reason why."

The air was cooling. With reluctance, they shifted, snuggling next to one another beneath the comforter. The condom had vanished just as magically as it had appeared. So had the cum which should have grown cool and sticky on their bellies.

"More perks to being a sorcerer?" Andrew asked.

Caius grinned.

"Is this where our fairy tale ends?"

Caius shook his head. "We don't get a turn of the page and the words 'happily ever after,'" he said. "We get a future."

"I like that better anyway."

"Me too."

They were both grinning like fools as they looked at each other.

"You do realize that was only round two, yes?" Caius asked.

Andrew laughed. "Do I get a few minutes to recover before you wear me out again?"

"I suppose. As long as you don't make me wait sixty years for round three. Orgasm denial is *not* one of my kinks."

"You have others?" Andrew teased.

Caius grinned. "Maybe."

"I look forward to finding out."

Andrew leaned forward and brought their lips together. Despite their flirting, the kiss was slow and sweet. The connection he'd felt was still there between them, making this kiss more powerful than their spell-breaking one. This was a promise of tomorrow, of tonight, and right now. It was the furthest thing from a story's end. It was the first page of a beginning.

ACKNOWLEDGMENTS

Special thanks to Anya for being such an amazing beta reader that Ghost House now has sequel that I never saw coming. Thank you to my wonderful editor Jenni Lea. This book would not be what it is without her guidance. And to Kiki for being a master at the comma when proofreading. Last, but definitely not least, a world of thanks to Kanaxa. A book is nothing without its face. Thank you for bringing Caius to life and creating an amazing cover for his and Andrew's story.

ABOUT THE AUTHOR

Jacqueline loves a good romance, especially ones that make her fall in love with the characters. She believes everyone has a right to be happy and enjoys seeing her characters find that happiness for themselves.

In real life, Jacqueline lives on an island on the east coast of the United States. She spends her time outside her day job juggling her many interests, which include reading, writing, and drinking tea.

You can find Jacqueline on Facebook, Twitter, Goodreads, and Pinterest, or you can email her at JacquelineGreyBooks@gmail.com.

Visit her website at www.jacquelinegrey.com.

facebook.com/JacquelineGreyBooks

twitter.com/jacqueline_grey

pinterest.com/Jacqueline_Grey

ABOUT THE AUTHOR

Jacqueline loves a good romance, especially ones that make her fall in love with the characters. She believes everyone has a right to be happy and enjoys seeing her characters find that happiness for themselves.

In real life, Jacqueline lives on an island on the east coast of the United States. She spends her time outside her day job juggling her many interests, which include reading, writing, and drinking tea.

You can find Jacqueline on Facebook, Twitter, Goodreads, and Pinterest, or you can email her at JacquelineGreyBooks@gmail.com.

Visit her website at www.jacquelinegrey.com.

facebook.com/JacquelineGreyBooks

twitter.com/jacqueline_grey

pinterest.com/Jacqueline_Grey